# TERROR'S CRADLE

DUNCAN KYLE was born in Bradford, Yorkshire, a few hundred yards from the house where J. B. Priestley grew up.

He started his career as a junior reporter on the *Bradford Telegraph and Argus*, later going on to the *Yorkshire Post*. In the mid-fifties he joined *John Bull* magazine – which later became *Today* – in London and from there he went to become editorial director at Odhams where he wrote his first novel, *A Cage of Ice*.

It was the success of this book which persuaded him to become a full-time writer and to fulfill his long-held ambition to live deep in the country. He now lives in Suffolk with his wife and three children.

He has written six novels, each more successful than the last: *Black Camelot* (published by Collins in 1978) is the latest.

DUNCAN KYLE

# Terror's Cradle

FONTANA / Collins

First published in the UK in 1975 by William Collins Sons & Co Ltd
First issued in Fontana Books 1976
Fifth Impression May 1983

© 1974 by Rupert Crew Ltd

Made and printed in Great Britain by
William Collins Sons & Co Ltd, Glasgow

This one for Robert
with my thanks

# CHAPTER ONE

I like working for the rough ones. Human nature being per-
verse, that's true of most of us. Give us a considerate, liberal
boss and after the first start of surprise, we gradually take
ever greater liberties and finally begin to call him an
amiable weakling as we linger over idle lunchtime drinks.
But show us a real brute, an untrustworthy, ruthless, slave-
driver who hounds men to heart attacks and mental collapse,
and there's something in us that makes us prance excitedly
to every tune he plays. Even his vicious quirks are somehow
transmuted into almost affectionate jokes.

I work for one such, I'm usually glad to say. His name is
Alex Scown and he's a bastard of the *premier crû*. Everybody's agreed on that, but when they talk about him, it's an
inadequate description. There's always something else to
add. They say, he's a bastard, *but* . . . but talented, but
shrewd, but brilliant. But watch your back.

Brooding about Scown, I half-listened to the interrogation
of the witness, aware that there would now be no revelations.
The big Senate committee room was handsome, woodwork
and lawyers were polished, witnesses and atmosphere were
sweaty, but the earlier tension had gone. The sharks had
escaped the net and were swimming gracefully away to off-
shore sanctuaries, grinning shark grins and thinking about
their next sharky bites.

'Did you,' an amplified voice with a strong Southern
accent demanded with truculence but no hope, 'transfer those
bonds yourself, in a suitcase, from Boston, Massachusetts
to Mexico City?'

I watched idly as the witness thought about it. He thought
for perhaps thirty seconds, then leaned away from the microphone and listened to the whispering lawyer beside him.
He'd say what they had all said; he'd have to, and the Con-

stitution of the United States had once been amended to ensure that he could say it. He cleared his throat and uttered the standard words. 'I stand on the Fifth Amendment.'

I nodded to myself and made a note. The trumpets had sounded, the great confrontation had taken place, the inquiry had had the promised vigour but nobody was incriminating anybody. In particular, nobody was incriminating a neat and elegant English gentleman who was in this smelly financial dunghill up to his aromatic armpits. He could retain his places in the City and Parliament and sue anybody who even dared to hint that his standards were less than knightly. Nor was he the only one. Discreet sighs of relief were audible from just outside territorial waters on both sides of the Atlantic.

I'd phoned London the night before to tell Scown all was virtually over. He'd been disappointed. He'd hoped for blood, thought he actually sniffed it, had planned gleefully to help place the elegant English gentleman in a specimen jar labelled 'crooked politician' and display it for ten million readers to examine, thereby laying one more banana skin on the Government's already perilous path. But now Scown's intended victim was clear and clean. The air around him would smell once more of sweet violets, or more likely Brût. I'd told Scown it was a waste of time for me now to hang on in Washington, and that the Congressional inquiry wore a hopeless look. Did Scown want me back in London?

He'd said, 'Hang on another day or so, John. See what happens.'

Well, nothing had happened. I closed my notebook, nodded to my fellow observers and began to thread my way through the yawners at the back of the committee room, already thinking about afternoon flights from Dulles International and the two weeks' holiday that kept on vanishing. Scown didn't believe in holidays. If Scown didn't take holidays, and he didn't, why should anybody else take them? He'd already done me twice, first with the Moscow trip, then with this sortie to Washington. I grinned to myself. If they'd both been glittering Scown-type triumphs, I'd never have seen water or sand again, except from thirty-thousand feet. But Scown in defeat has never placed a reassuring arm around the dejected soldier; he looks pointedly in another direction until the next little victory comes along. In London tomorrow I would say, 'I'm off for a few days,' and he'd say, '*That's* a bloody good idea. Try Ireland. Full of donkeys. You'll feel at home.'

I'd already checked out of my hotel, so I collected my bag and briefcase from the correspondents' room and took a cab to the Washington Press Club. Before the flight there was time for lunch and before lunch for a couple of valedictory Martinis. I cabled London with the glad news of my impending return, then went to visit Harry. He's the barman, and Harry's loving care and legerdemain arouse the same appetite for the Martini as the Martini itself is supposed to awaken for food. I watched him fondly and sipped his product with proper appreciation; also with a kind of sadness because the fine American Martini is like the fine Italian olive: it's never quite the same anywhere else and this would be the last for a while.

The club's an amiable and welcoming place and I've been around long enough to know people in most Press Clubs, so lunch was pleasant, gossipy and rather long and would have been still longer if flight time hadn't been ticking threateningly nearer. So finally I detached myself and left for Dulles Airport with that sorry-to-be-leaving-yet-glad-to-be-going-home feeling I always seem to get. Alsa says it's charming sentimentality when it's not maudlin insobriety, but then Alsa is a clear-eyed lady for whom one drink is refreshing, pleasurable – and enough.

At Dulles International voices of velvet filled the place with my name. Would John Sellers, passenger for London, please report at the double to the British Airways desk where, though they didn't actually say so over the Tannoy, bad news awaited. One just knows these things. I shouldn't have cabled London, that's what I shouldn't have done.

The girl smiled as she handed me the cable: FLY VEGAS RHODES EXCLUSIVE BOUGHT STOP REGISTERED

DIME PALACE SCOWN.

I sighed, told the girl I would not, after all, be a passenger to London and humped my bag over to the news stand in search of the key to Scown's cryptogram. They sold me the early afternoon edition and it was all on page one, brightly displayed. Superstars sell newspapers. The story said that one Susannah Rhodes, film actress, was in a state of some embarrassment and the state of Nevada. A corpse had been discovered in her hotel bathroom. The message was perfectly clear. Scown, bless his border-reiving ancestors, knew I hated doing showbusiness stories. I could almost hear the underlying pleasure in his subdued snarl as he dictated the cable. No story, Sellers? I'll send you on a bloody story. Also there was the implicit heavy sarcasm of the words EXCLUSIVE BOUGHT. In Scownese they meant: even *you* can't foul this up.

So not many hours later I was standing a few thousand miles away at the bar of the Flamingo, Las Vegas, waiting for the film company PR man, with my sweat drying too quickly in the air conditioning. Washington had been crackling cold; Las Vegas was going through one of its occasional winter heat waves, with temperatures around ninety.

I'd been waiting an hour, but at least I was reasonably sure he'd be along. Strings must certainly have been pulled. Scown sat on the board of a TV company which had diversified into films and was the principal backer of the Rhodes vehicle, so I had my little edge on the army of assembled press and television boys who'd been there hours before me.

From the bar I could see most of the gaming room, with its careful lighting, low enough to flatter the women and strong enough to let the staff keep its wary eyes on everything and everybody. Sweet Muzak was playing: heavily orchestrated and optimistic strings to keep the mind off the losings, yet loud enough to overlay the endless cranking of handles and whirring mechanical money swallowers.

The man didn't stop as he threaded his way across the gaming room. He was big and slim, wearing casual clothes so immaculately new and pressed they'd have made a marine warrant officer look wrinkled. He also wore, on what I could see of his face, the kind of set, non-committal, negative expression you see on mildly-hostile bank managers. His eyes were hidden behind big square sunglasses with mirror lenses and all I could see in them was a couple of reflections of myself.

He glanced along the bar and came straight over. 'You Sellers?'

'Yes.'

'Dave Spinetti.' He didn't offer to shake hands.

'Drink?'

'Coke.'

I ordered. Drinks are easier to order and delivered faster in Las Vegas than anywhere else on earth.

He beat about no bushes. 'How much you paying?'

I shook my head. 'Fixed in London. My paper and her agent. All agreed. I'm just here to talk to her.'

The corners of his mouth turned down. 'You and a million more.'

I said, 'But.'

'Yeah, I know.' He didn't like it. This time his palm wasn't to be crossed with gold. The deal had been done. There were no big percentages to be played. Perhaps he'd find a few scrapings, but they'd be small.

I said, 'Tell me about it.'

'You've seen the afternoon papers?'

I nodded. 'Very bald. Very careful. Very uninformative. What happened?'

He took a pull at his Coke, almost as though it were whisky. No thirst there – just the need for a crutch. 'When she woke up there was this dead guy in her bathroom. That's all there is.'

I said, 'With a bullet through his head and she didn't hear the shot.'

He nodded grimly. 'Right.'

'And she didn't know him?'

'Yeah. She didn't know him.'

'There can't be many like that.'

'Like what?'

'Men she didn't know. Four hundred million Chinese, perhaps. A few Russians and Albanians.'

'Cut that out!'

'Who was he?'

Spinetti shrugged. 'Who knows? His name was Bruzzi.'

'Where from?'

'Vegas.'

'And the gentleman's occupation?'

'Bartender.'

The picture wasn't even remotely fuzzy. I said, 'She was high. Drugs or alcohol?'

He shrugged again. Smooth creases slid about the beautiful knitwear jacket as his shoulders moved. 'You won't print it.'

Preserve the public's illusions. *Miss Rhodes, tired and sleeping soundly, didn't hear* . . .

I said, 'The only question is, who actually shot him?'

Spinetti grimaced. 'That's what the sheriff's office is asking.'

'Romantic quarrel over beauteous actress,' I said. '*Crime passionel*. Between a bartender and a gunman. And ten feet away, on the other side of a plasterboard wall, she's overtired as a newt and hears nothing.'

'You've got the picture.' His voice was suddenly a little weary.

'You've had a hard day,' I said. 'Relax. Have a real drink.'

'Just Coke.' Confirmation: reformed alcoholic and it still hurt.

'Has she talked to the sheriff's office?'

'Not yet.'

I said, 'But you moved quickly.'

'Sure I moved fast. She was in a state of collapse. The doctor wouldn't – '

'That would be the film unit doctor?'

'Yeah.'

'And how long does the tame doctor say it will be?'

'Coupla days.'

'Excellent,' I said.

'Excellent it's not, bud.'

I said, 'All publicity's good publicity. Remember *Cleopatra*. Don't worry about it. Meanwhile she's where?'

'Staying with friends.'

'Well, she always had plenty of those. New friends wherever she goes. Some nicer than others, but not much. Do I see her tonight?'

Spinetti shook his head. 'Tomorrow.'

'In Las Vegas?'

'No. Not in Nevada.'

'Arizona or California?'

He'd had enough. 'I'll call you tomorrow. Early. Where are you staying?'

'The Dime Palace.'

Above the mirror lenses his eyebrows lifted. 'A motel?'

I said, 'Pounds convert into dollars in a most unfavourable way. Legacy of war, and things.'

'Yeah. Call you tomorrow.' He turned and walked away.

He was stuck with the mucky end of this stick, and I didn't feel sorry for him.

The Dime Palace wasn't quite as cheap and nasty as it sounds. Las Vegas, and the people who run it, take a simple attitude to visitors: they encourage them, tempt and flatter them, house them comfortably, feed them well and cheaply – and concentrate on removing their money at the gaming tables. So the Dime Palace was a twenty-dollar motel and charged ten. Included in the ten was a free drink and a free meal and the pool and the rest, plus a colour TV set in the room and free local phone calls. I've stayed in places, in Paris and Stockholm for instance, and in Russia, that gave a quarter the value and charged four times as much.

I was back there, about half-past ten, taking off my tie and adjusting the air-conditioning, when the phone rang. I stared at the instrument for a puzzled moment, wondering who the hell was ringing me. Then I picked it up.

'John Sellers?'

'Speaking.'

'Message for you, bud. Leave Vegas. Don't come back.'

'Who – ?'

'You hear what I said?'

'I heard. You've got a wrong number, I think.'

'Just go, Sellers. Go now.'

Then he hung up. After a stupefied moment I realized I was still holding the phone, so I replaced it and lay back on the bed, thinking. Very few people knew I was in Las Vegas: Alex Scown was one, and not only had he sent me in the first place, he'd go off like fulminate if I left without the interview with Susannah. Then there was Spinetti, to whom I'd given my number not long before. But the caller hadn't been Spinetti. Some friend of Spinetti's? I grinned suddenly, imagining the conversation, the delicate little plot. Get Sellers out and you get the London *Daily News* out, too. Once they're out, the story's yours for two thousand bucks. Hell, Charlie, you can even pretend to *be* Sellers. Fifteen hundred. Two thousand I said, Charlie, and that's cheap. Okay? Okay.

I switched on the TV set to look for a newscast, and when I found it, Scown's editorial judgment was neatly confirmed. I had to wait for item nine, newscaster's head and shoulders only, for the senate inquiry. But item one had been Susannah. They'd had the county sheriff, niggled that he hadn't seen Miss Rhodes, but By God he would, yessir, 'cause when it came to justice in this here county, movie stars weren't no different to nobody else, and she'd better show for the coroner, collapse or no collapse.' Patently neither the sheriff nor anyone else had the faintest idea where she was.

I picked up the phone, dialled Western Union and dictated a cable to London to let Scown know that things were set for morning then opened my bag to get out pyjamas and shaving case. No shaving case. A thing isn't lost when you know where it is and I knew exactly where the shaving case was. It was in the bathroom of my Washington hotel room. I swore. There'd be no cleaning of teeth tonight; no morning shave; and worse, my new electric razor was in the damned thing, the one Alsa had given me to replace the one I had left in Russia.

'I want a call to Washington,' I said into the phone, 'The Drake Hotel.' You can do things like that in America. In Britain you spend half an hour waiting for Inquiries to answer because you have to have the number. Anyway, they told me the razor had been found and they'd send it on to London. Nice of them. Our pleasure, sir, and there was a call for you after you checked out.

I listened as he told me the call had come in from Gothenburg, Sweden, at 3 p.m. Washington time. From a Miss Alison Hay. They'd told her I'd gone, but she'd left a message just in case. Would I call her back and the matter was urgent. He gave me the number she'd left.

I hung up and looked at my watch. It would now be four in the morning in Gothenburg, I calculated, and urgent or not, a barbaric hour to telephone her. As it happened, I got the arithmetic wrong; by that time it was seven o'clock in the Swedish morning. Not that it would have made any difference . . .

## CHAPTER TWO

When Spinetti telephoned I was still asleep. I came to reluctantly and stretched out a dopey arm to pick up the receiver.

He said, 'Be out front in ten minutes.'

'Where is she?' The dopeyness slid away.

'We talk outside.'

'Hold on a sec.' I picked up my watch and scowled at it. Half-past six. Then I said, 'Food. Breakfast. Don't I get any?'

'Thought you were on a story.'

Some people have that idea. Reporters need neither food nor drink. All news editors believe it, in the same way they believe there's a telephone under every blade of grass. I said, "Twenty minutes,' hung up and crawled out of bed and under the shower.

I dressed quickly, grabbed my cassette recorder and notebook and hurried through to the snack counter in the fruit machine hall, drank a glass of orange juice, took two bites of a ham sandwich and a mouthful of coffee and hurried outside.

Spinetti had changed his clothes but the expression was limited as before. He was sitting inside a big white Oldsmobile and I watched myself hurry towards him in the twin mirrors of his sunglasses.

'Seventeen minutes,' I said. 'Not bad.'

'C'mon, huh?'

I climbed in beside him. 'What's the hurry?'

'Long ways to go,' he said. The engine was running and he was already easing the Olds into the traffic on the Strip as I was closing the car door.

'Arizona or California?' I was chewing the remaining mouthful of sandwich.

'You handle a boat?'

I frowned. 'What kind of boat?'

'Power boat.'

'Suppose so.' I'd mucked about the Solent and the Blackwater occasionally with water-struck friends.

'Like driving a car.'

'In that case I can handle a boat. But why?'

He didn't answer, concentrating on swinging the car through the early traffic. The road we took had three numbers, so presumably others branched off it. A sign pointed to Henderson, Boulder City and Kingman.

'The boat,' I reminded him gently. 'Why the boat?'

'Susannah's on the water. Hiding out on a cruiser. You rendezvous for the interview.'

I nodded, sat back, lit a cigarette, and watched the desert roll by. It's not a sand desert, just greyish stone and shale and mountains in the distance; the oases have petrol pumps, not palm trees.

After a while, I said, 'Some damn fool phoned me last night. Told me to get out of town pronto. It made me feel like John Wayne.'

I'd turned a little in my seat to watch his reaction and it wasn't quite what I'd expected. His jaw actually dropped, which meant he was either a very good actor or wasn't involved. He said, 'Who was it?'

'Didn't say. They just told me to get out of town.'

After a moment he said rustily, 'Why didn't you?'

'Serious, is it?'

'Have you . . . crossed some guy?'

'Frequently. But not in this country. Certainly not in Las Vegas. I only got here last night.'

Spinetti's jaw was tight. He reached into the dash and produced a Coke can, flipped the top open and drank. 'You thought it was some newspaperman playing tricksy, right?'

'Right.'

'Well, maybe.' He sounded far from convinced and I watched his eyes flicker to the rearview mirror.

'But you think not? Who usually tells people to get out of town?'

'How do I know? Listen –' he interrupted himself to take another swig from the can. 'Who you think runs this town?'

'Tell me.'

'Sure I'll tell you.' Spinetti's eyes darted again to the rearview mirror. 'The Mob runs it. For the Mob's benefit. Understand?'

I said, 'I wouldn't know a mobster from a Joshua tree. And they wouldn't know me. Why should they?'

He shrugged. 'Who knows?'

We drove on in silence, but his knuckles were whitish on the steering wheel and though it was morning cool, there was a shine of sweat on his tanned brow. After a while I began to feel it too, and turned to look back, but the road behind was empty.

We swung off to the left at a junction for Boulder City and the Oldsmobile slid along the wide highway at an easy

15

seventy that would have been pleasantly relaxing if there hadn't been all that tension in the driving seat. Spinetti was brown and broody, but at last he broke the silence. 'In your shoes, Sellers,' he said, 'I'd do like the man said. Right after the interview, I'd go. Maybe I'd go before.'

I nodded. A grey goose stamped on my grave somewhere and a little shudder ran across my shoulders. I said, 'When I've seen Susannah, there's nothing to keep me.'

'Not if you're wise.'

I was getting brown and broody myself. I was almost certain by now that Spinetti had had no part in the call and could think of nobody else, newsmen apart, who might have reason to want me out. Unless . . .

I said, 'Susannah. Who's she been involved with?'

'Just some guys. Like always.'

'People who wouldn't want her to talk to reporters?'

He thought about it. 'Maybe. I doubt that. But maybe. She chooses rough company some days.'

We came over a ridge, driving downhill towards a great sheet of smooth water. In the sunshine it looked cool and shiny-blue and beautiful, like a scene from a travel brochure, but better. We were dropping down towards the shore, where a lot of boats rode quietly at a marina. Spinetti said, 'Lake Mead.'

I looked at it with interest. Big things impress me, even if I try to resist, and this was, almost unbelievably, a man-made lake; water stretching away into the distance and desert and canyon walls all around.

I said, 'Where do we meet her?'

'Not us, Sellers. You.'

I had hoped I'd misunderstood him earlier. Clearly I hadn't. Suddenly the cool flat water looked a lot less inviting. 'All right. Where do *I* meet her?'

'Show you the map.' He pulled the car into an almost empty car park, climbed out and set off towards one of the marina's board walks where a man was crouched at the bow of some boat. As we approached, the man rose.

Spinetti said, 'You got a reservation for a boat hire.'

'Name, sir?'

'Sellers.'

The man pointed. 'This boat here, sir. All set.'

'Gas?'

'She's full.'

'Got a map?'

'Right aboard, sir. You got a credit card or somethin'?'

Spinetti turned to me. 'You have?'

I fished my trusty Diner's Card out of my wallet and followed the man into the office, signed the slip and returned to the boat with the information that it had a range of about a hundred and twenty miles.

Spinetti was already aboard. As I climbed after him, he spread the chart. 'Due north-east,' he said. 'See here. The entrance to Boulder Canyon.'

'How far?'

He shrugged. 'Twenty miles. Can't miss it. Just keep going. She's aboard a big cruiser called *Dragonfly*. Okay?'

'Okay,' I said. 'And when I come back, how do I get to Las Vegas?'

'Plenty of buses.'

'Well, thanks!'

'Look, bud, I got other things —'

I nodded and watched him step on to the boards and set off towards the car. As he moved away, my sense of loneliness increased; the wide water looked hostile rather than welcoming. It all seemed so crazy. Just another show business interview: two thousand words of bromides. And a joker who thought it was funny to warn me off. That made me think of telephones and reminded me of Alsa. I climbed out of the boat and went back to the office.

'Telephone?'

'Right over there.'

I searched my pockets but the little piece of paper wasn't there. Damn! I must have left it at the Dime Palace. I'd have to call Alsa later in the day.

I remember wondering why in hell Alsa was calling me from Sweden, anyway. I don't know about presentiments.

But I sensed something was wrong and as I walked back to the boat in the rapidly warming air and watched the bright sun bouncing off the lake, the world seemed to me to be quiet and peaceful and very beautiful – and yet haloed with inexplicable menace. I stood for a moment on the boards, watching a few big lake trout nosing around just under the surface, and thinking about Scown, trying to imagine his reaction if I ducked out and tried to explain why. He'd sit and stare at me in silence, but the words would come across telepathically, and the message would be: *Over the hill.* Then there'd be a ritual burst of anger and the rest of my life tied by one leg to a desk. Scown himself could, would and had walked through walls chasing stories. There'd been wounds as a war correspondent, arraignment at the bar of the House of Commons for well justified contempt, and all the time the steady upward climb. Finally the thought of telling Scown I'd been scared off by a bright lonely morning and a trick phone call actually made me grin to myself and I walked across to the boat and got in while the mood held.

For a few minutes the unfamiliar mechanics of handling the boat in a confined space kept my mind off everything else. There were some large and expensive toys parked in the marina and I have a phobia about damaged paint and insurance companies and negligence, but finally I was nosing out on to Lake Mead with the engine burbling happily and the water swishing beneath. There wasn't a cloud or a breath of wind. All that was missing from the whole adman's set-up was the blonde and the long cool drink, and both were waiting twenty miles up the lake. If I knew that particular blonde the long, cool drink would already be in her hand, and it wouldn't be the first of the day. Susannah Rhodes breakfasted off Bloody Marys.

A bit more throttle and the boat tucked her tail down determinedly. I glanced round. I was still alone on the water. More throttle still; the engine snarled happily, the bow lifted and quite suddenly I was enjoying myself. It's funny how the mind changes gear; the thoughts of a few minutes before had been blasted away by nothing more concrete than the roar of a healthy engine and the hiss of flying water. No wonder supermarkets use sweet sounds to sell groceries.

I sat back, consciously straightening my arms against the steering wheel like a grand prix driver. If Alsa'd been there she'd have said, 'Your great baby!' and laughed at me. I'd have purred like a kitten and asked her to marry me and she'd have refused again and said, like someone reciting Tennyson, that her heart belonged to another. She'd said it so many times I was beginning to believe it, in spite of the mock nineteenth century earnestness.

The sheer exhilaration of driving that speedboat was inducing its own kind of weird optimism and it occurred to me suddenly that she might have phoned from Gothenburg to say yes. But it wasn't true and I knew it. If Alsa'd intended to say yes, she'd have spent the money the phone call cost on a table cloth for her bottom drawer and written a quiet letter.

So why had she phoned? To let me know she'd actually reached Gothenburg, perhaps. A feminine cry of triumph – I've done it, and you didn't! Well, if she was in Gothenburg, it must be true; she'd worked Scown's little deal for him without being slung out of Russia the way they'd heaved me out. Two hours to pack and an escort to the plane, because I'd got a little tight and made a few mildly uncomplimentary remarks.

Scown's Russian scheme was typical of him. He wasn't content that the *Daily News* sold four million in Britain; he had his eye on larger horizons: Common Market editions, electronic print-out news eventually and a curious little quirk of ambition that made him want his to be the first Western newspaper on open sale in Russia. You could tell him the Russians wouldn't allow it in a million years, and he'd say, like a stockbroker, that it was a matter of confidence. As a start, he'd cornered some visiting Soviet Minister and offered to publish a magazine about Russia in Britain, using Russian material. Naturally enough they liked the idea and made very faintly encouraging hum-and-ha noises about the *Daily News* going on sale in Russia. One of these days. Eventually. So I'd gone out to rifle the files at the Moscow Number One State Magazine Publishing House for suitable stories and pictures. The scheme looked like lapsing when they threw me out, but Scown had breathed fire and life back into it and sent Alsa to pick up where I'd left off, in the certain knowledge that the Russians, like everybody else, would lay down their coats in icy puddles so Alsa could keep her feet dry.

Well, good for her! And if I were the woman's editor of the *Daily News,* I'd start watching my back. Alsa wouldn't stick a knife in anybody, but Scown would see Alsa as deserving of reward and he was as quick with a blade as D'Artagnan, without the same fine line in scruple.

I also felt a sharp stab of envy for whichever slick young Swede at the Gothenburg printers was assigned to look after her while the magazine was produced. No, on second thoughts, I felt no envy at all, because in a few days he'd find himself waving goodbye at the airport and wondering why the world was so empty and forlorn all of a sudden.

I returned my attention to my own empty world, feeling the need for a cigarette, and crouched behind the windscreen to light it. Then I straightened and looked around. A couple of big concrete towers had come into view behind me, presumably part of the works at the Hoover Dam, which banks up the water to form Lake Mead. Over on my right, what looked like a sheer rock wall rose away from the lake shore, but I didn't look that way too long because the sunlight flashed more dazzlingly by the minute off the shiny water. And still there was nobody on the lake. The only sign of man was a high white contrail rigid as a ruler in the substratosphere.

After about another twenty minutes, the lake began to narrow and the high walls marched towards me. I seemed to be heading directly for the end of the lake, but the chart told me the water swung to the right into the neck of Boulder Canyon a few miles ahead. I began to keep my eyes skinned, feeling a reluctant admiration for Spinetti for choosing to hide Susannah Rhodes here on the lake, where comfort, privacy and a first-class means of escape could exist in the single convenient shape of a big, fast boat.

Soon there was a giant rearing rock bluff to my right and I swung the boat around it, waiting for Susannah's floating hide-out to come into view. My course seemed to make the bluff move aside like a curtain, unveiling ever more of the shadowed water behind, and it kept coming until there was no new water to see. There was no sign of a cruiser either, or any other boat for that matter; just the vast, precipitous gorge of Boulder Canyon reaching emptily to the north-east, with sunlight high on one rock wall and the other darkly shaded.

I throttled well back until my boat was barely nudging ahead and looked around, but there was nothing ahead, nothing behind. I hadn't passed the cruiser on the way, so maybe she was coming from the other direction, down the canyon from the upper part of the lake. If so, perhaps I should go ahead and rendezvous in the canyon. I set the boat moving fast ahead and slid rapidly in between the towering walls, leaving the vee of my wake to wash against them.

Ten minutes later I was still going fast, the canyon was funnelling wider and the great sweep of the upper lake was spreading before me. But no cruiser. I shrugged. This wasn't where we were supposed to rendezvous. She was late, that's all, and I'd better go back to the right place.

I spun the steering wheel to bring the bow round, and five yards ahead of me something plucked at the water. A fish, probably, rising for a fly. But a second later the same thing happened again and it was no fish. Above the engine's burble I heard sharp cracks echoing between the rock walls. Christ, was it an avalanche? I looked upward scanning the cliffs anxiously, and saw a man's coloured shirt way up high. Then there was another crack. Something smacked my bow and there was a sudden tiny hole in the white paint. Bewildered, I looked upward again and saw the figure on the cliff extend an arm to point up the lake. His other hand held the rifle.

# CHAPTER THREE

I gunned the throttle and spun the wheel to try and get in beneath the cliff, but rifle bullets are faster than speedboats and another one smacked into the superstructure warningly. I glanced up at him again. The distance wasn't much more than eighty yards and I was worried the boat would already be taking water. Maybe that was what he intended: to sink the boat and let me drown. But no, he was pointing again, pointing up to the huge sheet of the upper lake.

There was no alternative; I brought the boat round again and began to move obediently out of the canyon's funnel mouth, wondering where the hell I was supposed to be going, and why and who was sending me there. Presumably this all fitted in with last night's phone call. It also seemed to involve Susannah Rhodes, but for the life of me, I couldn't see why. Susannah was a mixed-up, stupid blonde who happened to have been neatly assembled to a genetic pattern of current public appeal, but she had neither the will-power nor the reason to be involved in this kind of situation. Spinetti must be involved, though. A lot of fingers pointed to Spinetti. But I couldn't understand why, in that case, he'd been so surprised when I told him about the warning.

Glancing back, I could still see the rifleman, a dwindling figure now, high on the cliff, waiting to make sure I didn't turn and make a dash for it. But suicidal I'm not. War correspondents have to chance their lives; so sometimes do crime reporters and air correspondents; showbusiness writers never risk anything but cirrhosis. And for the moment, though not by choice, I was pure showbiz. I kept moving forward, swivelling my eyes across the water in the unjustified hope of finding some clue to what was happening. But there was nothing for several minutes. Then, from a dark gap in the rocks, two boats appeared behind me, power cruisers with rakish lines. They took up station perhaps half a mile back. Was one of them *Dragonfly*? Perhaps this whole stupid rigmarole was part of the rendezvous arrangements? Nonsense! Film stars do have bodyguards, but not to take pot shots at reporters arriving to keep an appointment for a story on which money is changing hands.

All the same, I slowed. When the boats came near, my eyes would tell me if one was *Dragonfly*. They didn't, though. It must have been a moment or two before they realized what I was doing, because the gap closed a little, but then they slowed, too. All right. What would happen if I speeded up? I opened the throttle and my speedboat surged forward, bow rising to skim the water. In a minute or so I must have been doing forty miles an hour. But so were the cruisers.

That answered another question anyway. I couldn't outrun them. But why on earth were they just keeping station? I reached for the map and began to examine possibilities. There was something called Bonelli Landing more or less due south and ten miles away, but the indications were that it was just a place to go ashore and was surrounded by desert. For the rest, three places lay ahead. The names were Echo Bay, Rogers Spring and Overton Beach and none of them meant anything to me. Apart from them there was nothing but the water and empty desert country.

All I could do was to keep heading north.

After a few minutes I rounded a sharp foreland and the whole length of the upper lake came into view. I'd been heading east. Now I swung more or less due north and for a moment I entertained a faint and fatuous hope tht I was wrong about the cruisers, that their presence half a mile behind me was just coincidence and that they'd sheer off elsewhere. But the way they swung smoothly after me, they could have been under tow.

How far to Echo Bay, then? Twelve or thirteen miles. All right, we'd see what happened there.

What happened was that a couple of miles short of Echo Bay one of the cruisers tore up on my left and inserted itself between me and the shore. A man then appeared on the decking. He was holding a long thin something that was presumably a rifle and his arm pointed northward. So there *was* a purpose of some kind to all this! I tried to understand where and why, but the equation was insoluble; query plus query equals plus or minus query. Who the hell were those bastards!

Whoever they were, they had control. I'd turned the boat's nose a bit. Now I turned it back again and continued up Lake Mead. The cruiser between me and the shore remained between me and the shore; the other had moved out slightly. Four or five miles later Rogers Spring came and went. That left only Overton Beach. Beyond there, so the map told me, the lake forked in two: left fork blind, right leading into the Virgin River. Well, they'd want me to steer one way or the other; no doubt they'd let me know.

Now the cruiser to my right was closing, the other one dropping back, and Overton Beach was visible maybe a mile and a half ahead. The two cruisers were perhaps six hundred yards behind me, the three of us making the points of a neat equilateral triangle on the water.

It occurred to me that on sudden full throttle I might nip into Overton Beach before them. I stared ahead, wondering what I'd do when I got there. The cruisers wouldn't be far behind; there was at least one rifle aboard one of them, and perhaps more. On the other hand, north of Overton Beach the lake shore was uninhabited and there'd be nowhere to run. Along the Virgin River there wasn't even a road for twenty miles.

Should I? Dare I? In the end it wasn't really a conscious decision at all; some instinct made the movement for me and the throttle was snapped open, the engine roaring and I was creaming in towards Overton Beach as fast as the speedboat could go.

I crouched low, making as small a target as possible, uncomfortably aware that the petrol tank was squarely behind me. As the boat blasted towards Overton Beach I made out a jetty of sorts and a long, low modern building behind that looked like a motel or restaurant or both. With the roar of the engine in my ears, there was no way of knowing whether anybody was shooting; I'd only know that if I, or that damned petrol tank, were hit. But I'd made my choice: I was running and now I had to decide where I was running to!

It would be stupid to try to land on the jetty itself. There I'd be ludicrously exposed. I decided to drive the boat directly on to the beach. Unless I was desperately unlucky, the speedboat's shallow draught would make that possible for *me*, but the cruisers would sit deeper in the water and have to approach the jetty.

Something fizzed by me and I didn't need two guesses at what it was. Then I actually saw, ahead of me on the smooth water, the angry little splash of another bullet. It was mad to run; suddenly I knew how mad it was to run. But wouldn't it be equally mad to slow down, to let them catch me again, to offer myself tamely for whatever they had in mind?

I swung the steering wheel from side to side, zigzagging towards the shore, hoping that made me a more difficult target. Now the wooden jetty was leaping towards me and beyond it the grey desert shale sloped upwards from the water's edge. I tore in a wide arc towards the end of the jetty, then snapped the throttle shut as the boat raced towards the beach. Also, I bloody nearly killed myself. I realized suddenly that hitting the beach at that speed would be almost like hitting a wall, and swung up my legs to brace them against the edge of the front decking. The boat struck with a sudden, murderous grating sound, and the stern swung round like a whip, catapulting me into the shallow water. If it had flung me on to the shale, I'd have been skinned; as it was I was merely soaked and shaken and only a few feet from the edge.

Getting to my feet, I splashed wildly out of the water and began to run towards the building. A rapid glance back showed the two cruisers moving quickly towards the jetty. And up ahead, the building seemed deserted. I'd maybe sixty yards to cover and before I'd gone twenty I realized just how hot it was. On the water, moving fast, I hadn't felt the heat; here on land it was as though I'd stepped into an oven. God but I'd been stupid!

My soaking clothes clung to my skin as I raced up the slight incline. The whole place looked deserted, too; windows reflecting the sun back seemed both blind and blinding. I was out of the pan and into the fire with a vengeance. Another glance back as I came close to the building. The two cruisers were approaching the jetty now, one on each side, and men were poised aboard them to jump ashore and come after me.

I ducked quickly round the corner of the building and saw the glass doors with the 'closed' sign hanging discouragingly. I looked round wildly, frantically, for some kind of bolt hole, but there was just the bare asphalt of the approach road. In a few minutes, I thought despairingly, I'd be trapped, held firmly in the sights of a rifle with the bleak choice of surrendering or being shot. If they gave me the choice!

I sprinted across the front of the building and turned the corner. A car park. Two cars. And a man getting out of one of them twenty yards away. Probably he ran the place and was just arriving to open up. He turned inquiringly as he heard my running footsteps.

'Happened to you?'

'I'm being chased. Hunted,' I gasped. I knew how stupid it must sound. 'There are men with rifles! Help me, for God's sake!'

He stared at me for a second. I said, 'Quickly. Please. Get me away from here!' – wondering what I'd have done in his place.

"Kay. Get in!' He flung the door wide and I more or less dived across the front seat, scrambling to the far side. Rapidly he slid in beside me. The motor spun and the tyres squealed as the car tore out of the park towards the road.

'Thanks. Christ, thanks!' I stared across him, waiting for my pursuers to come into view round the angle of the building. And they did; four men, moving fast. One raised his rifle and fired as the car lurched on to the approach road, but we weren't hit. A few seconds later they were out of sight as the car tore over a little rise. I began to explain: 'I don't know why. They just – '

'Save it.' He was concentrating on what he was doing, whamming the big car along the shimmering tarmac with skill and judgment, hands easy on the wheel. The soft suspension bounced us, but he took the bends easily, sun-tanned face still but watchful.

After three or four miles there was a crossroads. Signs pointed left to Echo Bay and Las Vegas, right to Glendale. We took neither, ploughing straight on. As I stared ahead the scenery changed with startling suddenness from greyish shale to weird reddish rock. Another sign came up SCENIC RIM DRIVE: VALLEY OF FIRE STATE PARK and he swung left, away from it, plunging down a lesser road among the red rock formations.

We'd both looked back pretty often, he through the mirror, I by turning in my seat. So far I'd seen nothing. But now I did. A blue car was racing over the rise behind us. I watched it in dismay. The empty car at Overton Beach had been blue, too . . .

That was when he began to brake. I turned in surprise, but the braking was sharp and the big car slowed suddenly, fling-ing me forward, almost out of my seat. By the time I'd grabbed the padded ledge and was pushing myself back, he'd stopped. Also a revolver had appeared in his hand and was pointing at me.

'Out,' he said.

'But – '

'Out.'

The tanned face was expressionless. I said, 'They're right behind – '

'I'll count to three.'

I forced my eyes away from him, looking back up the road. The blue car was closing fast. I said, 'They'll kill me.'

'One.'

'Christ!' I reached behind me, for the door handle.

'Two.'

I pulled the handle, swung the door open and lurched out. The blue car was only a couple of hundred yards away and slowing. I looked round me desperately. There was a gap of sorts in the rearing rocks at the roadside. I flung myself towards its doubtful shelter.

## CHAPTER FOUR

As I stumbled quickly between the sheltering rocks, I heard the car stop and doors open and close. Then there was silence. I kept going, frantic to get space and distance between myself and the road. Already I was disturbingly conscious of the heat. The sun blasted down out of a brilliant sky; there was no wind; the spaces between the rocks were filled with air so hot it was uncomfortable to breathe. In the open spaces it was worse. I tripped and fell, then dragged myself to my feet and plunged on between two red, rock outcrops. Within fifty yards sweat was streaming off me. Then five more yards and a bend in the narrow passage and I was faced with a blind end, a massive lump of red sandstone ten feet high, blocking the way. But it was fissured, there were big cracks. Maybe I could scramble up . . . I tore at it, jammed my foot into a low crevice, grabbed for handholds, and forced my way up. Seven or eight feet above ground was a narrow ledge and I strained to reach it, managed to haul myself up. From there to the top was simple: two easy footholds and I was standing, then flinging myself flat as a bullet sang by.

The rock was intensely hot to the touch; I could feel it even through my soaking clothes and it was too hot for my bare hands. All the same, I had to get off the flat top of that rock. I turned, rolling over across the bumpy, scorching surface towards the far edge and glanced down. The drop was a good fifteen feet into a rough fissure strewn with stones. I swung my legs over the edge and eased my body backward, trying to grip the smooth rock with hands that demanded relief from the burning contact with the red sandstone. Then my feet found a ledge, but there was nothing for my hands, no way down but to jump and pray I didn't break leg or ankle.

The jar as I landed hammered at joints I scarcely knew I had, and drove the breath out of me, but at least there was a passage now and it seemed to offer a route away through the stone jungle. I staggered bone-achingly on, threading my way along the defile.

'Over here!' The shout came from behind me, and not so far behind at that. I looked over my shoulder and saw a man standing, not fifty yards away, on top of a rock. He was raising his rifle. I flung myself sideways into the shelter of a boulder and heard the crack of the shot. Now if I moved it would be into the open into his sights. But no, there was another gap, dark in the sweltering shadow, four or five feet away. I took a deep breath, launched myself into it and found that a rocky track led steeply upward. By now I could scarcely breathe; the heat was unbelievable, the air itself seemed to scorch my lungs, sweat cascaded out of my hair and off my forehead and ran saltily into my eyes. Valley of Fire the sign had said, one place in the burning Nevada desert that had been singled out for its heat, one place hotter than all the others. Oh God!

I staggered up the narrow track, my heart beginning to hammer frighteningly. Then I blundered out into the open, where another defile crossed mine and instantly a rifle cracked and I heard the bullet fizz by, smacking into a rock to my right.

I dived forward, flinging my body headlong into the defile ahead, scraping knees and elbows painfully on the rough sandstone. It was like diving on to emery paper. But I was up quickly and driving my body forward because there was nothing else I could do. It couldn't go on. I'd travelled only about a quarter mile and I was almost exhausted, my energy was being drained away fast by the murderous combination of heat and height. Up there, three or four thousand feet above sea level, the air is thinner. I was flogging along with my sea-level lungs and a body accustomed to temperate climates, in a high-altitude desert.

Trying to move fast, I knew I was slowing with every step, forcing each leg forward with my hands on my knees, not even aware until I heard the shot that I'd left shelter and was exposed again. Blindly I flung myself flat, but on to a lump of rock that smashed against my ribs and sent a tremendous flash of pain through my body. I glanced back dizzily. I could see nobody, but that didn't mean a thing; they could be in any of a hundred places, waiting to pick me off as I rose. I didn't rise. I edged my body agonizingly forward across the baking rock until I could slide into a dark, protected crevice and crouched there, gasping, knowing I was done. I no longer had the strength to run, barely the strength to crawl. I was bruised and beginning to suffer from oxygen starvation; sweat was sluicing out of me and the sun was hot as hell. What lay ahead, if I lived that long, was heatstroke.

That was when the thought struck me. I don't know why it hadn't hit me before. It came in the form of a question, and the question was: if they were hunting me with rifles, why in hell hadn't they hit me? Because they were bad shots? Hardly. At forty or fifty yards it's not difficult to hit a man-sized target. Then why? Even to think was appallingly difficult. I felt as though I were crouching in a furnace and my mind seemed to be only a quarter my own. I forced myself to concentrate. On the lake I'd been forced along, shepherded, driven northward. And then, at Overton Beach, there hadn't been a cruiser between me and the shore. And in the car . . . the shot that had been fired at the car had missed. From fifty yards it had missed a car? A *car*! The driver had been in cahoots too, waiting for me. That's why they hadn't hit the car. But up here? Among the red rocks? A rifleman need only go high, wait for me to show myself and pick me off.

True or false?

It could only be true. So why was I still in one sweaty piece? There had been at least two easy chances.

I thought I knew the answer, but still I weighed it carefully. The only possible answer seemed to be that they hadn't shot me because they didn't want to shoot me. But *was* that the only possible answer? It seemed to be, unless they were all blind and their hands trembled as badly as mine. Which couldn't be true. They could stroll in the heat, come slowly and easily towards an unarmed man. Also, they'd be accustomed to the temperature, to the high land.

No. The first answer must be the right one. They didn't want to shoot me. Next question: what *did* they want? No answer; no way of guessing. I didn't begin to comprehend what was happening. But . . . I clung to the one thought: they weren't going to shoot me!

Slowly I forced myself to stand upright and looked round for a way to the top of the rocks. If I was wrong, they'd shoot me now instead of ten minutes from now, by which time I'd be a sweating, semi-conscious wreck a short distance farther on.

Over there. Over there it would be easier. There was a worn rock forming almost a staircase upward. I began to climb, awkwardly because my strength was almost gone, making each upward step with an audible grunt of effort. One more yard and I would be in clear sight. I hesitated. What if I were wrong? But I already knew the answer to that. I took a deep, gasping breath and forced myself higher.

*Crack!* The bullet smacked into the sandstone a yard from me and instinctively I almost dived for cover again. I was trembling so much I could hardly keep my balance, but I forced myself to straighten and turned my head to look in the direction from which the shot had come. A man was standing there, atop a rock, rifle at his shoulder, perhaps forty yards away. As I watched he moved his head to sight and fired again and red stone chips flew from the rock a couple of feet away. Two shots at forty yards. Two shots

31

that missed. I struggled one weary step higher, straightened and stood with my hands loose at my sides, staring across at him.

Then a movement caught my eye. Another man, another rifle, off to my right. The next shot came from him and it, too, flew by. I looked round. There were two more of them, an arc of four men, all with rifles at the shoulder, all close. And quite suddenly they all started firing at once. God knows how many shots there were! And God knows why I didn't fling myself down on the blistering rock! From four directions the shots whistled past, one after another, a stutter of firing that sounded almost like a machine gun. I remember closing my eyes, clamping my teeth together, waiting for one to hit me. It seemed impossible that among all that rifle fire not one bullet should touch me, even by accident.

Then, suddenly the last sounds had bounced away among the rocks and I was standing in an incredible flat silence, uninjured, looking across that weird landscape from one man to the next. For all of a minute it stayed like that. Then one of them shouted, 'Okay, let's go!' And they turned their backs to me and began to move slowly away, back down towards the road.

Maybe it was the relief, perhaps sheer weakness, but I was suddenly dizzy and almost passed out. I know I stood swaying in the burning sunlight until the sheer heat of it reminded me that to collapse on the spot would be more certainly lethal than the rifle fire.

It took me nearly an hour to pick my way back to the road and even though it was downhill, I wasn't recovering at all. Sweat still flooded out of me, breathing was difficult. I remember glancing at my watch and being astonished that it was still only eleven, and realizing that the worst of the heat was still to come. The two cars had long gone, of course, and the road was deserted. I stood beside it for a little while until I realized just how hot the sun was on my head and neck, so I found myself a shady place beside a big boulder and crouched there, waiting. It was forty minutes before a vehicle came along and I must have been half-dozing because I almost missed it. In a panic I staggered out of the shade on to the road, waving my arms, and forced it to stop or run me down.

I blinked at it. The car was bright and clean and shiny and the blazing sun shone blindingly off its chromium. Then the door opened and a middle-aged woman got out. When she spoke, there was a quaver in her voice.

'Is something wrong?'

I almost laughed, not because the words were funny, or even because they were conventional, but because I was close to hysteria.

I said, simply, 'I got lost.' My mouth was so dry it hurt to speak.

'Lost?' The quaver was still there. She was torn between a wish to help and fear of this unknown stranger on a lonely road.

'Lost,' I croaked. 'I've been out in the sun. Have you water?'

'Water? No.'

'Could you give me a lift?'

'You're British?'

'Yes.'

The quaver disappeared. Nobody's afraid of the British, I suppose. She said, 'I'm going to Vegas.'

I managed a grin of thanks. 'Perfect!'

Only two miles along the road we came to a building labelled Visitor Center and she stopped. 'There'll be water in there.'

There was. I drank about six pints of it and walked back to the car feeling it switching round inside me. I'd also washed and I felt better.

We talked a bit on the fifty miles or so into Las Vegas. However had I got lost? I told her a little lie about setting off for a walk from Echo Bay. Walk! She was horrified and gave me a long, solicitous lecture on the manifold dangers of walking in the United States. It wasn't she said, like England. She was right there.

She was a nice woman, her ancestors came from Noocastle,

and she insisted on driving me right to the Dime Palace, where she warned me again with some severity about walking, and drove away with a wave.

I walked into the foyer, and a large man in a uniform that would have stifled him five yards away from the air conditioning, looked at my dishevelled state as though he was contemplating throwing me back on to the street.

'Four-one-oh-five, please.'

'Here it is, sir.' The smiling girl handed me an envelope along with my room key. I looked at it for a moment then ripped it open with my thumb. A single sheet of paper, folded once, no signature, type-written. It read: 'Take three o'clock United Airlines flight Chicago. Connect direct to London. You will be watched. If you do not go, you will be killed.'

I swallowed. The message was clear enough, the morning's horror recent enough. I still didn't understand why, couldn't see how I could be a danger to anyone, or why it should be necessary to somebody to get me out of the US. But evidently it was, and Susannah Rhodes certainly wasn't worth staying for. Not at the price I'd pay. Alex Scown would be annoyed or worse, but Scown at least wasn't a killer. Not in the short term, anyway.

I said, 'My account please.'

'Cashier's counter is right over there, sir.'

I waited for my bill and paid it, went and had a cup of coffee and a hot pastrami sandwich at the casino snack counter, and then went up to my room. I hesitated before going in but when I finally summoned up the courage it was empty. There weren't any message lights on the phone either. Presumably they thought I'd have got the message now, loud and clear. And so I had.

When I'd showered and put on some clean clothes, I sat on the bed and tried to phone Alsa, but there was an hour and a half's delay on calls to Gothenburg. I then tried to telephone Spinetti but he was out. His girl didn't know when he'd be back. She knew nothing about me, nothing about the arrangements and sure wasn't interested. Nor, by that time, was I. I used my cable card to send a message to London. There was no point in phoning because I was telling not asking, and not even Scown would change my mind for me. After that I slung my goods in a bag, and winced as I remembered the tape recorder I'd left in the boat. Not that Scown would mind; it wasn't his machine. But my possessions were certainly getting scattered.

I waited out front until a cab arrived, my suitcase ostentatiously at my feet to proclaim to the world at large and watching eyes in particular that I was in fact departing, then rode out to the airport.

At the United Airlines desk, I inquired whether any seats remained on the three o'clock flight for Chicago.

'I'll see, sir. What name?'

'Sellers.'

'One moment, please.' The clerk looked at his list. 'Sellers *is* the name?'

'Yes.'

'Already a reservation for you, sir.' He wore that patient look given to idiots by people paid to be polite.

'Thanks.' I handed him my ticket and my credit card and waited while the new ticket was made out. Then I handed over my suitcase, went along to the departure gate waiting room, and sat watching the other intending passengers in a furtive kind of way to see if I could discover which of them was doing the same to me.

I suppose somebody must have been there, but I didn't spot him. I didn't spot him in Chicago, either, which was hardly surprising because O'Hare International Airport's a big place and by that time three restorative Scotches were cutting down my powers of concentration a little. I added a fourth in the soothing coolth of the Four Seasons bar while I waited for the British Airways Chicago-Montreal-London flight to be called. There was still an hour's delay for Gothenburg and I hadn't an hour.

I've taken that flight before. At Montreal it fills up with parcel-laden, misty-eyed grandmothers heading back to Bristol or Bury St Edmunds, but the Chicago-Montreal leg

35

isn't exactly jammed. This time there were six of us scattered thinly around the cabin of the VC10. The captain, as captains will with an almost empty aircraft, gave a performance demonstration, taking it up like an express lift then levelling off to hot-rod through the airways, while the cabin staff kept the passengers amused. There were three stewardesses and a steward between the six of us, so the service was excellent and less starchy than usual. While I sipped my Bell's and water, a pretty blonde girl with shiny, much-brushed hair, chatted me up a bit, went away and came back.

'There's another journalist aboard,' she announced, all helpful.

I responded politely. 'Oh?' He could be one of the drunks from El Vino's and I'd be back in El Vino's soon enough, thank you. It's a bar in Fleet Street. *In El Vino's nil veritas*. Not much, anyway, and not often.

'Would you like to meet him, sir?' They maintain certain standards, these girls; people must be properly introduced. When there's time, anyway.

'What's his name?' I asked cautiously.

'Mr Elliot, sir. He's American.'

I said, 'I'm sorry to be finicky, but does he look the reminiscent type? I don't want ten hours of past triumphs.'

She smiled. A nice smile. 'He seems rather quiet, sir. He works for the National Geographic.'

She nodded towards the back of a head six rows nearer the nose. Another girl was talking to him, Presumably sounding him out about me.

'Well . . .' I hesitated.

She giggled. 'We're picking up a hundred and thirty war brides' mothers in Montreal. Not one much under seventy-five.'

'That settles it. I'll join him. Will you bring a pair of Bells, please.'

We were properly introduced, hand-shaking, smiling politely and sizing one another up in the usual kind of way. He was pleasant enough, a tall, rangy, bespectacled man, fortyish, lantern-jawed, with dark thinning hair and a worry line or two on his forehead. We didn't talk a great deal, just the usual mild arguments about who'd pay as glasses were replenished; the kind of argument that amounts really to keeping score.

We had dinner after take-off from Dorval, Montreal, not talking much because it would have been difficult to make ourselves heard above all the grandmotherly pride and the negotiations about exchanging seats and who was to look at whose snapshots first. Then, smiling at the noise and each other, we tilted the seats back and slept until we flew out of darkness into brilliant dawn sunlight above the clouds. When we woke up, we looked at each other sympathetically, both dry-mouthed from the whisky and I persuaded the shiny-haired girl to bring orange juice.

'Where are you going?' I asked after a while. The long day stretched ahead and he must be going somewhere.

'Lapland.'

'If I recall,' I said, 'National Geographic has done Lapland before.'

He grinned. 'Three hundred and eighty-two times. But it's a lot of territory. You?'

'Back to base.'

'Where've you been?'

I hesitated, then told him about Las Vegas. Not all of it; just that I'd been threatened and decided safety lay in flight.

He raised his eyebrows. 'You must have crossed somebody. The Mob's pretty sensitive.'

'But you're not surprised?'

'Not any more. Times have changed. You know, we've got a thing called Trick or Treat. The kids play jokes on people, knock on doors and run away. Kind of a sacred custom, right? People hand out candy and apples. Well, a little girl I know got an apple with a razor blade inside. Nothing surprises me any more. You were right to leave. Tell your boss I said so.'

'Hope he'll believe it.'

He laughed. 'Yeah. They never do. Who d'you work for?'

So we talked shop, gently and companionably, as the VC10 started its slow run in from somewhere over Northern Ireland, then shared a cab into London from Heathrow.

I went direct to the *News* building and up to Scown's office. Neither of his secretaries was there, but their coats were and voices could be heard faintly through the teak door. I put my suitcase down and sat down to wait. About ten minutes later the editor, Rowlands, came out looking worried, with the shreds of that day's paper in mournful hands. Not that that was in any way remarkable. Three hundred people sweated sixteen hours to put it together; Scown tore it apart in ten minutes of choice phraseology. Then the operation began again, six days a week. Rowlands glanced at me, shrugged, and gave a thin grin as he went by. But Scown must have seen me through the doorway, because a moment later Secretary Two appeared. 'Mr Scown would like to see you now, Mr Sellers.'

I swallowed and rose. Just a few hours earlier I'd been cringing, exhausted and terrified, in the Valley of Fire. My emotions, as I entered Scown's office were not dissimilar. The two secretaries exited slickly past me, getting out of range.

The stiff quiff of white hair with the wave in it bristled up from his forehead and the cold blue eyes looked me over. 'Well?'

I told him. Briefly. He likes short sentences, Scown does. Then I waited for the blast.

He said, 'Money up the spout. Good story lost.'

I blinked. It was like being tapped with a feather when you're expecting to be hit by a bus. There'd be more to come.

Surprisingly there wasn't. He said, 'Silly cow!'

'Susannah. Yes, she is.'

'Not her, you bloody idiot. Alison Hay.'

Alsa! That phone call. Damn! I said, 'Why? What's she done?'

He looked up at me for a moment and there was something in his eyes I hadn't seen before. He said, 'Christ only knows. She's vanished.'

# CHAPTER FIVE

'Off the face of the bloody earth,' Scown said. He was staring at me angrily, but the anger wasn't for me.

My whole body seemed to tighten, then shrivel. Alsa? Vanished? 'Where?' I demanded.

'She was in Gothenburg,' Scown was a Scot but the accent was usually neutral. At moments of stress he reverted a bit, and he was reverting now; the *o* of Gothenburg was contemptuously emphasized.

'When?'

'Night before last.' That was when she'd phoned me.

Scown knew what he was telling me, and what I was feeling. Alsa was something special in several people's lives, including both of ours. Her father had been Scown's only real friend and Scown had worked him into an early grave by way of gratitude. But long before that Joe had plucked me off the *Yorkshire Post* and opened his kingdom and his home to me. Like his daughter, Joe Hay had been the special kind, with heavy emphasis on the word kind. Though there wasn't much humanity left in Scown, what trace there was had been directed at Alsa since Joe's death. But he had weird ways of showing it, like sending her to Russia.

'What happened?'

'She phoned me. When she got in from Moscow. She was okay then. Night before last, fairly late, she rang the local police.'

'Why?'

'She said . . .' He paused. 'It's bloody stupid. She told them she was in danger. Asked for help. When they got to her hotel, she'd gone. No message. Nothing.'

'And nothing since?'

'No.' He exhaled hard through his nose in exasperation, nostrils widening. 'Not a bloody word.'

'What do the police say?'

'What do they ever say? Bugger all!'

It was rare to see Scown looking and feeling helpless. Another time I might have enjoyed the sight; now, somehow, it underscored the nastiness. 'Who's over there?'

'Nobody.'

'Why not, for God's sake?'

'Because the police said no. That's why.'

'And you're supine? You just say "yes, inspector." '

'Don't bloody well talk to me like that!'

I stared at him, astonished that I'd done so already. All right then, I'd go on. I said, 'Alsa Hay. Joe's daughter. And some copper says keep off and you do! Jesus Christ!'

Scown was angry now, too. Those pale blue eyes were very hard. He said, 'That's how it is.'

'Not for long.' I turned and headed for the door.

'Where d'you think you're going?'

I said, 'Gothenburg,' over my shoulder and kept walking.

He said 'No!' The familiar monosyllable with the familiar sound, like a steel shutter dropping.

At the door I turned angrily. 'There are two secretaries out there,' I said. 'One of them can type out my resignation.'

'Come here.' He sat behind his big desk like a not too-quiescent volcano. The habit of obedience to Scown was strong, but this time not strong enough. I didn't reply, just reached for the door handle.

Behind me Scown said, 'We're warned off.'

That stopped me. I turned to face him.

'By whom?'

He stood up suddenly, prowled over to the big floor-to-ceiling picture window, and stared coldly at the dome of St Paul's. 'Official circles.'

I set off back across the carpet. 'Which ones?'

'Big ones.'

'And you're – '

'I'm doing as I'm bloody well told. *I* don't like it either.'

'Otherwise you don't get your knighthood!'

He swung round at me, furious, but for once I got in first.

I said. 'The resignation stands. You do what you like. If you think you're bound, you're bound. But you don't bind me. Not where Alsa's concerned.'

'Accepted!' He was boiling. But he was also Scown. I was outside dictating the letter of resignation to Secretary One when the door opened again and he said mildly, 'Come back in, John. You'd better know.'

I followed him and waited.

He said, 'She told me something on the phone. When she left Moscow there was some kind of panic. They stopped her and searched her stuff. Very polite and proper, she said.'

I went suddenly cold. 'She was carrying something?'

He shook his head.

'She thought it was just funny. She'd got a pile of pictures and a lot of them were transparencies. The Russians said they thought she'd picked up the front cover of one of their magazines by mistake.'

'And had she?'

'She said not.'

'Official circles,' I said angrily, 'means MI6 or somebody, doesn't it? *You* let them use *her*?'

He didn't reply. Instead he walked to the wall, slid back a teak panel, opened a safe and took out two bundles. He always has a pile of tip-off money to hand. 'Here's five hundred. Let me know.'

There wasn't much information to be had, but I got what there was. She'd been staying at a hotel called the Scanda, and the printers were an outfit called Strom Brothers who apparently did good-quality work reasonably cheaply. Scown was trying them out on this to see whether it worked out good and cheap; if it did he planned to switch one of the women's magazines there, because Sweden was relatively free of labour troubles and he'd been strike-bound twice in a year.

After that I went back to my flat to collect a clean shirt or two and ring SAS. The next flight was a nonstop, just before five, which would do nicely, and it left me time to

nip round to the bank the *Daily News* used and turn some
of Scown's five hundred into kroner.

I landed in Gothenburg around six-thirty and took a cab
to the Scanda, a straightforward modern rectangle of the
type that adds nothing to the character of any city and very
little to the pleasure of the visitor. I registered, went to my
room, and sat down to think, which wasn't easy; I'd spent
too many hours in aeroplanes for my head to be full of ideas,
or indeed of anything but clogged cotton wool.

The first problem was that Scown had been warned off
and I didn't know whether the Swedes knew that. If they
did, there'd be no help. On the other hand, there had to be
some sensible basis for the questions I was going to ask.
I decided, in the end, that the best place to begin was with
the hotel staff. If there was a clamp on them, it would
show fast enough.

I went downstairs and into the square sideshoot that passes,
in hotels like the Scanda, for a lounge, and ordered some
coffee. The girl who brought it looked at me in a worried
kind of way when I mentioned Alsa's name, and said that
I should talk to the manager. The proffered kroner were
accepted but unproductive. Simple enough; the staff weren't
talking and my problem was clear: it was no good being
unofficial. I went to reception and asked to see the manager.

His name was Pederson and he was as neutrally modern
as his hotel: a medium-sized Swede, the darker side of fair,
with the kind of bland, smooth public face which kept his
difficulties decently out of sight.

'How may I help you, Mr Sellers?' He'd come to the
counter.

I said, 'Do you mind if we use your office?'

'Is it necessary?'

'I want to talk about Miss Hay, Alison Hay.'

'Ah. Of course. This way, please.' He had my registra-
tion slip in his hand and glanced at it quickly. I'd left the
Business or Profession space blank.

He sat me in an angular chair upholstered in French

mustard, then sat formally behind his desk, instead of taking my chair's partner. 'May I ask who you are?'

'I'm a friend of Miss Hay's.'

'A journalist?'

'As it happens, yes. But I'm not here as a journalist.'

'You have some authorization?' he asked carefully.

'Do I need any?'

He shrugged. 'It helps. Always it helps.' Then he smiled. 'We are a slightly bureaucratic people, Mr Sellers.'

So I showed him my passport, my Cable and Wireless card, my Press card and my Diner's Card. The Diner's Card seemed to impress him most. At least I existed and was credit worthy.

He handed them back to me politely. 'I know so little. Miss Hay had a booking for ten days. She slept here one night. On the following night she apparently telephoned the police, said she was in grave danger and asked for immediate protection. The police sent a car without delay. When it arrived, she had gone.'

'The phone call,' I asked. 'Was it made from the hotel?'

'Oh, yes.'

'You're sure?'

'Certainly. It was put through the hotel operator.'

'At what time?'

'At five minutes past eleven, I believe. The list can be checked if it is important.'

'She didn't tell you she was in danger?'

'No.'

'Or any of the staff?'

'No.'

'What about her room. May I see it?'

'I'm sorry.' He shrugged again, but with a touch of irritation. 'The room is locked. Instructions from the police, you understand. If you get their permission, then naturally . . .'

I said, 'Was there any commotion?'

'No.'

'What about her things. Were they disturbed?'

'By the police, inevitably. They spent much time in the room.'

'But there was no sign of a struggle?'

He sighed a little. 'These are questions you must ask the police, Mr Sellers. I am simply the manager of a hotel. We prefer –'

'Not to get involved?'

'Naturally. No hotel likes these affairs. If I can help, naturally I will. But I have told you all that I know. I really think you should talk to the police now.'

I nodded. 'I will, Mr Pederson. Thanks.'

He showed me out with the same neutral courtesy, trying to mask his distaste for the whole business, but it showed all the same.

'One more thing,' I said. 'She tried to phone me that night. I'd like to know what time that was.'

'Of course. I will ask the telephonist.'

I learned that Alsa had made, or tried to make, three phone calls that night. The first was to London, to the *Daily News*, but not presumably to Scown or he'd have mentioned it. The second was to me, the third to the police. It seemed likely she'd rung London to find out where I was, tried to reach me and finally, nearly three hours later, she'd called the police. What had happened in those three hours?

I'd have to get on to the police. I went up to my room intending to ring them but changed my mind and decided to go in person. I was putting on a raincoat when the phone rang. An Inspector Schmid was downstairs and would like to see me.

I told them to send him up, removed my mac and waited. Pederson had clearly called the police the moment I'd gone.

When the knock came on the door, I opened it and two men came into my room.

'Mr Sellers?' the first one asked. He was surprisingly small, no more than five feet six or so. I nodded. The size of policemen is in reverse ratio to the prosperity of a country.

'I am Inspector Schmid. This is Sergeant Gustaffson. I understand you are here about the case of Miss Alison Hay.'

'Sit down,' I said. Schmid sat. His sergeant apparently preferred to stand.

'How much do you know, Mr Sellers?'

'Not much. What the hotel manager told me.'

'We ourselves know very little more.'

'No news, then?'

'None.'

I said, 'People don't just vanish. Do you know how she left the hotel?'

'We are concerned,' Schmid said, 'because this lady had just returned from the Soviet Union.'

'I know she had. Why do you think it's relevant?'

He smiled. 'I prefer to believe everything is relevant until it is eliminated. May I see your passport?'

I handed it over and he flipped through the pages, then looked up at me. 'I see you have been to the Soviet Union recently, too.'

'Not too recently. Some time ago.'

'Yes.' He gave the passport back to me. 'I know, of course, the reason for her presence in Gothenburg. But not in detail.'

I said, 'The company she works for is producing a magazine about Russia for sale in Britain. She went to Russia to collect material and came here to put it together. The magazine's being printed here.'

'Why is that?'

'Usual reasons. Suitable printer at a suitable price.'

'Yes.' He looked at me for a moment. 'Why was a woman sent?'

'Because . . .' I hesitated. I didn't fully understand Scown's reasons myself. 'I suppose because she was the right person to do it. She knew magazine production.'

'But it would be unusual to send a woman?'

'A bit,' I said. 'We're male chauvinist pigs in Fleet Street.'

'You're what?'

'It's a man's world,' I said. 'The thing is, it wasn't just

"a woman" who was sent, any more than they'd send just any man. She went because she's damn good.'

'And very attractive? I have seen her photograph.'

'Then you know the answer.'

'Also, she has charm?'

'More than most,' I said. More than any was what I meant, but I was keeping things deliberately flat. Police forces the world over send worried lovers and husbands home for a cup of tea. It's a conditioned reflex.

He saw through me though. 'Your relationship with Alison Hay?'

'I've known her a long time. Her father was a friend. So is she. And we worked together for a while.'

He nodded, glanced down at his fingers, and muttered something I didn't quite catch.

'Sorry?'

He looked up, met my eyes deliberately and said quickly: 'Why did *you* go to Russia, Mr Sellers?'

If I hadn't been so worried about Alsa, I'd have laughed. The old interrogator's punctuation trick! I said, 'On the same thing.'

'The same magazine?'

'That's right.'

'Why? Why was it necessary to –'

I interrupted. 'Because I made a mess of things and they threw me out. She apparently did the job properly.'

Schmid nodded and rose. 'Thank you. If we have any news, you will be informed.'

'Not so fast,' I said. 'There are things I want to know.'

'Well?'

'I'd like to see her room.'

'No.'

'Why not?'

'We want nothing disturbed. It may be important, Mr Sellers.'

'There may also,' I said sarcastically, 'be something there that will help. Something you wouldn't see and I would. That could be important, too!'

'Possibly. However, that is the decision. As I said, you will be informed of any development.'

I wanted to hit him, instead I made myself speak quietly. 'It's forty-eight hours now, Inspector Schmid. Are you really telling me you've discovered nothing? Don't you even know where she went, who she saw, why she was afraid?'

Schmid said, 'One possibility, Mr Sellers, is that she was carrying something out of the Soviet Union. Had that occurred to you?' He was pulling the same trick again, looking me suddenly hard in the eye.

I said, 'Sure she was. She was carrying articles and pictures. Enough for six issues of the magazine. She was a journalist, not a spy.'

'Is the distinction always so clear?'

'She wasn't a spy,' I said. 'You can be quite certain of that. If she was carrying anything, it was planted on her.'

Schmid nodded. 'We are aware of that possibility, too.'

Then he slid out, without looking back, and the big sergeant followed.

I watched the door close. Appropriate. I faced a closed door, all right. I picked up the phone and gave the operator Scown's phone number, the line that wasn't intercepted by secretaries, and listened to the assorted clicks as the call was routed.

'What is it?' Other people give their names or numbers, or at least say, yes? Scown assumes the worst.

'The police aren't very co-operative,' I said.

'Who's *that*?'

'Sellers.'

'Are they ever?'

'They've closed the door,' I said. 'But I want to check one thing. She phoned the office that night. To whom did she speak and what did she say?'

'Your number?'

I told him and he put the phone down.

Miss Harrison, the editor's secretary, rang me back ten minutes or so later. She said, 'Miss Hay spoke to me the other night, Mr Sellers.'

'What did she say?'

'She wanted to know where you were. Whether I had a number for you. I told her where you were staying in Washington.'

'How did she sound?'

There was a pause. 'I don't quite see what you mean.'

So Miss Harrison didn't know! Scown was keeping the whole thing to himself! I thought angrily about those bloody official circles. 'Did she seem worried?'

'Well, I don't quite know. She just said she wanted the number. I don't remember anything unusual.'

I thanked her and hung up, wondering whether she'd gossip in the ladies'. But she wouldn't. Editors' secretaries are hired because they won't gossip, in the ladies' or anywhere else.

I stood at the window, brooding, for a while; wondering if Alsa was somewhere among all those lights. A couple of times another question flickered in my mind. Was she even still alive? I tried not to think about that. Instead I tried to think what I could do next. In the face of police non-co-operation I could do precious little, and my mind was now so weary and leaden I was incapable of thinking clearly. I hated the idea of going to bed and leaving it till morning, but knew I had to.

I woke at four. No, that's not quite accurate. I was awakened at four. There was no intermediate, dopey stage. One minute I was fast asleep; the next I was awake, alert and tense, and wondering why. Someone in the room? I lay still, listening hard, but I could hear nothing except my own heartbeat. I reached for the light switch, but carefully. If someone were in the room, bed was not a helpful place to be. With my thumb on the switch, I hesitated. Somewhere in my mind there was the memory of a small sound. Had I heard it, or had it been part of a dream? Was it the sound that had awakened me?

I switched on the light and looked round the room, blinking. Nobody there. Nobody in the bathroom either. Odd. I had a feeling it *was* a sound that had awakened me, but the silence was complete; few things are quieter than a hotel at four A.M. I began to prowl round, looking at things. Maybe it had been one coat hanger banging against another, something like that. I looked, but they all seemed still enough and there was no draught in the wardrobe to set them swinging.

Then my bare foot touched something moist on the carpet. Water? I glanced at the ceiling, but there was no sign of moisture up there, so I bent and rubbed the carpet with my fingers and found the moist spot. All right; where had the water come from? Was it, for instance, raining? I pulled back the curtain and it was raining cats and dogs. But it hadn't been raining when I went to bed, had it? No. I crawled round on my hands and knees wondering if there were other drops of water, and there were, several of them, half a dozen single drops more or less in a line from the door across the room, and two or three close together by my bed.

It was no longer a question of whether somebody had been in the room, but of who? And why? My scalp was still prickling; my heart thudding. There's nothing quite so alarming as the knowledge that somebody broke through and found you defenceless, even if he did nothing.

I thought about that for a moment. The intruder, whoever he was, hadn't come here to do nothing. He'd come to do something. What? My bag lay on the stand. I lifted the lid and looked at the contents, but they hadn't been particularly tidy to begin with; there was no way of knowing if he'd been through them, and it didn't really matter, because the' bag held only my clothes. My passport and wallet, then? Hotel thieves like to have passports and wallets, not just for the money, but because there may be credit cards and almost certainly things like driving licences and letters, and documentation of a personality can be useful to criminals.

But both were still in my pockets, so it wasn't a hotel thief. Those drops of water beside the bed puzzled me: had the intruder just stood there, looking at me – the thought made me shiver involuntarily — or was there something else?

The Bible lay in the drawer with the telephone directory; the phone on the bedside table. The phone. I picked it up, not just the receiver, the whole thing.

Then I turned it over and looked carefully at the screws that held on the base plate. Steel screws, and in two places there were small, shiny scratch marks on the screw heads. Fresh scratch marks.

I've been through the experience before, in one or two places. I'd been bugged.

## CHAPTER SIX

I'm no electronics engineer, so there was no way of knowing whether the bug only worked when the phone was used, or whether it was the nastier type that listened constantly. If it were the second variety, the listener would know I'd been handling the phone, and might be wondering if I'd inspected it. The best thing now would be to pretend to make a call, any call, and behave as naturally as possible. I picked it up and waited a while, deliberately mumbling and muttering to myself when there was no answer. The hall porter was presumably dozing in his cubicle somewhere; either that or he'd been paid to stay out of the way while somebody came up to my room. I held on for a couple of minutes, then swore softly, replaced the receiver and went back to lie on the bed and brood.

I was wiser about only one thing. The fact that somebody had me bugged was clear proof Alsa hadn't voluntarily gone off somewhere. But then I'd never believed she had. Apart from that, two hours' thought got me precisely nowhere. I wasn't even sure what to do next.

Around six I took a shower, shaved and dressed and went downstairs in search of nourishment. The hotel dining room wouldn't be open for another hour, so I went out, found a workman's café and had some breakfast. As I finished the second cup of coffee, I decided I'd start at the obvious place and went to look for a taxi.

Strom Brothers AB was about three miles from the city centre and still not open when I arrived. I hung about in the drizzle for a while, and then the gates opened and cars began to roll up. The usual thing: works people arriving half an hour before the office staff. I persuaded the watchman to open up the waiting room. At five-to-eight people began flooding in and exactly at eight a girl asked what I wanted. I explained and was taken to see the works manager, a man called Morelius.

Morelius was grave and sorry and said he understood my concern for Miss Hay. He, too, was concerned and he would naturally help in any way he could. I asked if he'd seen Alsa.

He told me she had spent just one afternoon at the print works. She'd arrived from Moscow, booked herself into the Scanda Hotel, then rung Strom Brothers and they'd sent a car to pick her up. The way I saw it, while she was waiting for the car, she must have rung Scown in London to say she'd arrived safely.

'Did she bring material here that afternoon, Mr Morelius?'

'Some, I think.' He frowned, remembering. 'She had a briefcase and one of those flat portfolios artists use.'

'Is any of it still here?'

'Yes.'

'May I see it?'

The corners of his mouth turned down. 'The police . . . unfortunately they insist that—'

I said, 'We're deeply concerned about Miss Hay, of course. But we're worried too about the production of the magazine, the schedule.'

Morelius was looking at me carefully. He said, 'We meet our schedules, Mr Sellers. Always we meet them.'

'Doesn't look as though you will this time.'

'No. But the fault is not ours. And there is a clause in the contract covering events such—'

'We're not thinking, are we,' I said pointedly, 'of just

one little contract?'

He blinked a couple of times, feeling the nutcracker squeeze, then said defensively, 'This is not fair. We—'

I interrupted him again. 'This contract is for six issues of forty thousand copies. *Woman's Week* is two million copies a week for the foreseeable future. That's number one. Number two is that Mr Scown is fond of Alison Hay.'

Morelius was blinking even harder. 'You mean, personally . . .?'

'Not like that,' I said. 'But it's as if she were his daughter.'

He hesitated. 'The police would be angry.'

I said, 'The police don't place two-million-copy print orders. Mr Scown will also be angry.'

Morelius thought for a moment. 'You will undertake to be most careful?'

'Certainly.'

Then, reluctantly he conceded. 'I show you. One moment please.' He picked up the phone and spoke in Swedish. When he'd finished, he said, 'I will be told if the police come here. If they do, you will have time to come away from the room. You will do that?'

'Of course.'

The room was plain and tidy. All magazine printers have places like it, where editorial production people can work. There were a couple of desks, a layout table, a frosted glass with a light beneath it for transparency viewing, a couple of telephones, a photo-copying machine.

'Thanks.'

He didn't want to leave me. I said 'You must have other problems.'

'Please. If the police come, you will—'

I nodded. 'Like a rat down a rope. So let's not waste time.' He left me to it.

There were a few rough layouts on the desk, some black and white prints in a wire basket, and that was all. Alsa must have taken the briefcase and the artwork portfolio back to the Scanda Hotel. I sat at the desk and began to go through the material carefully. The pictures were the usual Russian propaganda stuff: new cities mushrooming out of the Siberian vastness, kids at a ballet school, more kids doing exercises in a beautifully equipped gymnasium, watchmakers at work. A few had pencil marks on the back in Alsa's writing; she'd sized one or two up provisionally. It all seemed very innocent.

The layouts were roughs for various pages in the magazine, with type areas and pictures blocked in and not much else. A few were front-cover designs, with scribbled-in picture outlines and a few rough type styles for the title. *Russian Life*. They didn't look particularly exciting, though one was fairly striking: a rough map of Russia with flags sticking out of it. Alsa clearly intended to put a picture inside each flag. Nice idea if the artists didn't foul it up and the printers got the register right and didn't blur the edges.

I stayed for an hour or so, and went through the stuff carefully three times, but there was nothing I could see that might give me a lead. All the same, I made quite a few photo-copies in case there was something important I'd missed. When I'd finished I left everything as I'd found it, picked up the key Morelius had left on the table, locked the door behind me and went back to Morelius' office.

'No police?'

'No.' He managed a smile. 'It was useful?'

'I don't think so,' I said. 'Sorry about the pressure. I felt I had to look.'

Morelius smiled. 'Now it is over, I do not worry. I would like to help. If there is anything . . .'

I nodded. 'I'll ask. Thanks.'

'You tell Mr Scown we wish to help, please.'

'I'll tell him.'

'Where will you go now?'

I had no idea. 'Back to the hotel, I suppose.'

'We will send you by car,' Morelius said. He got up and opened the door. 'You will have spoken to Mr Marasov?'

I turned to look at him. 'Who?'

He looked surprised. 'You did not know? Mr Marasov came here with Miss Hay. He is a press attaché, I think anyway, at the Soviet Embassy in Stockholm.'

'What,' I asked, 'was *he* doing?'

'Miss Hay said he was helping her with some translation.'

'Was he, now?' I thought about that. 'Did they leave together?'

'Yes. In our car.'

'Where did they go?'

'To the Scanda Hotel. The police know this. They asked the driver.'

I asked the driver myself on the way back into Gothenburg and he confirmed it. He'd taken Alsa and the Russian to the Scanda and when he dropped them, they both went inside.

'What were they talking about?'

He shrugged. 'I not listen. My English . . .'

'You heard nothing?'

'No. Once he say he is sorry. I hear that.'

I wondered what he'd been sorry about, but there was no mileage in it. He could have been sorry about dropping cigarette ash.

I thanked the driver, watched the Volvo move away, and wandered into the Scanda's lobby. At least I now knew what to do next. I was heading for the lift and my bugged telephone when the porter called my name and hurried over.

'A visitor asks to see you, sir.'

'Oh? Who is he?'

'Over there, sir.' He nodded towards the apology for a lounge, where a man sat quietly, smoking a cigarette. He looked up as I approached and began to rise.

'I'm Sellers,' I said.

'Pavel Marasov. I am Press Attaché at the Soviet Embassy in Stockholm.' He offered his hand and I shook it: a cold hand, limp grip. He was a bit like his handshake, too. Rimless glasses of Glenn Miller vintage. Medium height, nondescript, in a slightly scruffy suit, but with a kind of intensity around the eyes. 'I came here to see if there was news and was told you are here.'

'And *is* there any news?' I sat down next to him.

'No. I asked the police. They do not know where Miss

Hay is. It is very worrying.'

I said, 'We're all worried.'

'The Ambassador himself is most anxious.'

We stared at each other for a moment or two. Then I said, 'Mr Marasov, I don't know much. The police are keeping it tight. But I understand there was some problem about a transparency.' I used Schmid's trick, watching his eyes and emphasizing the word transparency.

But he didn't hesitate. 'Oh yes. It was unfortunate. We were sorry Miss Hay was troubled, but – you are a journalist, I think?'

'Yes.'

'Then you will understand. In Moscow Miss Hay was at the Number One Magazine Publishing House.'

I said, 'I know it. I was there myself.'

He looked at me for a moment.

'So you are the, er – '

'I'm the one you threw out,' I said.

He nodded, even smiled a little. 'I heard of it, but – this is a neutral country, eh?' Then he frowned and returned to the subject. 'You understand that there is a central photographic laboratory. They do work on many publications.'

'I remember.'

'They were copying transparencies for Miss Hay. A great many transparencies, you know? She selected what she wanted and they were copied because it is the rule that the original transparencies are not released. You follow me?'

'Yes.'

'Well, naturally there was much material in the laboratory, including the transparency which had been selected for a special anniversary edition of *Soviet Industry*. Miss Hay had taken away a large number of transparencies and when it was found that the cover was missing, it was thought it might, in error, have been given to her. The matter was urgent for production reasons.'

I said, 'I'd still like to know what happened.'

'It was most regrettable. It was necessary to stop her at the airport and ask if her material could be examined.'

'Who stopped her?'

'I believe a message was sent from the publishing house to the airport police. Naturally it was not a police matter . . .'

'Naturally,' I said. I could imagine the happy moment: Alsa at Sheremetyevo Airport with a pile of transparencies and the sudden heavy hand of the Russian police. She must have been scared out of her wits.

'They search her?'

'No.' He looked at me reprovingly. 'She was a guest of the Soviet people, Mr Sellers. She was asked if the material could be checked.'

'And she agreed?' Of course she'd agree, I thought. With the plane on the runway and the Soviet police breathing heavily, anybody'd agree.

'She was most co-operative. Unfortunately the transparency was not found.' Marasov smiled again. 'They have to find a new cover now. It is most annoying for them.'

'I can imagine.'

'But these things happen. Miss Hay told me she understood and did not mind.'

I said, 'Alsa's a nice girl.'

'Very nice,' he agreed. 'I found her most charming.'

'Everybody does. Tell me, Mr Marasov, since Gothenburg's a long way from Stockholm, why're you there?'

He made a little gesture with his hands. 'She speaks no Russian. I speak English. I have instructions to help her in any way necessary. With additional information or material, translation. And so on.'

It was all plausible enough. Indeed it was more or less to be expected. Marasov would have been instructed to help, to keep a watching brief, and to try to make sure the official line wasn't transgressed.

'You have no idea where she is?'

'No.' Marasov shook his head. His regret seemed genuine.

'Or why she might have disappeared?'

He said, with a slightly weary air, as though he'd said it a lot of times: 'I know what you think, Mr Sellers. You believe *we* have kidnapped her for some reason.'

'I'm a reporter,' I said. 'It wouldn't be the first time I've come across the story.'

'I assure you it is not so.' The glasses glinted indignantly. He looked at me with an intensity that was almost pleading. 'We wish to see Miss Hay complete her work. We have regard for her. Also it is to our advantage. Please do not think otherwise.'

I shrugged. 'Okay. I'll try to believe it. One question, though. What time did you leave?'

'We had one drink. I left at five thirty o'clock.'

'All right. And we keep in touch?'

'Please. I am at the Hotel Nord. And Mr Sellers.'

'What?'

'If you hear anything at all, please let me know. We will help in any way we can.'

I watched him go, and tried to decide whether to believe him or not.

Marasov was an official of a country that had engaged for half a century in devious, determined and often horrific clandestine activities, a prime suspect if ever there was one. Yet he was apparently showing distress and wanting to help. One duckling missing from a pond; one ferocious pike in the pond, and the pike says, it wasn't me. I'm as anxious as you are. Who believes the pike? Why should I believe Marasov?

Oh, God, I thought despairingly, where *was* Alsa?

Schmid had used the don't-ring-us-we'll-ring-you routine, but it was difficult to imagine that Sweden's highly efficient police hadn't progressed a millimetre in more than sixty hours of investigation, so I telephoned the police from the pay-phone in the lobby. I'd assumed almost automatically that the bug in my bedroom was Russian. So it might be, but if Marasov wasn't lying, then it might be somebody else's bug and I preferred not to speak into a microphone without having some idea whose it was.

But Schmid was out, or so they said, and so was Sergeant Gustaffson. The duty inspector said he was sorry there was no news, and I'd be told the moment anything new turned up, if I'd leave my name and number. I told him Schmid had both, but he made a note all the same, and said don't ring us, we'll ring you.

I took the lift to the top floor and found the door of six-two-eight, the room Alsa had used. I tried the door handle, just in case, but it was locked. However, the door of the next room, six-thirty, was open and I looked inside. The twin beds were freshly-made, and the room clean. There was no communicating door. I strolled along the corridor. A chamber-maid was at work making beds, and several doors stood open. She seemed to be working from one end of the corridor to the other and hadn't reached six-thirty yet, so it was a fair guess the room hadn't been occupied the previous night. I wondered who'd been in it the night Alsa vanished. She must have been moved quickly, either out of the hotel or at least to another room, and presumably against her will. How had the trick been done?

I returned along the corridor, found the fire escape door, pushed it open and saw the stairs that could lead only to the roof. After that I took the lift back to the lobby and asked the reception clerk who had occupied the rooms on either side of Alsa's on the night she disappeared. He looked at me doubtfully at first and then gave me the information. Six-thirty had been occupied by two gentlemen.

'Who?'

'Frenchmen, sir. Mr Raoul Maisels and Mr Phillipe Cohen.' He pronounced them the French way and it was only because I could see the paper in his hand that something dawned on me. 'Jewish?' I asked.

'Possibly. I do not know, sir.'

'Okay. What about six-two-six?' That was the room on the other side.

'One moment.' He worked down the list. 'An American couple, sir. Mr and Mrs Paul C. Scott from Philadelphia.'

'When did they check out?'

'Next day, I think, sir. Yes, next day.'

'Both lots?'

'Yes, sir.'

I thanked him and walked away. Two people each side, and both pairs had packed and gone next morning. Coincidence or not? I wondered how rooms were allocated in the hotel; who drew up the lists?

Probably the reception clerk, unless VIPs were involved. At that point the manager would take over.

I turned to walk back to the lift and nearly fell over the feet of a workman. Two of them were doing repairs in the recesses of some kind of cupboard. I skirted them and pressed the lift button. When it came and the doors opened, I checked the inside buttons. They were numbered one to six, and the bottom one was for the garage beneath the hotel. I pressed it and went down a floor. It wasn't exactly difficult to see how Alsa could have been removed from the hotel. The door to six-two-eight upstairs wasn't ten yards from the lift; the garage had free and open access to the road.

If Inspector Schmid hadn't worked that one out he must be pretty stupid, and he hadn't seemed stupid, so why hadn't he mentioned it, at least as a possibility? To hell with it, I'd go round to the police now, see Schmid if he was in, and start asking questions about Maisels, Cohen and Mr and Mrs Scott and their movements.

When I got there, Schmid was still out. I was asked if I was a relative of Alsa's and what my interest in the matter was anyway, then told to sit on the hard wooden bench they obviously kept for the people they wanted to discourage. When Inspector Schmid returned, he would perhaps see me. He would, at any rate, be informed. The decision was his.

I sat there for an hour and a half with corns developing rapidly on my rear end, but watching the comings and goings carefully. I was determined that when Schmid came in, he wasn't going to slip past and then refuse to see me.

At long last the desk sergeant, who'd been studiously ignoring me ever since I'd first sat on the bloody bench, beckoned with his finger. Schmid would see me now. He told me how to get to the second floor office and I went up in the lift, found it and knocked. The door was opened by somebody I hadn't seen before. 'Mr Sellers?' he asked politely.

'Yes.'

'Please come in. This is Inspector Schmid.'

I glanced at the figure behind the desk, then turned to the man who'd opened the door. 'Are you Sergeant Gustaffson?'

'Yes.'

I'd never seen either of them before.

## CHAPTER SEVEN

There could have been two Schmids, of course. But that possibility was disposed of quickly. This was the real Inspector Schmid, the only Inspector Schmid, the genuine article. And he was far from amused: impersonating a police officer was a very serious matter. Presumably impersonating two was doubly serious. Schmid demanded immediate descriptions of the impostors and sent Gustaffson off as soon as I'd given them, to make sure the descriptions were circulated *at once* to the whole Gothenburg force.

When that was done, he looked at me grimly. 'I have here a note to telephone you, Mr Sellers. I would have done that.'

'I had a feeling the other man wouldn't,' I replied. 'And I was right.'

'Okay.'

We went over the whole business and Schmid was very far from happy. I got the impression he was accustomed to clearing his cases quickly and efficiently, and liked continuing mysteries no more than I did. When I told him about the rooms on either side of Alsa's and the lift direct to the garage, he said yes, he was aware of the possibilities and was pursuing inquiries with some vigour. Messieurs Maisels and Cohen were, it seemed, salesmen. He'd spoken to both next morning; they'd known nothing and said they had heard nothing, and were leaving for home forthwith. He'd had no reason to keep them in Sweden and had had to let them go. Mr and Mrs Scott were tourists and had stayed only one night, leaving for a Lake Vättern resort next morning.

It was all very pat. I said so and Schmid didn't disagree. Schmid was a familiar type, a hard-nosed and patient professional, not especially happy to see me, but perfectly prepared, since I was there, to find out if there was anything I knew that he didn't. We went over the whole ground several times. Then he said, 'You think she was carrying something, do you not?'

'Depends what you mean. I don't believe she was a courier. Certainly not intentionally.'

'Intent is not involved. She may have been carrying something.'

'If she was, she didn't know,' I said.

'You are wrong. Okay?'

'Go on.'

He looked at me speculatively. 'You are also right.'

I said, 'Just tell me.'

'You are right about part of the time. Wrong about the other part. Look at it this way, Mr Sellers. She had spent nearly two weeks in Russia. I am told there was no trouble.'

I nodded, thinking about the sudden search at Sheremetyevo Airport. Maybe Schmid didn't know about that.

He went on. 'She arrived here in Gothenburg and behaved perfectly naturally?'

'Yes.'

'For a while. Describe to me what she did.'

'All right. She went out to the printers'. To Strom Brothers, with Marasov.' I was watching him as I spoke. Marasov's name wasn't news to him. 'They worked for a while, then she left and returned to the Scanda Hotel with Marasov. They had one drink, then Marasov left.'

'Your deduction from all this?'

I said, 'All right, she was behaving normally.'

'She was. But afterwards, no. Afterwards she telephones London. She even telephones to America. To a Mr Sellers, person-to-person. Okay?'

'I didn't get the call,' I said. I didn't enlarge on it.

Schmid nodded. 'Does she often telephone you like that?'

'No.'

'You are her lover? Fiancé?'

'Neither. A friend.'

'Okay. She is not able to speak to her friend. She leaves the hotel. Alone.'

'Where did she go?'

'I do not know. But she was out for quite a long time. Nearly three hours.'

'Having dinner?'

'Perhaps. But not in any restaurant in Gothenburg.'

'You've checked them all?'

'We are thorough. Not inspired, perhaps, but thorough. If she left the city it was not by taxi. We checked that, too. When she returns, she goes to her room. Half an hour passes. Then she telephones the police and says she believes her life is in danger. What does that mean?'

I said, 'You believe it means she had found something?'

'Exactly.'

'When?' I asked. 'If she'd found something, when did she find it? Before she went out, or after?'

'That,' he said, 'is a problem. Logically it was when she returned. It is sensible? She returns, finds what it was she carried, and telephones the police.'

'Because her life is in danger. But what made her think that? Why did she believe she was in danger?'

Schmid said, 'Perhaps it was the fire.'

I must have looked as surprised as I felt. 'What fire was that?' I demanded.

'At the Scanda Hotel. The letter box. A small quantity of phosphorus was placed in the letter box, Mr Sellers. All the letters were burned. You did not know.'

'No,' I said. 'I didn't know. Had she posted a letter?'

'We do not know. The heat of burning phosphorus is intense. Nothing was left except small ash.'

I remembered the workman in the hotel foyer, working on a cupboard. I said, without thinking. 'She'd phone. She wouldn't write letters.'

'No? A birthday card to a relative? A postcard? The British send many postcards.'

I said, 'Or whatever it was she'd found. Perhaps, when she found it, *if* she found it, she put it in an envelope and posted it. Postal services are secure.'

Schmid nodded. 'Very secure in Sweden, as in most countries. But not until the letter is collected. The letter box was not secure. Okay?'

'Okay.'

'Okay. *If* she posted the thing she found. *If* it was destroyed . . .' He paused and left me to finish.

'You mean, why was she kidnapped?'

'If she *was* kidnapped.'

I said lamely, 'Yes.' I could see his problem very clearly. 'So you see.'

'Were there,' I asked, 'any indications at all that she had been in another room? The ones on either side, for instance?'

Schmid shook his head. 'No trace. We took what we believe are Alison Hay's fingerprints from some papers. There were no such fingerprints in either room, though there were many in her own.'

'Americans one side, Jews the other.'

'Frenchmen,' he corrected. 'Possibly Jewish. You have thought they were Israeli? Why?'

I shrugged helplessly. 'No reason. I'm trying to find some reason for it all. You've had trouble with Arab terrorists in Sweden.'

'We have trouble with Germans and British and Americans, too. Also with Russians and Greeks, Norwegians and Danes. This is a cosmopolitan city.'

'It's not the same thing!'

'No, Mr Sellers, it is not. But conclusions cannot yet be

reached. There are too many possibilities.'

I said bitterly, 'Okay, it's a bloody fine intellectual exercise. Meanwhile, where the hell is she? Who's got her? And why?'

His answer didn't help. 'We have a small population and a big country, Mr Sellers. There are more places to hide than could ever be searched.'

'All right then. Let's start at the beginning. Who could have used her to bring something out of Russia?'

The question was rhetorical and stupid and a product of frustration.

Schmid answered counting on his fingers. 'American, British to begin. Sweden, since this is where she came. France – we have Frenchmen, okay? The Russians themselves.'

'Why the Russians?'

'Who knows,' Schmid said, 'why the Russians do things?'

'All right. I'm sorry.'

'Do not be. We are not inactive, Mr Sellers. I wish you to believe that.'

'I believe it. Can I see Alison's room?'

'No.'

'Why not?'

'Because that room is all we have. I have examined it. There appears to be nothing – '

'There may be something I'd notice that you wouldn't.'

'Agreed, Mr Sellers. But I think not. Understand please that my work is progressive. We find one thing, then another. Perhaps something in the room will be step two, useful when we have taken the first step.'

'All the same – '

But he was wearying of it. He said, 'Do the British police allow journalists to examine important evidence during an investigation? I think not. Neither do we.'

I left him then and set off back to the Scanda Hotel, walking for once. There was no hurry; there seemed to be nothing I could do. If Gothenburg's police hadn't been able to trace where Alsa went, the night she disappeared, it was unlikely I could. Equally, if they'd found no clue as to where she'd been taken, I hadn't much chance either. But the stuff locked up in her room was different and I wanted to see it. The more I thought about it, the more I was certain there'd be something there. Alsa had made the phone call to the police because she was scared. But at least she'd had time to make the phone call. But why had she made it from her room. Why hadn't she gone down to the lobby where there were people? Because she daren't? Because she knew somebody was waiting, either outside or in the adjoining rooms? She'd returned to the hotel, spent a while in her room, then rung the police. Why hadn't she telephoned immediately, the moment she'd come in. Why had she waited? Because something must have happened after she went to the room. Either that or she'd found something.

I knew Alsa. She might have been scared, but she wouldn't have panicked. She'd think, tightly and clearly, before she acted. She wouldn't reach instantly for the phone the way I would. Alsa used to tease me sometimes. You, she'd say, are a telephone reporter, too idle to use your feet. It wasn't entirely untrue.

I didn't realize it then, but I'd almost got on to something with that train of thought. The train, however, was derailed when I reached the hotel. I was crossing the lobby to the lift when a voice said, 'Is that Mr Sellers?'

I looked round and he was walking towards me, grinning, apparently as surprised as I was. Damn it, what was his name? Then I remembered. I said, 'This is a surprise, Mr Elliot. What are you doing here?'

'Just gonna ask you the same thing.' He laughed. 'Buy you a drink?'

As we walked towards the bar, I said, 'The odds against this are rather large.'

'Yeah. Good to see you. I'll say they're large, Mr Sellers. I thought you were staying in London.'

'I thought you were going to Lapland.'

'Still am. Question is when. My cameraman's been re-called, so I'm stuck.'

'But you were flying to Stockholm.'

'Yeah. Bell's Whisky, right?' I nodded and he ordered.

'There's another cameraman been photographing the Nor-wegian Skerries or some such. He's due back in Gothenburg. Doesn't know I'm waiting, poor bastard. What brings you?'

I said, 'It's a bit difficult. You know!' One reporter-to-another talk, I'm on a story and I'm not telling you, so don't inquire.

'Hell. I don't work for the wire services!'

'There are people in the newspaper game,' I said, 'who don't let their left hands know what their right hands are doing.'

'Okay, okay. If it's that good. Skol!'

'Skol.'

I sipped the whisky, making myself smile at him but remembering Schmid counting on his fingers. Who'd be likely to be interested in things brought out of Russia? The Americans for one, and more than most. I wondered whether Elliot really did work for National Geographic and probed gently as we talked, but he was technically sound and full of Charlie this and Fred that and how pleasant it always was to return from foreign fields to the manicured head-quarters in the Maryland countryside. Whether he worked there or not, his cover was too good even to dent, so I stopped trying.

He'd just said, 'How 'bout dinner tonight, John?' – by that time we'd reached the John and Harvey stage – when my name was paged over the hotel Tannoy.

At the desk I was told there was a phone call for me and I went into the foyer kiosk to take it.

'Hello?'

'Mr Sellers. Mr John Sellers?' It was a man's voice, possibly a trace of accent.

'Yes.'

'You will be interested in a house at Storgatan forty-one, Gothenburg.'

Yes, there *was* a trace of accent. Swedish, I thought, at any rate Scandinavian. 'Why will I be interested? And who's speaking?'

'Storgatan forty-one,' he said, and hung up.

I replaced the receiver and went to fetch my raincoat from the bar. Elliot had gone and his glass was empty. I put on the coat, went out to look for a cab and there was Elliot on the steps. He smiled. 'Stuffy in there. Thought I'd get a breath of air.'

'Fine,' I said meaninglessly, staring angrily across at the empty taxi rank. I crossed the pavement and stood at the edge, looking up and down the road for a cruising cab.

'Drive you somewhere?' Elliot called. He was holding up his car keys invitingly.

I hesitated. I didn't want him with me, but impatience was the dominant emotion at the time. 'All right. Thanks.'

He walked towards a blue Saab 99 parked just off the road and opened the door. 'Don't worry,' he said as I joined him. 'I'm not horning in on your big exclusive. Just bored; that's all. Where'd you wanna go?'

'Storgatan forty-one, wherever that is.'

He laughed. 'It's okay. There's a street guide in the pocket here. You look for it while I get this thing moving.'

Storgatan was a dismal street off the main Gothenburg-Möludan road, about three miles away, and we cruised slowly along it until I saw number forty-one. Most of the houses were empty and it was probably a demolition area. The house was old, or at least middle-aged, one of a terrace, three stories high. I told Elliot to stop the car and walked back to the house.

There were eight or nine stone steps leading from the iron gate up to the front door and I went up them slowly, already aware that Storgatan forty-one was empty. The windows were dirty and the only curtains were a couple of tatty rags hanging limply at one upstairs window. The paint of the door and the wooden front was more peeling, it was almost peeled. The house was fast becoming derelict. Perhaps there wasn't much point in knocking at the door, but

I knocked anyway, as much from habit as anything else. The knock echoed hollowly: the unmistakable sound of an empty house.

I gave it a minute, then tried the door. Peeling and dirty it might be, but it was also strong and locked. There was an iron rail to the steps and I held on to it as I tried to peer into the ground floor window. All I could see through the grubby pane was old floorboards with a few bits of yellowish newspaper lying about.

'No luck?' Elliot called. He'd climbed out of the car and was leaning easily against it.

'I'll try the back,' I said. As I came down the steps I stopped to look in through the cellar window, but that room, too, was deserted; empty and filthy like the rest of the house. As an afterthought, I went back to the door and had a look at the locks, wondering whether they'd been used recently, but it was impossible to tell.

'Do I come along?' Elliot asked.

'If you like.' I was marching urgently down the street, wondering who'd sent me here and why. The house must hold something, and it must be something to do with Alsa's disappearance. Suddenly I felt bile rush into my throat at the thought of what the secret of Storgatan 41 might be.

The street at the rear was cobbled and the yards – nobody could call them gardens – were full of broken-down outhouses and sour earth. From the rear, number forty-one looked even more dismally decayed than from the front.

'Realtor's dream,' Elliot said sardonically as I pushed open the bent, wooden gate. A few weeds were fighting their battle for survival in the hard-packed ground. I walked first to the cellar window, rubbed away some of the muck with my hand, and looked in. There was a chipped stone sink and a few rags hanging on nails on the walls. Nothing else.

The back door, too, was locked and what I could see of the ground floor back room was simply a repeat of the front: dusty floorboards and old newspapers.

'How bad you want to get in?' Elliot asked.

'Badly enough.'

'Well, I reckon that window there's just waiting for a jack-knife blade.' He was pointing to the cellar window. 'And I just happen to have the jack-knife. '

'Give it to me, then.'

The window was the sliding sash type, with a turner-bar securing the two halves. As Elliot had kindly pointed out, it was easy with the jack-knife. I poked the blade between the top of one frame and the bottom of the other and pushed. The bar turned. Now, would the window slide? The top half wouldn't move, but the bottom half did, with a bit of effort, creaking upward awkwardly. When I'd raised it, I held it carefully in case it crashed down again.

'Coming?'

'Why not! What's a little burglarizing matter?'

Strangely enough I hadn't thought of the illegality; now he'd mentioned it, I didn't care anyway. 'Coming?' I asked again.

'Sure. I'll take the weight while you go through.' A second later we were in the house.

We looked at the cellars first but they were empty. So were the ground floor rooms. As I started up the worn, wooden stairs, Elliot asked, 'Just what do you plan to find?' There was no answer I could bear to make.

The first things I found were in what had been a bedroom. A few paper food bags lay crumpled in a corner with some plastic cups that still contained the dregs of coffee with the remains of a film of cream white on the surface. I'm not inexperienced in the matter of dirty cups and at a guess the liquid was no more than a day old. There was nothing else on the first floor.

That left the attic rooms and I looked up the gloomy stair in trepidation. It was possible Alsa was up there. And if she was . . . well, if she was, there hadn't been a sound. The stair rail must have been well polished in its time by dedicated Swedish housewives, because it was still shiny brown in patches where the dust had been disturbed as somebody held on to it to go up or down.

I took a deep breath and hurried up. There were two doors on a little landing at the top. As it happened I opened the wrong one first. That room was empty. The other room was not. In there, two men lay on the floor, both wearing suits, both in early middle-age.

Behind me Elliot said suddenly, 'Jesus!'

I stepped forward and went to look at the man nearest me. His face, mottled with tiny skin haemorrhages, was already darkening, and round his neck was a deep, heavy red mark made by the ligature that had been used to strangle him. The other man had died in exactly the same way.

## CHAPTER EIGHT

I recognized neither of the two dead faces. As I crouched beside them, my heart thumping, I wondered whether they'd be unknown to Schmid. Somehow, I thought they wouldn't.

A moment earlier, Elliot had said in astonishment, 'Hey, those guys are dead!' But the rising inflection in his voice seemed tinny and forced.

I turned my head and looked up at him. The sound he made wasn't consistent with the expression he wore. Elliot may have been surprised to find the bodies but he wasn't shocked at the sight of them.

'Who in hell are they?'

'I don't know.' I lifted the jacket of one of them and felt in the inside pocket, looking for papers. The pocket was empty. All the pockets were empty.

Elliot said, 'Hell, you're on this story. You got to have some idea!'

'You too!' I said. He looked at me in surprise, and somehow that wasn't convincing, either.

'Me? What do you mean, me? I'm just the guy who drove you here!'

I said, 'Christ, I'm not stupid. The first time we meet, we just meet. The second time it's coincidence. But this – !'

'You're crazy!' he said. 'I'm just waiting. I told you –'

'Don't wait any longer,' I said. 'Get the police.'

'Okay,' he said angrily. 'But Jesus!'

'Ask for Inspector Schmid.'

'Inspector . . .? Listen, what is this?'

'Get Schmid first, then *you* can tell *me*.'

He nodded and clattered away downstairs. Twenty minutes later there were feet on the wooden steps. Two pairs, at least. Would there be three? Would Elliot have left? No, he'd stayed.

Schmid glanced at the two bodies, then looked at me grimly. 'Strange, is it not, Mr Sellers?'

'Do you know who they are?'

'Do you?'

I said, 'I have an idea. Just instinct. They could be those two Frenchmen, Maisels and Cohen.'

'You have not seen them before?'

'You know I haven't. Are they?'

He nodded. 'I should like to know how you found them. Here in Storgatan, I mean.'

'A telephone call,' I said. 'Somebody telephoned me at the Scanda and told me to come here. I don't know who it was.'

Schmid was watching me carefully, but he didn't comment. Instead he turned his head and spoke in Swedish to Gustaffson who promptly went away down the stairs.

Then Schmid asked, 'Did you touch them?'

'I looked in their pockets.'

'That was wrong. And the rest of the house?'

'I opened the doors. There's nothing. A few paper cups. They'd been here a while.'

'And this man? Mr . . .'

'Elliot. Harvey Elliot.'

'Why are you here, Mr Elliot? You are American?'

'I am. I drove John Sellers here, that's all.'

'So.' Schmid listened to the feet on the stairs, waiting.

Gustaffson came in, panting a little and spoke softly to him. 'The doors were locked. You broke in?'

'I did,' I said. 'That didn't seem important.'

'Perhaps.' He looked again at the bodies on the floor. 'I can hold you for that. Perhaps for more than that.'

I said angrily, 'For Christ's sake! You know why I'm here?'

'I know,' he said, 'why you say you're here. I know why Mr Elliot *says* he's here.'

'I told you. I had the transportation,' Elliot said. 'That's all.'

'Not *all*, Mr Elliot. You also entered the house. A criminal act.'

I was watching Schmid's face carefully, but there was nothing in it to indicate whether he was just going through formalities, or getting ready to be unpleasant. Schmid had made it clear enough a couple of hours earlier that police business should be left to him. He might feel it useful to keep me out of the way for a while.

I said, 'Can I talk to you privately?' I didn't want Elliot there. There had to be more to Elliot than there seemed.

'Later,' Schmid said. Then changed his mind. 'All right, Mr Sellers. Downstairs, please.'

He stood at the ground floor window looking out at the street. 'Well?'

'Alsa . . . Miss Hay must have been here!'

'Why do you say so?'

I said, 'My God, they were in the next room the night she disappeared! The same night there was a fire in the hotel!'

'I know that.' Schmid was extraordinarily impassive. He missed very little, that was clear, but he hardly seemed to react at all. And always the same maddening pat-back of everything I said to him.

'Then let's speculate a little,' I said savagely. 'If she was here, with those two upstairs, and she isn't here now, it means somebody else has taken her!'

'No. It could mean two other things. Even three. One, she killed them herself – '

'For Christ's sake!'

'Oh, it is not probable, certainly. Though she could have had assistance, or been party to the killing. No, it is a possibility from a police point of view.'

'But –'

'Secondly, she may have been released.'

'And third?'

'Thirdly,' Schmid said, 'she may not have been here at all.' Then those greyish eyes crinkled a little at the corners. 'However, I think you are perhaps right. We will examine –' Outside, tyres squealed and two cars disgorged men with equipment. Schmid moved to open the door and added, 'We will examine the evidence and the facts. I promise you that.'

Men carrying equipment poured past him towards the stairs and he gave rapid instructions, then turned to me again. 'This man Elliot?'

'I don't know,' I said. I told him briefly about our first meeting on the plane, our second in the hotel and how we'd come to the house together.

Schmid listened quietly and when I'd finished, said, 'I am a policeman, Mr Sellers. If I met a man who said he was also a policeman, I would know quickly if it was the truth. Is Mr Elliot a journalist?'

'What else do you think he might be?'

'I do not know. Answer my question, please.'

'He seems to know quite a lot about it. '

'But you are not certain?'

'Not certain, no.'

'And the question arose in your mind before I asked it?'

I said, 'He says he's with the National Geographic Magazine. A cable to them would confirm it.'

'It might, Mr Sellers. It might.' Then he walked towards the stairs, adding almost as an afterthought, 'Stay here, please. A statement will be required. I am sorry but it may take some time.'

It took a hell of a while and all the time Schmid kept me carefully apart from Elliot. We were driven to the police headquarters in separate cars and interviewed in separate rooms. It was after nine that night before Schmid produced the typed statement and told me I could go when it was signed. He also told me there was nothing in number forty-one Storgatan that suggested Alsa had been there.

'You're sure she wasn't?'

'No,' he said. 'I simply have no proof Miss Hay was in the house.'

'Would there be proof, if she had been there?'

'I cannot say.'


I walked back to the Scanda alone and deeply depressed. The streets were brightly lit and there were quite a lot of people about. I looked at them sourly. A few nights before, Alsa had been here, somewhere on these same streets. She'd been out three hours. Why? Not, apparently, for dinner. So what the hell *had* she been doing?

The door man at the Scanda opened the swing door with a flourish and I muttered my thanks, then stopped as a thought struck me.

'Were you,' I asked him, 'on duty the night Miss Hay disappeared?'

He looked at me carefully. 'I was. But you should see the manag –'

'I know,' I said. I gave him twenty kroner and he palmed the money with a practised hand. 'Did you see her go out?'

'I open the door when she go and when she come back.' He seemed almost proud of it; a big moment in his life.

'Did she speak? To you or anybody else?'

'She ask about cinemas.'

I blinked at him. Alsa didn't like cinemas much. 'You're sure. Cinemas, not theatres?'

'Cinemas. I tell her.'

'Did you tell the police this?'

'No.'

'Why not?'

'They not ask me. Just when she go out. When she come back.'

74

Schmid and his bloody thoroughness! 'What did you tell her?'

'The near one. This street. Three hundred metres.'

He was glancing round a bit guiltily. 'The manager has told you not to talk?'

He hesitated, then, 'Yes, sir.'

'Don't worry.' I gave him another twenty for encouragement. 'Did she go that way? Towards the cinema?'

'Yes, sir.'

'What was she wearing?'

'Sir?'

'Her clothes?'

'Ah. A coat.'

'Colour?'

'White.'

I knew that white coat.

'She have bag, and . . .' He mimed pulling on gloves.

'Gloves?'

'Yes. Glove.'

'When she returned. What then?'

'The same. A pretty lady.'

'Very. You remember anything else?'

'She look . . . mmm-m . . . not happy.'

'When she went out, or when she came back?'

'Both times, sir.'

'Thanks.' I went out through the swing doors again and turned right, the way Alsa had gone, walking until I found the cinema. It was showing two Swedish films and I looked into the lighted foyer for a moment or two, feeling very puzzled. Alsa didn't enjoy the cinema much; I knew that. Theatres, yes, but she had an idiosyncratic dislike of films and TV. I like, she said often, to be entertained by live people, not manipulated images. She hardly ever went to the cinema and certainly wouldn't go alone, not in a strange city. In addition, this place was showing films of no great importance and in a language she didn't speak.

Everything about it was odd. I tried to think of some reason, any reason, why Alsa might have gone alone to the cinema, but nothing suggested itself.

Finally I took Alsa's photograph out of my wallet and went in. Infuriatingly, the box office was closed. I swore to myself. There'd be a manager, but he wasn't likely to be much use; the girl at the box office would have seen all the people go in and out, would perhaps have remembered a striking redhead in stylish white. The manager would spend only part of his time in the foyer. All the same, I went to find him.

He was bald, round-headed, wearing a worn dinner jacket and blinking owlishly. I said, 'I'm looking for —'

'You are English?'

'Yes.'

'My English bad. Something . . . ah . . . lost? Lost things we keep.'

'Not things. A lady.'

I showed him Alsa's photograph and he frowned. 'Lady is lost? No. I not see.'

'You're sure?'

'I not see.'

'Thanks anyway.' He was obviously telling the truth; he wasn't used to lost people, just lost property. But something struck me then; cinemas must have a system about lost property: all those gloves and umbrellas and handbags people left behind. I said, 'I understand she may have left something behind.'

'Ya. It was . . .?'

'Gloves,' I lied quickly. 'Brown gloves.

'Come please.'

We went into his little office, with its rolled posters in one corner and film cans in another. He opened a cupboard and pulled out a cardboard box. In it lay a lot of gloves, a couple of purses tied round with string, a lighter, a copy of Strindberg. I turned them over, but everything was well-worn, lost-looking, rather forlorn. It had occurred to me that Alsa might have left something in the cinema deliberately, but all this stuff was ordinary, the litter of a passing trade.

Back at the hotel, there was a note asking me to tele-phone Marasov at the Hotel Nord. I went up to my room, thought about the telephone bug, and decided to ignore it. If Marasov wanted to say anything important, I'd ring off and phone from somewhere else.

He didn't. He asked whether there was any news of Alsa, and when I said there wasn't he said he was sorry and hoped there'd be better news soon.

'I hope so, too,' I said tersely. 'I'll let you –'

'My superiors,' Marasov said quickly, 'are anxious to know about the publication of *Russian Life*.'

'They what!' Suddenly I saw red. 'Well, you can bloody well tell them it can wait, as far as we're concerned, until – '

'I am sorry,' he said quietly. 'We understand, naturally. I was simply instructed to ask you.'

'Well, you asked!' I slammed the phone down angrily. Sorry to hear she's disappeared, but would you mind getting back to more important matters! The bastards! They could stuff their piddling magazine. So could Scown, sitting com-fortably in his half-acre office, also with his mind on more important matters. Meanwhile, Alsa was God knew where, and anything could be happening to her. Schmid could play his verbal games, with hair-splitting answers and tricky questions, but he wasn't getting anywhere either.

Marasov had triggered it, and now the fears, the frus-trations and the depression of the last few days boiled to-gether inside me. I was furiously angry, and determined, suddenly, to be put off no longer. There was one place where I felt sure I'd find some clue to what had happened, but I'd even been denied that!

Well, I'd be denied no longer. I went out of the room, on to the end of the corridor, summoned the lift and pressed the button for the sixth floor. When the gates opened I headed for the fire-exit door to the hotel roof.

The roof was flat. There was a big water tank and con-duits of one kind and another, and a parapet waist high round the four sides. I went to the edge and looked over, but I was on the wrong side. Not for long though. A few seconds later I'd found the right spot and was looking down on the concrete balconies of the floor below, calculating which belonged to Alsa's room.

It would be the fifth one along. Fine. One, two, three, four, five. The drop was about twelve feet, but so be it; it was a direct drop, the balcony would stop me from falling out into space and I was in no mood to be put off, especially since by hanging by my hands, I could cut down the distance by more than half.

As I climbed over the parapet, though, my resolution was evaporating. It might be only a short drop to the balcony but it was a hell of a long one to the street below; not just long, fatal if I missed.

You'll just have to be bloody careful, I told myself savagely. Careful about the drop and careful, too, that I should not be seen from the street below by some public-spirited Swede who'd howl police. Clinging to the parapet, I lowered one foot into space and reached down with my right hand for the edge of the roof. This was the moment, and I hesitated. Once my left hand left the security of the parapet, I would be committed, unable to climb back, because my other foot would be levered out into space; I forced myself to relax my fingers, and held on desperately as my whole weight swung downward, jerking brutally at my grip. Now there was no changing my mind. I could only go down. I turned my head to squint awkwardly down at the balcony, to be sure I was correctly positioned, then let go.

I landed where I intended to land, smack in the centre of the narrow balcony, but I fell awkwardly, jarring my knees, hips and right wrist and for a moment or two the pain convinced me I had broken bones all over the place. I lay still for a while, then the pain began to ease and I pulled myself shakily to my feet. The sound I'd made seemed to have attracted no attention; surprisingly, because it had seemed very loud to me. When the pain began to recede, I started to examine the double doors that led from the balcony into the room. Inevitably they were locked, which meant I'd have to do damage to get in, which meant in turn that it would be known the room had been entered. Even Schmid, I thought, wouldn't have much difficulty in guessing who was responsible.

But I wasn't going to let that stop me. It wasn't difficult to tell which of the two doors were bolted and which held by the tenon of the lock. I looked cautiously round in case anyone might be out on one of the other balconies; at that time of night it was unlikely, but I checked. Then I looked down at the street. I watched for a minute or so and no-one seemed to look up at the hotel.

Right, then. I leaned back against the balcony rail, gripping it tightly, and smashed my heel as hard as I could at the point on the door frame where the lock was housed. There was a splintering sound, frighteningly loud in the stillness, and I ducked down quickly in case it attracted attention. A couple of minutes later, certain that it hadn't, I smashed my heel at the door again. This time it gave and I slipped inside quickly, pushing the door closed behind me.

The pale moon gave precious little light; certainly not enough to read by, and the pile of paper I could make out on the little corner desk fitment would need examining with care. I stood for a moment weighing the alternatives: should I take it all and leave, or risk switching on the light? Removing evidence would be a felony, no doubt about that, but then it was a crime to be in the room at all. What decided me was the realization of the futility of taking the stuff away. Schmid might need it to find Alsa. I had no doubt he was searching genuinely enough, but I was beginning to doubt his capacity, or mine, or anybody else's, to find her. Still, Schmid might find her, and to do so he might need the papers. All right, then, I'd have to examine them here.

The curtains weren't thick. Light would show through them. I stripped the heavy candlewick bedspread and draped it from the curtain rail, then switched on the bedside light and looked around. Alsa's handbag lay on a chair, presumably exactly where she'd left it. I opened it and looked at the contents. There were the usual impedimenta: lipstick, powder, nail file and scissors in a little case, a couple of Russian picture postcards that she hadn't used; a couple of ball point pens and a magnifying glass with a little stand for transparency viewing. It was no help. Suitcase, wardrobe and chest of drawers held only clothes. I crossed the room and started looking at the papers.

There were a few layouts, but just roughs with pictures and type areas blocked in. They told me nothing. Then I started on the typewritten material: about a hundred articles of one kind and another, about a whole spectrum of Russian activities. Each had a note attached saying which Russian magazine it had appeared in and when. I began reading them, but to go through the lot would take all night and I hadn't got all night. So I flicked the pages of each one and got nowhere. Only a few pages showed anything apart from plain typescript, but there were one or two on which Alsa had begun to work; she'd made sub-editorial corrections and marked the type in which she wanted the text to be set. I looked at the familiar markings: twelve-point Medium Gothic lettering here, ten-point Metrolite capitals there, eight-point Times Roman for the bulk of the setting. It was all normal and ordinary; familiar, rabid marks, many indecipherable to the lay eye, but passing effective instructions from sub-editor to typesetter. My eyes ran over the markings absorbing and dismissing them quickly. There were marginal query marks here and there, too; *SEE OD,* which means she intended to check a spelling in the Oxford Dictionary; *SEE Britannica,* and so on. I stopped suddenly at one of them. *See myopic.* Myopic? What the hell was myopic? Hardly a standard reference book, anyway. I made a mental note to try to find out and continued my examination of the articles with a new urgency. A minute before, I'd seriously been doubting whether there was anything at all in the papers. Now instinct told me that there was more.

I found the second oddity on a torn page of one of the articles that had been partly sub-edited. Paragraph one was Metrolite, twelve-point; paragraph two was ten-point Times.

Paragraph three eight-point Times? But it wasn't. The type marking was one I'd never seen before. It said, ten-point Aggie Waggie, but the 10pt had been struck through, invalidating the type instructions. I stared at it. Aggie Waggie? There are literally thousands of type faces, and in a long career I'd come across many of them, some with very weird names indeed, but I'd never heard of Aggie Waggie. Some novel Swedish face, perhaps? But worth checking.

Ten minutes later, I found a third thing: a pencil note on top of one article said, 'No contacts. Check.' Contacts are contact photographic prints, made with the negative in direct contact with the photographic paper, and Alsa had none, either here in the room, or at the printers. I puzzled about it for a while, but could make no sense of it at all, partly because I had, by that time, been in the room about forty minutes and was getting jumpy.

I'd have to leave soon. The sooner the better, in fact. With luck it would be next day before Schmid discovered I'd been in there and in the meantime I could try to work out what the three strange references meant.

I rose and softly switched off the light, then tiptoed to the door. There was no possibility of leaving the room by any other route. Dropping down from the roof had been difficult enough; getting up again would be impossible. I waited until my eyes adjusted a bit to the darkness and noticed that the bedspread I'd draped over the window had slipped at one corner. A triangle of light would have been showing, damn it! If anybody had noticed *that* . . .!

I swallowed. There could now be somebody in the corridor outside, waiting for me, yet it was impossible to know until I opened the door. I'd just have to take the chance. With my hand on the doorknob, I thought of a tiny bit of insurance, went back and carried the little upright chair from the desk to the door and balanced it on its back legs so that the chair back would move beneath the handle as the door opened. Holding it steady with one hand, I turned the handle gently with the other. When the handle was fully turned, I began to ease the door slowly open, leaning to peer round it. With the crack an inch wide the corridor seemed empty. Another inch revealed nothing. I moved it a little more, until the door touched my fingers where they supported the chair. All well so far. It looked all right.

But it wasn't all right. Suddenly there was a hand holding a gun, pointing at me from behind the angle of the door frame. Then Elliot's voice said, 'Hold it, Sellers. Hold it right there!'

## CHAPTER NINE

'Step back and open the door,' he said. 'Don't put on any lights.'

'All right. 'As I took a step backward, I remembered my right hand was still holding the chair. I disengaged it successfully and took another step and the gun followed me round the door. As Elliot's head came after it, I whipped the chair upward hard, hitting the gun hand from underneath, and simultaneously smashed my foot against the door. The gun spun upward and fell with a thud on the carpet; the door cracked hard against the side of his head.

With my foot jammed against the door to stop it opening, I flipped on the light and reached for the gun, then snapped the light off again. I'd never fired a hand gun in my life, but I felt a lot safer holding it, if only because Elliot was unlikely to have another. I moved the chair out of the way, reached for the handle, opened the door quickly, and stepped back. Then, I hurled myself out of the room into the corridor.

It was empty. Elliot had gone, or if he hadn't gone, at least he wasn't anywhere I could see him. He could be waiting anywhere though, behind a door somewhere, in the lift, in my room. Or he might not be waiting at all, might have disappeared once he'd lost his advantage.

I decided I'd get out of the hotel, if I could, and then

stay out. Perhaps find myself another hotel; certainly get away from the immediate area. But first I had to get out. Available alternatives were the lift and the fire escape. If Elliot watched one, presumably he couldn't watch the other. Unless he had help. In any case, I had the gun, though I couldn't quite see myself using it.

I chose the lift. It came up empty and I punched the Garage button, keeping a careful finger on the Doors Closed button as the lift descended. I stepped out into the sharply-shadowed light of the garage with the gun held inside my jacket, and looked round. The place was deserted and a concrete ramp, two cars wide, led upward to the street. I went up the side of it close to the steel guard rail and examined the street outside. There were a few people in sight still, but no obvious sign of Elliot, though he could easily be standing quietly in any of a hundred doorways.

I came out sprinting, racing for the first cover, my bruised knee and hip joints protesting. As I ran, I rounded every corner I came to, every time I came to one. After two hundred yards I'd put three corners between myself and the Scanda Hotel and was standing in a doorway myself, trying hard to breathe without gasping noisily. I waited five seemingly endless minutes, then decided to take a chance, and walked quickly towards a brightly lighted thoroughfare fifty yards away. There I was lucky. A taxi was cruising towards me as I emerged in the street and I flagged it down.

Somehow or other, amidst all the exertion, an idea had come to me and I wanted to investigate it while I had the chance. While the taxi was heading for the cinema I'd visited, I kept a careful watch through the rear window to see whether anybody was following. Nobody seemed to be, at any rate not obviously, though among the fairly heavy late-night traffic it could have been done discreetly. At the cinema, I paid off the cab and began to walk back towards the hotel.

It was Alsa's word *contacts* that interested me. *No contacts – check*. That was what Alsa's note had said, and I'd assumed, naturally in the context of articles and pictures, that it meant contact prints. But it could refer to something else. Alsa wore contact lenses. They hadn't been in her handbag, where she would normally keep them. Nor were her ordinary glasses, the heavy ones with the black library frames there either. It could mean nothing, of course; just that she'd left them somewhere else in the room and I hadn't noticed. Or it *could* mean something else entirely.

I remembered the little case in which she kept the contact lenses: a small, plastic tube about two inches long and one in diameter. She'd shown it to me once, a couple of years earlier, when the lenses were new. The case had a lid at each end. The lids were marked L and R for left and right, so the lenses didn't get mixed up, and the tube itself was filled with some protective fluid. There was one further thing about that little plastic case: it had a small transparent window for the owner's name and address in case it got lost. *No contacts -- check.*

It all fitted. She'd phoned me in America. She knew how I felt about her, knew that if anything happened to her, I'd be there come hell or high water. The note itself would mean nothing to anybody unless that person knew that Alsa wore contact lenses and perhaps not even then, because it was a commonplace thing to find written at the top of an article. I walked slowly along, looking at those buildings whose lights were on. There were a few restaurants still open, a cigarette kiosk, a news stand. Then a chemist's and I hurried across the road, but the lights were display lights and the place was closed. I swore to myself and moved on.

The shop, when I found it, wasn't in the main street and I almost walked past. It was tucked away perhaps fifty yards down a side street and it was the glowing pair of spectacles, neatly executed in red neon, that caught my passing glance. And this shop was open! There was a woman at the counter and a back room which must be the dispensary.

I said to the woman, 'Good evening. My wife thinks she mislaid her contact lenses here the other night.'

'One moment.' She disappeared through to the room at

the back and a moment later a man in a white coat came out and spoke to me.

I said, 'I'm sorry. I don't speak Swedish.'

'English?'

'Yes. My wife thinks she may have left her contact lenses here.'

He smiled. 'Ya. On the counter she leave them. Tell her she not worry.'

I manufactured what I hoped looked like a grin of relief and put out my hand. 'Can I have them please. '

'I am sorry. I send them away by post. I not know where the lady is. I was most careful. I put them in a box with cotton wool to protect them. You see? Then I copy address from the case.'

I said, 'Oh, that's marvellous! Thank you. Just one thing. Which address was on them?'

His eyebrows rose. 'You have more than one?'

I smiled. 'Two. Plus her office address. She wasn't quite sure which . . .'

'Ah . . . mmm . . . I think . . . was Norway, I remember.' He looked at me suddenly in surprise. 'Norway? You are English?'

'My wife's Norwegian,' I lied quickly.

'Ya. It was Norway.' He smiled. 'I remember exactly! Jarlshof, Sandnes G.B., Norway, Mr Anderson. You see how well I remember.'

I could hardly ask him to write it down, but I'd got most of it. I thanked him, trying to remember every detail until I got outside.

'Ya. She came to buy Kleenex, I remember. She must have leave it on the counter. I find next morning.'

'Thanks so much,' I said, repeating: Anderson, Sandnes G.B., Norway in my mind. 'It was very kind.'

I took out a few kroner and offered them. 'Postage?'

'No, no. A pleasure. To lose them would be bad, eh?'

'Very bad. She'll be very glad to have them back. Thanks again.' And I was off, walking away from the shop, then stopping to write it down.

At last I knew something more about what Alsa had done! I tried to think what I did know. One, she'd left the hotel, quite deliberately, to get rid of something. Two, it had to be something small to go into that little lens case. The lens case and the optician's shop made an obvious enough connection: Alsa could have been reasonably sure that an optician of all people would take the trouble to return contact lenses to their owner. But why the cinema? I pondered for a while and decided she might have intended to leave the case in the cinema, for the cleaners to find, but had decided against it in case the cinema people weren't too meticulous about lost property. But what was *in* the case? It was ludicrous to believe she'd taken all that trouble about the cover transparency for *Soviet Industry*. If she'd found that, she'd simply have returned it to Marasov. All the same, I was prepared to bet on a transparency. The Russians had detained her in Moscow to search for one. My God, I thought, what *had* Alsa been carrying? Already two men had died for it, and Alsa herself had been kidnapped once and probably twice and was now either somebody's prisoner or dead.

I went back to the open news stand and bought a Scandinavian guide book, then took myself for a cup of coffee. I found Sandnes, Norway, easily enough near Stavanger, but Jarlshof wasn't big enough to show on the map or be mentioned in the guide, and I didn't know what G.B. meant in relation to Norway. Could it be the Norwegian equivalent of 'and Company Limited?' Like AG in Switzerland and GmbH in Germany? That was the likeliest explanation, but who was Anderson, and why had she sent the damn' thing to Norway? To the best of my knowledge Alsa knew nobody in Norway. She might, of course; anybody can know anybody anywhere; Anderson could be an old schoolfriend, or a distant relative.

I looked at my watch. It was now close to midnight. If Sandnes was where the trail led, then I was going to Sandnes. But clearly, there'd be no transport that night.

I ordered another cup of coffee and a sandwich; the sight of the café's menu had reminded me I'd eaten nothing for hours and though I wasn't hungry I forced the sandwich down. Then I fished the bit of paper out of my pocket and stared at it until *Anderson, Jarlshof, Sandnes G.B., Norway,* was so fixed in my mind I'd never forget it. After that I burned the scrap of paper in the ash tray, powdered the ashes and thought about the three things I had: that Norwegian address and the words *myopic* and *Aggie Waggie*. The clue to Alsa's disappearance lay in them somewhere, but for the life of me I couldn't see what the clue might be. Myopic means short-sighted. Shortsightedness was the reason Alsa wore glasses – or the contact lenses she'd disposed of so carefully in the one place she'd be fairly certain they'd be found and forwarded. But so what? The thing led round in a circle. And the address in Norway was no more helpful. She wouldn't normally have a Norwegian address on the lens case and her name wasn't Anderson. So why had she put *that* name and *that* address on the label? She'd obviously done it deliberately, and the whole business of the visit to the cinema, followed by the visit to the late-night chemist/optician, where she'd left the case on the counter to be found after she'd gone, indicating that she knew she was being watched and followed. She'd done it because it was the *only* way to get rid of the thing!

All right. But it still didn't tie up. That fire in the mail-box at the Scanda Hotel was the odd item out. It suggested she'd posted something that must be destroyed and had in fact been destroyed. But that had been *before* she left the hotel; *before* she took the lens case to leave it in the shop!

I didn't want to go to Sandnes. All my instincts were screaming to me that Alsa was still in or near Gothenburg, and the idea of leaving Gothenburg to travel into another country felt badly wrong. Still, logically it was the only thing to do; I must follow the only lead I had.

In the meantime, what? It was now after midnight and I dared not return to the Scanda. I'd pay my bill later, by sticking money in an envelope and sending it. All I'd left at the hotel was a few clothes. Everything that mattered was on my person, including the bulky wad of photocopies that had been forcing my suit out of shape since early morning.

I decided I'd take a cab to the airport and wait there for the first morning plane to Norway. That way, with luck, I'd stay out of everybody's clutches. Schmid was unlikely to know, until morning, that Alsa's room had been entered. Unlikely, anyway, unless Elliot told him, and considering the nature of Elliot's activities, I felt I could rule out the possibility.

I paid for the coffee and sandwich and went out to look for a cab. There wouldn't be a lot of direct flights, if any, from Gothenburg to Stavanger, but there was a strong possibility of very early feeder links to Copenhagen, hub of the Scandinavian Airlines System. After that, well Copenhagen-Stavanger was probably well serviced. Or maybe I could go via Oslo; I didn't mind which, as long as I could get to grips with *Anderson, Jarlshof, Sandnes, G.B., Norway.*

At the airport I paid off the cab and took a seat in a quiet corner of the lounge. The place was still quite busy. The Tannoy system was going on about a flight from New York that had been delayed and wasn't due in Copenhagen for another hour, and quite a number of people were pulling long faces about it because they were clearly destined to wait half the night for relatives and friends to arrive. It suited me fine; the last thing I wanted was to be the sole occupant of an otherwise deserted lounge, eyed by airport coppers wondering who and what I was, and, with time heavy on their hands, deciding to find out.

From where I sat I could see the departures board. There was a Copenhagen flight at 6 A.M. and after the next announcement I joined the angry crowd at the SAS Information desk and fought my way forward to speak to one of the two harassed girls who were trying to explain that they hadn't exactly delayed the transatlantic DC8 themselves and everything possible was being done. The girl I spoke to seemed relieved to deal with a rational inquiry and I learned that the six o'clock Copenhagen flight connected onward at seven-ten to Stavanger. I went and bought a ticket, then returned to my seat.

The New York people came in at four, to the accompaniment of sighs of relief, not least from the girls on the information desk, who departed promptly, still looking remarkably self-contained, for what was probably a relaxing cup of coffee but may have been a necessary schnapps.

In a few minutes I was alone. It would probably be an hour before the place became busy again, as passengers arrived for the Copenhagen and other early flights. A couple of cleaners mooched around in a desultory kind of way and one or two people in uniform crossed the lounge occasionally, but otherwise the place was too still and quiet for comfort. Sitting there I felt exposed. I'd committed felonies and Schmid would want me. And not only Schmid, either. As the minutes ticked by I became progressively more uncomfortable. To sit like a statue was to attract attention; to move was to attract attention. After a bit I decided I couldn't stand it any longer and headed for the door bearing the silhouette picture of a man. With all these women in trouser suits they're going to have to find a new international sign before long. I went into one of the cubicles sat down and began to watch my watch. Five-thirty was flight check-in time and I hoped that by five-twenty there'd be enough bright, early-morning faces around to lose myself among. At five-fifteen I rose, flushed the toilet for the benefit of nobody in particular, and had a wash and shave by courtesy of one of those coin-in-the-slot electric shavers that are labelled Hygienic but don't always look it, then straightened my tie, combed my hair and stepped out.

As I did so, a policeman not ten yards away glanced at me, did a swift double-take and marched purposefully towards me. I looked round for somewhere to run, but there were several other policemen about and they looked young and fit and I'd never have got away with it.

'Passport, please,' the policeman said. I sighed, reached into my pocket and handed it to him.

'Come with me, Mr Sellers.'

So I went with him. As I did so, the loudspeaker was reminding intending passengers for the first morning flight to Copenhagen to check in. I tried once. 'I'm booked on that flight,' I said, with what innocence I could muster. 'Will this take long?'

The young policeman didn't smile, didn't even reply. He took me to the airport police block and phoned. I could distinguish only two words of what he said. The words were: Inspector Schmid. When he put the phone down, I expected to be loaded into a car and taken to the main police station to see Schmid, but nothing happened. After a while I said, 'What now? My plane's still waiting.'

'You wait, too.'

The plane was long gone before anything more happened. I'd been given a cup of coffee and had twiddled my thumbs extensively, but nobody spoke to me and all my conversational overtures were rejected.

Then the door opened and Schmid came in. It was a quarter to seven and he looked morning grim. News of my capture must have dragged him from beneath his down quilt and he was angry about it.

'Come with me,' he said. Just that.

I rose and followed him out of the room. Outside a police Volvo stood, but he didn't walk towards it. Instead he headed for the departure gates. I walked along with him, puzzled.

When we reached the gate he produced a ticket and handed it to the official who glanced at me and asked for my passport. A moment later I was through and walking with a still-silent Schmid along the corridors. Finally we turned right at Gate Four and I stopped and stared. The board above the gate said SK 463 Gothenburg-London. And outside on the tarmac stood a nice, shiny DC9.

Schmid escorted me aboard, took me to a seat in the tail, and handcuffed me to it. I'd asked him what-the-hell once or twice and he hadn't responded. Now I said it again and he still didn't respond. He merely slid into a seat on the other side of the gangway, opened a copy of the *Svenska Dagbladet* and began to read. He glanced at his watch from time to time as though expecting somebody.

Outside, ground crews and fuel trucks swarmed round the DC9 and I watched them without seeing. I was trying to work out several things. One was why I hadn't been searched when there was a gun weighing down my jacket and the thick wad of photocopies bulging in my inside pocket. The second was why Schmid was hustling me out of Sweden.

It must be, I thought, because I was just a damn' nuisance to him, getting in the way of his inquiries. But that seemed pretty thin. Schmid was a policeman, a policeman's job was to apprehend and bring charges against lawbreakers; I was a lawbreaker. So why this?

I found out at about a quarter to eight, when footsteps sounded on the boarding ladder outside and two men entered the aircraft. At the sight of them, Schmid folded his paper, gave me a hard glare, and rose.

The two men came towards me, squeezing past Schmid in the narrow gangway, and sat in my row. One I didn't know. But the other was Elliot.


CHAPTER TEN


Ten minutes later the rest of the passengers came aboard. We must have looked a bit odd, the three of us, sitting in silence, shoulder to shoulder in a single row of seats with the rest of the cabin empty. One or two people did give us the kind of mildly curious second glance reserved for privileged travellers who don't have to wait at gates.

Elliot and his companion sat like statues, not talking either to me or to each other. I'd asked Schmid what was happening several times, and he hadn't told me, so I'd no reason to expect anything from these two. I'd save my breath.

Then the hostess came along the gangway, looking at seat

belts, and noticed mine. 'Fasten your seat belt, please, sir.'

'I can't,' I said, raising my wrist. 'I'm handcuffed to the seat.'

Her eyes widened briefly. 'I see, sir. Perhaps one of these gentlemen . . .?'

'Would you be so kind,' I murmured to the silent bloke next to me. 'Regulations do require it.'

He leaned over without a word, fastened the clip and jerked the strap brutally tight across my stomach.

'I think they're here to guard me,' I said loudly, to the hostess and everybody in general, 'But I'm not certain and they won't tell me.'

She smiled uncertainly and went away. A few heads half-turned to look, but aircraft seats aren't designed to assist the curious. Soon the engines wound up for the taxiing and again for take-off.

I ate breakfast one-handed as the DC9 headed for London and tried to decide who Elliot's companion might be and why I'd been handed over. There was a powerful smell of official co-operation on a fairly high level, and that alone finally confirmed that Elliot wasn't a National Georgraphic writer. I'd been suspicious of his credentials anyway. And so, I realized, had Schmid. That thought made me blink for a moment, but the answer to the riddle must be simply that Elliot had had to declare himself to Schmid and Schmid had had to co-operate. Government stuff.

I looked hard at the man in the next seat. He was as English as Elliot was American: a darkish suit of some tweedy mixture, Tattersall check shirt, club tie, brown, well-polished Tricker shoes and that kind of fair tight-to-the-skull curly hair that somehow always says army officer. Sometimes wrongly, but not often. Official circles! I grinned mirthlessly to myself.

When the seat belts sign lit up again as the aircraft began its descent towards Heathrow, there was no need for further action; the belt had been left fastened and my guts felt badly constricted. But having sat quietly through the journey I felt entitled to one more try. I reached up and quickly pushed the 'Call Hostess' button with my free hand. As she approached Elliot waved her away, but she looked at me inquiringly. I said, 'I am not certain that these men are properly authorized. I wish to surrender to the British police at Heathrow. Will you ask the captain to radio that message ahead, please. My name is John Sellers.'

'I think, sir,' she began hesitantly, 'that . . .'

'Please give my message to the captain.'

She nodded, turned and walked away up the aisle. She didn't come back. It had been pretty feeble, anyway. Elliot and the other man continued to ignore me. A car was waiting at the airport and the passengers were kept in their seats while the three of us disembarked, my handcuffs having been unfastened by Elliot's still unidentified companion. Not much more than half an hour after landing, I was being hurried from the car across the pavement into a building in Northumberland Avenue. We entered a lift and went up two floors, along a corridor and into what looked like a company board room. There was a long, polished table, with seats round it, an Indian carpet on the floor, a couple of dark, old, unidentifiable and unlabelled portraits on the walls.

Then the one with the wavy hair spoke for the first time. He said simply, 'Your clothes.'

'What about them?'

'Take them off.'

'Not until I know who you are and what all this is about,' I said. 'For all I know, you're just some sadistic poofter – '

'You can be held and stripped forcibly.'

'I can be shot, too, I expect,' I said. 'But unless you do that, you're going to have to let me go, sooner or later, and when you do – '

'A D-Notice will cover these matters,' he said, almost contemptuously. D-Notices are issued by the British Government to gag the press on matters of supposed national security. A while ago they slapped one on a railway magazine to stop it publishing a story about a proposed reduction in rail services.

'Not in America, Germany and a lot of other countries,' I said.

His neck muscles tightened. 'I am an official of the Ministry of Defence. This is a matter of national security.'

I pointed to Elliot. 'But he's not. I want names and reasons and documentary proof.'

He stared at me grimly for a moment. I stared back, unimpressed. I've met them before once or twice. There's usually at least one in British embassies abroad, and they're characterized by their satisfaction at being in many respects, above and outside the law. The British like to think they haven't a secret police, and that there's protection for all under the law etc. etc. It's not wholly true. These people operate on terms and budgets not approved by or even submitted to Parliament, except as part of a lump estimate, and where the law is concerned, they're the ones who make sure the trial is *in camera*. That's if the matter comes to trial.

Elliot said, 'Can't you – ?'

'No, he can't,' I said. 'Not without asking his superiors. If he goes high enough, of course, these things can be fixed, but he's not high enough. You can tell by his suit.'

The man glowered at me for a moment, then went to the telephone and talked into it quietly. A few minutes passed silently, then another man came into the room. I recognized this one, which probably annoyed him. His name was Wemyss (pronounced Weems) and he'd conducted Ministry of Defence briefings for defence correspondents in his time.

I said, 'Good morning.'

He nodded. Black jacket and striped trousers, high level professional civil servant doing his three years in this rather distasteful organization before promotion to yet higher things. 'I understand you're being unco-operative, Mr Sellers,' he said, in a rather pained way.

'I'm not doing anything,' I said. 'Neither co-operating nor otherwise until I know who I'm talking to and why.'

'I should have thought it was obvious,' he said mildly. He turned to the man with the wavy hair. 'You told him who you are?'

'Yes, sir.'

I said, 'He says he's an official of the Ministry of Defence.'

'So he is. Such officials do not normally disclose thei names.'

'Or authorizations?'

'I see. Very well.' He snapped his fingers.

I saw the card briefly as it was flashed resentfully under my nose. It was headed Ministry of Defence and said the bearer was a duly authorized . . . I said, 'I have a feeling this militaristic clown and I don't speak the same language.'

'Your choice of words is offensive.'

'As F. E. Smith once said, I am *trying* to be offensive. He can't help it.'

The mildness was wearing thin. 'You know who I am?'

'I know your name. Alastair Wemyss. '

He sighed. 'You shouldn't know even that. However . . . all right. Mr Elliot here is an official of the National Security Agency of the US Government.'

'That's not how he introduced himself to me. '

'No.' Wemyss looked at me for a moment. He was an abstracted, scholarly man, and his dislike for his current position showed. He'd much prefer to be back at Oxford, or out in the glowing light of Civil Service day again. 'You'd better leave us.' The DI5 man left reluctantly, badly wanting another go at me. Elliot remained.

Wemyss said, 'Would you mind telling me what you know?'

'Precious little. I didn't have much chance. I was only there thirty-six hours.'

'All the same. If you please.'

'Alison Hay has disappeared,' I said, 'and nobody knows where to start looking for her, including me. Including Elliot, and including a Swedish police inspector called Schmid. I was trying to look.'

'You shouldn't have been there at all.'

'Why not? Because you tied Scown's hands?'

He said patiently, 'In these matters it is sometimes necessary. How did you discover Miss Hay was, er, missing?'

'She rang me up.'

Wemyss frowned. 'I understood she failed to get through. Elliot?'

'That's right.' Elliot was totally unemotional watching me through his shiny glasses. 'She didn't get through.'

'I do wish you'd help voluntarily, Mr Sellers,' Wemyss said in that pained manner.

'If I don't?'

'Let's avoid that attitude.'

I said, 'Correct me if I'm wrong. I think you've been *using* Alison Hay. Without her knowledge. As a result she's deep in something she can't handle and probably in very grave danger. Or even dead. Why the hell *should* I help you.'

'You have a duty to your country.'

'Certainly. But not to Elliot's.'

'We have an alliance. You may have noticed. Your plain duty is – '

'No,' I said. 'Not that way. You tell me what this thing's about and if I can I'll help. But *not* if it involves further risk to Alison.'

'That decision is not yours to make.' He kept glancing past me at something and now he did it again. I turned my head. There was a clock on the wall.

'Unless we're back to the days of rack and thumbscrew it's my decision,' I said.

'Yes. Please empty your pockets.'

'You're charging me?'

'I hope it won't be necessary, Mr Sellers, but you are impeding, quite deliberately, an important matter of state security. As you say, I can't put you on the rack, even if I so wished . . .' Wemyss gave a thin smile. 'But I am entitled to ask to examine your effects.'

'All right. Start with that.' I laid a none-too-clean handkerchief on the table. Then the rest: Elliot's gun, my passport, wallet, press card, money, cheque book, keys, notebook, pens, finally the layout photocopies. Elliot recovered his gun with a long, easy arm. Wemyss picked up the passport and said, 'There is no entry relating to all this currency.'

'No.'

'A technical charge, of course, but –'

I said, 'Don't threaten. I'm interested in Alison Hay. Just Alison. I don't give a damn what she was carrying and I think to make her carry it, whether she knew she was doing it or not, was bloody disgraceful. If there's some way of getting her out of whatever she's in, then I'll help. For the rest, you can get knotted!'

'It's a natural viewpoint,' Wemyss admitted. He looked up at me and then his eyes flickered past me to the clock. 'But a difficult perspective for –'

I said, 'If time's as tight as it seems to be, you're wasting quite a lot of it.'

'Perhaps.' He'd gone through most of my things and was now unfolding the photocopies. 'What are these?'

'Layouts. They're innocent enough.'

'Why did you copy them?'

'Because they were there. Because I thought they might tell me something.'

'And they didn't?'

'No.'

I folded my arms and decided to say no more. I knew that at least one of those layouts had been done before Alsa left Russia. She'd also brought something out and got rid of it. These men wanted it, whatever it was. But having got rid of the thing, Alsa was part of the past, expendable, perhaps already expended. Except that Wemyss kept watching the clock.

Wemyss glanced at me, then said to Elliot, 'Did you bring Miss Hay's belongings?'

'No.'

'Better get them sent over.'

Now Elliot glanced at the clock. 'Okay, but –'

'Please be quick.'

'Okay.' Elliot moved to the telephone.

Wemyss said, 'It means, Mr Sellers, that we must confide in you. At least to some extent.'

'Good.'

He shook his head. 'Hardly that. This is extremely important information.'

'I shan't pass it on.'

'No?' He shrugged a little. 'Well, perhaps you won't. Let me ask you this: why are you so sure Miss Hay was, as you put it, carrying something?'

I stared at him. 'You mean she wasn't?'

'It was open to question. Now I'm no longer sure there's any doubt.'

I said, 'You know it all, surely. The phone call saying she was in danger. The two alleged Frenchmen in the next hotel room who got murdered. Then she vanishes. And the business of being searched before she left Russia.'

Wemyss said, 'People are sometimes searched before they leave Russia.'

'To me it adds up.'

'And to me.' He gave his thin smile. 'I wish it didn't.'

Elliot replaced the phone and crossed the room towards us. 'They'll try for the afternoon plane. Swedish police won't like it, though. They weren't too happy in the first place.'

Wemyss' manner changed abruptly. His voice was suddenly crisp. 'Sit down, Sellers. And listen.'

I obeyed, watching him. The scholarly air had departed. He said, 'There is a writer in the Soviet Union whose work is disapproved by the authorities.'

I said, 'There are quite a number.'

'Please do not interrupt. This man's name is Daniel Kominsky. You know about this?'

I nodded. Kominsky was Jewish and had a daughter. He wanted to emigrate to Israel but wouldn't leave his daughter behind in Russia and his daughter was being kept there because her mother wanted her to stay. The Kominskys were divorced. A nasty tangle. The official Russian line was that Kominsky was free to go, but meanwhile he had no job in Russia and no income and survived on the charity of friends.

It was rumoured that his wife was an officer of the KGB. Nobody knew the daughter's view because she was in a training camp on the Black Sea. The Russians said she didn't want to leave her mother behind. Kominsky said she did. The story had been in and out of the newspapers for months.

Wemyss said, 'A group of Russian Jews, admirers of Kominsky, apparently decided to exert direct pressure upon the Soviet Government, other methods having failed. In spite of what you may have heard to the contrary, there are still many highly-placed Jews in the Soviet Union. What they did was to acquire a piece of important military information. They then made arrangements to take it out of the country. The plan was to inform the Soviet Government that unless Kominsky and his daughter were allowed to leave the Soviet Union, this information would be passed to the Americans. Clear so far?'

'Perfectly clear.'

'Very well. It was not intended that the information should actually reach the Americans. The group of Russian Jews were neither espionage agents nor traitors to their country.'

I said, 'In that case, how do you know? '

'There are sources.'

'One of them talked. There *was* a traitor among them.'

Wemyss said, 'I repeat, it was learned in the West that this . . . ah . . . plan existed. It seems the first courier, carrying the information in some physical form, was on a Russian aircraft which crashed on landing at Vienna three weeks ago. Another means had to be found.'

'Alsa was the other means?'

'It seems likely.'

'What form did it take, this information?'

'We believe it was photographic. We're not certain.'

'What's wrong,' I asked, 'with word of mouth?'

Wemyss looked at me for a moment. Then he said, 'I don't know.'

'What was the information?'

'We don't know that either.'

I said, 'This is bloody stupid!'

'So we thought at the time. Arrangements had been made by . . . ah, by Mr Elliot's organization, to intercept the courier on the plane at Vienna. The crash, of course, made that impossible.'

'The crash wasn't accidental?'

He hesitated. 'The courier *was* on the aircraft. If the aircraft was deliberately destroyed, the need must have been extraordinarily great.'

Elliot chimed in. 'A hundred and sixty-three people died.'

I whistled. 'Surely not. Not even the Russians – '

Wemyss said, 'The violence of the Russian reaction was enormous. There were a great many arrests inside Russia. We know that. But the Central Intelligence Agency learned, indirectly, from a source within the Soviet Union, that another attempt was being made to smuggle the information out via State Publishing House Number One. It seems likely that Miss Hay was the chosen method.'

'Why?'

Elliot said, 'She was there by government arrangement. She was carrying large quantities of photographic material.'

'And you still don't know what it was?'

Wemyss lifted his hands and let them fall. 'No, Mr Sellers, we do not. But there can be no question now of its importance.'

I turned to Elliot. 'These two men in Gothenburg, Maisels and Cohen? They were Jewish. They were part of it, right?'

He nodded. 'We don't know how they originally planned to get this thing, but it's obvious they finally had to grab her.'

I said savagely, 'And they were murdered! Who by? Your people? The two Americans in the other room at the hotel?'

Elliot said tightly. 'No, sir. My people missed the whole damn' thing. But whoever killed Maisels and Cohen snatched your Miss Hay. That's for damn' sure.'

I said, 'And who was that?'

But I knew the answer before he told me. Alsa was now a prisoner of the Russians.

I shuddered. She'd tell them; she'd have no alternative. They'd find out where she'd sent the thing and then finish with her.

Wemyss said, 'You were right about the pressure of time.'


# CHAPTER ELEVEN


Wemyss was looking at me uncertainly, as well he might. We both knew the way my thoughts were running and that the slight improvement in the atmosphere since the DI5 man's departure hadn't affected the basic issue. His difficulty was that I might know something important; in fact, he was sure I did. He also wanted to know, quickly, what it was.

I didn't know what the snippets of information meant, and I wasn't going to find out sitting there talking to Wemyss and Elliot. Furthermore, even if I could somehow discover the meaning of *Aggie Waggie* and *myopic*, I wasn't going to pass on the information without copper-bottomed guarantees. The Russians in Gothenburg had had Alsa for a whole day now, and wouldn't have been wasting time or sympathy on her. They'd know, by this time, precisely where and how she'd got the lens case away and would have made arrangements to collect. Indeed, the little packet would almost certainly have been delivered already. I groaned inwardly. Alsa was safe only while the Russians did not have the packet. As soon as they had it, they'd dispose of her. They'd have to. They couldn't afford to release her and let her broadcast what they had done.

But if I told Wemyss and Elliot what I knew, I had no illusions about the action they'd take. They were after the information Alsa had carried. No more, no less. If a means of persuading the Russians to release her were to arise, they'd probably take it. But that wasn't likely. The result was that nobody but me gave a damn what happened to Alsa. No, perhaps I was not quite alone. Scown would care in his own weird way, but even to get to Scown would be difficult and if I did, what could he actually do? It was imperative that somehow I get clear.

I said, 'Why do you suppose they grabbed her?'

'You know as well as I do,' Wemyss said quietly.

'Tell me.'

Elliot said, 'She got the thing away. That's why Maisels and Cohen grabbed her, and it's why the Russians followed suit. The question is, where did she hide it?'

'What's she like?' Wemyss asked me gently. 'You know her. Have you any idea what she'd do?'

I thought for a moment, trying to manufacture some mental lever. 'She's cool,' I said. 'Doesn't panic.'

'Resourceful?'

'I'd say so. She's a damn' good journalist.'

Wemyss looked at me thoughtfully. 'You're in love with her?'

I avoided it. 'I've known her since she was a little girl.'

'Was she in love with you?'

I ducked that one, too. 'How the hell would I know?'

'To whom would she run in emergency?'

'Well, she phoned *me*.'

'What about Scown?'

'The wrong man,' I said. 'He thinks only about newspapers. She wouldn't approach him, anyway.'

'He paid for her schooling. '

'You've got a file, have you?'

'A poor one. Assembled too quickly,' Wemyss said, regretfully. 'We'd like you to add to it. We'd like to know who her friends are; whether she knows people in Sweden, or anywhere in Scandinavia for that matter. You know her friends?'

I shrugged. 'Some. The usual Fleet Street people. Her flat's been searched, of course.'

'Of course.'

I thought of something suddenly. 'What about the office?' I asked carefully.

'No. We spoke to Scown –'

I said, 'A lot of journalists just about *live* in the office. Home is somewhere to rest your head.' But I knew why the office hadn't been searched: because Alsa's disappearance was supposed to be secret. So if I could get to the *Daily News* office . . .

I said, 'She'll have a contacts book. Phone numbers and so on.'

'In her desk?'

'Probably.'

'Let's go,' Elliot said quickly.

'You're nuts!' I said.

'Why's that?'

'Because the moment you show your face in the *Daily News* reporters' room, a lot of professionally sensitive noses will begin to twitch.'

Wemyss said, 'But if we go through Mr Scown?'

'If Scown descended from his eyrie into the reporters' room, the whole place would start wondering why.'

'What you mean,' Wemyss smiled thinly, 'if I understand you, is that your own presence would cause no comment?'

'They don't even know,' I said, 'that I've resigned.'

He looked at me doubtfully, but his eyes flickered involuntarily to the clock. I waited while he thought it out; he was eyeing me speculatively, and wondering exactly what I knew. Finally he said, 'You'll have to be accompanied. '

I rose. 'Come with me yourself.' Knowing he wouldn't.

He said, 'I think Mr Elliot.'

'Not Elliot,' I said.

'Then it will have to be Wil –' he stopped.

'Williams, is it?' I asked. 'Or Wilson, or Wilkinson or Wilton?'

'Willingham,' Wemyss said tightly.

'All right.'

He looked at me in some surprise.

I said, 'At least I don't have to talk to *him*!'

Sitting in the car with Willingham a few minutes later, moving along the Strand and with my property back in mv pockets, I was trying to work out how he could best be handled. Wemyss had given him firm instructions to remain inconspicuous, but Willingham would be watching me closely all the same. It was now noon, and Jimmy Caulfield, the features editor, would be in the King and Keys having a revivifying drink. Morning surgery, he called it. Caulfield's office was glass-partitioned and looked out on to the newsroom, and Alsa's desk was about twenty feet away. Also, I had been serious about her desk, if not about her contacts book. If there was a clue to *Aggie Waggie* and *myopic* anywhere, that was where I'd find it.

I let Willingham pay off the cab and went into the *Daily News* building, nodded to the commissionaire, picked up the house phone and dialled Scown's number. His secretary intercepted, then put me through.

'What is it?'

'Bad,' I said. 'Probably very bad. I've got an official circle with me and I'm going to search her desk.'

'Want anything?'

'No. If I do, though – '

Scown said, 'Let me know. I mean it. '

He wasn't surprised I was back, but then he wasn't often surprised about anything. I turned and found the commissionaire blocking Willingham's way.

A big man. One of two big men who stop undesirables moving beyond the foyer. Both of them ex-Marines, in their fifties perhaps but still formidable. I said, 'Okay Tom, he's with me.' Tom nodded and stepped aside, allowing Willingham to follow me to the lift.

Caulfield's office was, as expected, empty. I sat Willingham in it, pointed out which was Alsa's desk and left him. He wasn't happy, but I scarcely expected him to be happy. As I crossed to the desk, his big face was glued to the glass, watching my every step.

After a couple of minutes the assistant news editor wandered over. 'Borrowing a lipstick?'

I forced a grin. 'An address Alsa promised me, that's all.'

'She doesn't set up dates for me.'

'I'll speak to her about that,' I promised. He smiled and wandered off.

I found Alsa's contact book in the right hand top drawer, where most people keep them, and leafed through it without taking it out of the drawer. No *Aggie Waggie*. No *myopic*. No Society for the Short Sighter. It may exist, but it wasn't listed.

I began to take out notebooks and work through them. There were twenty or more, all dated, all full of the usual miscellany of shorthand notes and phone numbers from Batley to Bognor that fill all reporters' notebooks. After a few minutes, though, it occurred to me that Alsa wouldn't have pointed me in the direction of twenty notebooks. It would be something a damn sight more positive than that.

But what? I sat drumming my fingers on the desk top, wondering. She'd aimed the information specifically at me, no doubt about that. Therefore she intended me to look somewhere specific. Somewhere I'd look because I knew her and knew the way she thought. I glanced round the office. Willingham's angry face was still pressed gargoyle-like against the glass partition. Telephones were ringing, reporters were typing, gossiping, using telephones. The tea boy was wandering round with a big enamel teapot. A messenger was carrying a cuttings file from the library to the news desk.

The library? Surely not. It held literally millions of cuttings and pictures, harvested for half a century and carefully filed away. But there could, I supposed, be a file labelled *Aggie Waggie* in there. I half rose to go and look, but changed my mind, because an idea struck me then. It wasn't the library cuttings I wanted, but Alsa's own cuttings. That might be it! She'd kept cuttings of the stories she wrote since she was a beginner – her father's idea, and perhaps a bit old-fashioned these days, but . . .

I found them in the bottom left hand drawer. Three fat volumes. I was careful to be casual as I lifted the top one on to the desk top, careful not to glance towards Willingham. I began to turn the pages, reading each story carefully. After forty minutes or so, I'd worked back in time to the point where she'd joined the *Daily News*. Before that she'd been on a woman's magazine for a while, doing production, not writing very much except a weekly books' page. All the same, I felt the cuttings book *was* the likely place. Somehow I was certain the clue lay somewhere among the carefully pasted-in pieces Alsa had written.

The reviews were the usual women's magazine stuff, memoirs of a country midwife, flower arrangement, dressmaking, medical and pseudo-medical stuff, how to bring up kids. None of them more than a few paragraphs. There was an office style, a way of setting out the salient details: title, author, publisher's name in brackets, price, in that order.

Perhaps I saw it because the name was unusual. I don't know. Perhaps my senses were just sharply tuned. Anyway, a name suddenly seemed to stand out in a mass of type: Opie. I looked at the book's title: *Children's Games in Street and Playground* by Iona and Peter Opie (Oxford University Press) £2. I kept turning the pages for Willingham's benefit, but I was thinking furiously. My Opie? Myopie? The word had been hand-written, and *c* and *e* are easily confused in handwriting. *See myopic* made no sense at all; *See my Opie* might. The intervening capital letter needn't be important. What I needed was a sight of the book. Would there be a copy in the library?

I put my head round the door and told Willingham I was having no luck and that if he didn't mind terribly, I was going to the gents. He scowled at me and watched me go.

'Have you,' I asked the librarian quickly, 'a copy of a thing called *Children's Games in Street and* –'

He said, 'Opie. Up there. The blue one.'

Thirty seconds later I knew about *Aggie Waggie*. It was, naturally, a children's game. But it was more than that; the game was played all over Britain, under various names. It was called *Aggie Waggie* is only one place, and a remote one at that; in the Shetlands.

I returned to Alsa's desk, trying hard to look relieved and frustrated at the same time, and picked up the cuttings book again. There'd been a story in there about the Shetlands, and those islands rang a tinny bell in my mind for another reason. Alsa had taken a holiday or two up there and she always came back shiny-eyed and enthusiastic talking with a kind of laughing provocation about strong, silent Vikings, so somewhere inside me a worm of jealousy had long tunnelled around. In the cuttings book were two pieces she'd done. I read them carefully. The first was about the first impact of the discovery of North Sea oil on an isolated community, the second about a local character who spent his life among the islands' sea birds, climbing wild crags to count eggs and so on. Maybe he was the Viking type, I thought sourly, but it was his name that made my scalp tingle. Anderson. James Anderson. *Anderson, Jarlshof. Sandnes G.B. . . . Norway?* But where did Norway come into it? The coincidence of the names was too strong to be ignored, but Norway was completely inexplicable. I looked for a while but the cuttings book contained nothing about Norway and the other two books pre-dated the one I was looking at.

Finally I put the stuff away, all except the contacts book, and went back to Willingham.

'Anything?' he demanded sourly.

'Not that I can see. Here's her contacts book. Let's see if it means anything to Wemyss.'

He grunted and rose and we walked together to the lift. On the way down I needled him deliberately and hard about his clothes, his manners and his appearance. He didn't reply, but he was visibly fuming. Just as the doors were opening at the ground floor, I kicked his shin hard.

'You bastard!' he said loudly. He was red-faced with pain and anger and Tom the commissionaire looked round interestedly.

'Tom,' I said. 'We're having trouble with this one. Wants to horsewhip Mr Scown. Don't let him through again, will you?'

'Course not,' Tom said. 'This way, sir.' He took Willingham's elbow with a large firm hand and blocked the furious Willingham's punch deftly. As I ducked back through the doors, he was saying, 'Now we don't want any trouble, do we, sir?'

I raced downstairs, through the machine room, quiet at that time of day, and out through the despatch bays where the papers are loaded for distribution. Two or three minutes later, I was cutting up Chancery Lane across High Holborn and into Bedford Place, heading for the Holborn Library. I'd have preferred the available resources of the *Daily News*, but Willingham had been at only a very temporary disadvantage and the *Daily News* building would be dangerous for me now.

I went up to the second floor reference library and helped myself to a book, the telephone directory for Northern Scotland. Andersons weren't exactly uncommon, and there were numbers of James Andersons, several of whom could have been the man in Alsa's story. I put the phone book away and searched the shelves until I found the *Survey Gazetteer of the British Isles*. There was an interesting entry under 'J': 'Jarlshof (Earl's Court) ruin, in S. of Mainland, Shetland.' Then I tried Sandnes, and there it was, 'pl, 8 mi NW of Walls, Shetland, PO. TO.'


CHAPTER TWELVE


I stared grimly at that formal little entry in the Gazetteer. It was true that at last things were coming together, but it was happening in a faulty kind of way. For a start, Sandness in the Shetlands wasn't spelled the same way as Sandnes, Norway. Anderson, oddly enough, was a name common to both countries. I got out an atlas and found that Jarlshof and Sandness were a long way apart. I tested the breadth of the library's available material and found a Norwegian

Trade Directory to see what the letters G.B. meant. They meant nothing at all. G.B. was not, as I had supposed, an indication of a company's legal set-up.

I was standing by the window, which overlooked Theobald's Road, with the book in my hand, when a pair of white police cars appeared outside. Shutting the directory with a snap, I headed quickly for the door and stairs and went down to the street, startled that the Metropolitan police had been called in so quickly. I emerged from the library cautiously, only to realize I needn't have bothered. If I'd thought before moving, I'd perhaps have remembered there was a divisional police HQ almost next door, but by now I was decidedly jumpy and simply hadn't thought. I decided not to go back inside. The police would certainly be asked to look for me. Wemyss already suspected I had facts I hadn't told him about, and it was clear enough from what I'd done with Willingham that I'd picked up more in the *Daily News* office. If this was as big as he and Elliot believed, they'd now want me very badly indeed.

So what next? Christ, there were three places I ought to be: Gothenburg; Sandnes, Norway; and Sandness, Shetland! Of the three Gothenburg was the one that called most strongly, simply because that was where Alsa was. But she'd fixed things so the lens case would be sent to Sandnes, Norway, then deliberately pointed me in the direction of the Shetlands. Why? The only answer I could see was that she wanted me to go and see this man Anderson. I wondered where he came into it: an ornithologist working in wild and remote islands; one of those dedicated, away-from-it-all people who find satisfaction in the simple life. That, at any rate, was the picture Alsa had painted in her piece about him.

I soon realized it was all very well thinking blithely about heading for the Shetland Isles, and a lot less easy to do it. They were nearly a thousand miles away and accessible quickly only by air. I had no doubt, either, that there would be people watching for me at Heathrow.

I kept walking, trying to think what other arrangements

Wemyss and Co. might be making to get their hands on me. Tapping the wires into the *Daily News* for a start, though that alone would keep them busy: there were sixty general lines into the switchboard and private phone lines all over the building. The first one they'd tap would be Scown's. I wondered how long it took to tap a telephone. Probably not long if the job were being done officially, so it might be dangerous, now, even to try to speak to Scown. The realization that I was completely alone hit me then and I felt momentarily slightly sick. On one side there was Wemyss, with the resources of his immensely powerful department ranged against me. Plus Elliot, and *his* agency. On the other side were the Russians, determined to recover the thing that had been smuggled out. In the middle, two tiny, insignificant figures in the giant pincers, were Alsa and me. Of the two of us, only I had liberty of action and even that liberty was rapidly being curtailed.

I came to the corner and glanced along Gray's Inn Road at the *Sunday Times* building, its metal cladding gleaming dully in the cloudy sunlight. I thought about it, and dismissed it. I had one or two friends on the *Sunday Times*, but none was close enough for me to seek help there.

But what about the other papers? I knew plenty of people in Fleet Street, for Heaven's sake, and there'd be somebody among them, surely . . . Walking up Gray's Inn Road, I thought of names, some of them powerful names in the business, and dismissed them one by one. What I needed was a plane, and there were plenty of people I knew who could charter one with a phone call. I could myself, normally, but this time I daren't risk using my own name. The trouble was that all the people I knew would want to know *why*. They'd be after the story. And the story couldn't be told.

All right, then. Did I know anyone who could fly? Plenty, of course, who'd flown years ago, but I needed someone with a valid, current licence. Then I remembered a little Australian on the *Daily Mirror*. What was his name? Hinton, that was it. Bruce Hinton. It had to be Bruce, all Australians of his generation seemed to be called Bruce.

I found a phone booth near the top end of Gray's Inn Road, close to King's Cross, and rang the *Mirror*. When the switchboard put me through to features I put on a fake Australian accent and asked for him.

'Just a sec,' said a busy voice. I swore softly to myself. Hinton was actually on duty, damn it, I'd hoped it might be his day off and that I could persuade somebody on the *Mirror* to give me the home number.

'Bruce Hinton.'

I said carefully, 'I think we may have got something that might interest you. Can you meet me?'

'Who is it?'

'John Sellers.' I hoped he'd think it was the offer of a job coming up.

'S'pose so. Where?'

'I'm up near King's Cross.'

'Bloody hell, mate!'

'All right,' I said. 'If you feel like that.'

'No, no! I'll come. 'Bout twenty minutes, okay?'

'Right.' I told him where to meet me and filled in the waiting time buying myself a blue donkey jacket, a cap and a pair of sunglasses at an army surplus shop nearby.

I had talked to Hinton, or more accurately been one of a drinking group that included him, a few times. I didn't know him well, just well enough to be aware that flying was his private obsession. He had a one-third share in a small Cessna. He'd have a fair salary, but nothing like enough cash to indulge a hobby like flying as much as he'd like. I was banking on that.

A few minutes before he was due to arrive I went looking for a taxi, cruised round in it for a couple of minutes, then went to the rendezvous. He was there, waiting.

I shouted his name and he came across and got in. As he closed the door, he said, 'This is bloody mysterious!'

'It gets worse. Is your plane flying today?'

He blinked at me. 'It was this morning. Not sure now. I think it will be free. Why?'

'Because I want you to fly me somewhere.'

'Jesus, John. I'm not licensed for bloody charter! They'll have my licence so fast it – Anyway, I'm on the desk today.'

'Pity. I thought a couple of hundred quid might tempt you to give an old friend a demonstration.'

He looked at me quickly. 'It bloody well does, too. Where d'you want to go?'

'Lerwick.'

His eyes widened. 'You joking?'

'No.'

'Sure? You're not pulling the old Pommie –'

'I'm sure,' I said. 'Two hundred in cash. Plus fuel and maintenance charges.'

He grinned suddenly. 'What the hell you up to?'

'My business.'

'Yeah. Jesus, if they heard at the *Mirror*!'

'Why should they?' I said persuasively. 'Your old Auntie Rainbow just blew in from Woolloongabba. Wants you to show her round London.'

'So she did. Good old Auntie Rainbow.' He thought for a moment. 'Listen, it's not Lerwick, you know. The airport's at Sumburgh. Christ, it's five, maybe six hours!'

'Are you on?'

'Have you two pence for the phone?'

I gave him some coins. 'Better check the plane's there, too.'

I waited in the cab while he phoned his office and the airfield from a pub. When he came out his walk was spring-heeled.

'All right?' I asked.

'They don't think it's funny, but I've still got my job, I think.'

'And the plane?'

'Okay.' He settled back in his seat. 'Better than work, sport. Tell him Elstree. I'll direct him when we get there.'

I made one phone call from Elstree: to Scown on his private line. I didn't care now who overheard. I said, 'Tell the official circles to look for Anderson, Jarlshof, Sandnes, Norway,' and hung up.

We were off the ground within an hour. His flight plan was accepted straight away, which was a bit of luck, and I watched the metamorphosis of a slightly bolshie Australian journalist into a hard-nosed precise pilot. He seemed to my untutored eye to have a lot of experience. I said, 'How many hours?'

'Five-fifty. Five fifty-six to be accurate. Average cost about fifteen quid an hour, I reckon, by the time it's all in. Comes expensive. That's why this trip's tempting. What in hell did you say you're doing it for?'

'I didn't say. But not for fun.'

'Not at that price, sport. Must be a good story. Maybe I'll hang on. Work myself back into favour at the *Mirror*.'

I said, 'When we land, you get a cup of tea and turn round. If you have to stop over, do it in Scotland somewhere. You're not staying on Shetland.'

He laughed, 'Okay, blue. Now do me a favour. Shut up and let me fly.'

Obediently, I shut up and watched the cloud patterns beneath us. I also thought a good deal, to no great purpose. After a while I took out the layout photostats I'd made at Strom Brothers and stared at them hopefully for a bit. Nothing emerged, though, and I put them back in my pocket again; but the feeling persisted that there was something there, if only my purblind eyes could see it. We came down to refuel at Dyce, Aberdeen, then flew on. The clouds had disappeared as we crossed the Pentland Firth. Once we'd passed the Orkney beacon, Brucie Hinton talked to Sumburgh control then turned to me looking pleased. 'There's a twenty-knot bloody crosswind. Have to be bloody careful, sport. Glad I came!'

It must be nice, I thought sourly, to have nothing on your mind but the challenge of landing in a dangerous crosswind. 'Well *be* careful.'

'I've got a one-third share of this bastard. You watch how soft I put her down.'

But he didn't. He came in one-wing low and didn't ease her across properly and we bounced sickeningly four times.

But he was happy.

'Well, I tried, sport. I'll do better next time.'

'I hope there won't be a next time.'

'Pity.' He pocketed the two hundred and I told him to send the hangarage and maintenance bills to Scown.

He said, 'Now *there's* a useful guy to know.'

'I'll introduce you, one day,' I said. I hoped I'd have the chance.

'Do that!' He climbed back into the Cessna, yelled, 'Thanks, sport,' and started the motor. While I walked across to the airport building, he roared off south.

There was a four-sheet Ordnance Survey map of the Shetland Islands pinned up in the terminal building and I stopped for a minute to get some idea of what the place was like. I'd intended to take the first available transport to Lerwick, the island's capital, but something I saw on the map stopped me. There was the single word 'Jarlshof', in the Old English typeface used on Ordnance Survey maps to indicate antiquities. Furthermore, Jarlshof was no more than a mile from where I stood.

I left the terminal buildings, looked around me and set off walking down the road. After a while it forked. The main road led away to the east, but a smaller road signposted Jarlshof. I followed it and quite soon the archaeological site came clearly in view.

It looked deserted. The day was dying and the tourist season probably over. Overhead a small twin jet screamed down towards a landing at Sumburgh, incongruous in the stillness. I swore to myself, turned to walk back and in doing so noticed a car. Well, at least somebody was here. I began to walk round. Notices set out the history of the place, and I read one cursorily. Excavations had revealed habitation there from mediaeval times right back through the Viking Age and the Iron Age to the Bronze Age. But I was wondering where this collection of ancient stones came into my own problem.

The place was well cared-for, grass neatly trimmed to the bases of the walls, paths carefully marked and I walked round aimlessly, thinking, until a voice said, 'Can I help you?'

The man who'd spoken was sixty-ish, tall and slightly stooped and with a scholarly air. A grey-haired woman stood beside him.

'So this is Jarlshof,' I said, meaninglessly.

They smiled at one another, and the woman said, 'It's lovely, isn't it.'

'Lovely,' I agreed.

The man must have sensed my puzzlement. 'Not what you expected?'

'I'm not sure what I did expect. I'm looking for somebody.'

'At Jarlshof?' He was a little puzzled.

I said, 'It's part of the address I have. I saw the sign at the airport, and walked over here.'

'If I can help?'

'It's a Mr Anderson,' I said, 'Jarlshof, Sandness, Shetland.'

'Sandness? Dear me, that's a long way from here. It must be forty or fifty miles. Are you on holiday?'

'Visiting, anyway.'

The woman said, 'Everybody thinks the Shetlands are tiny. I think it's because maps always show them in a separate little box, quite out of position. But they're very big really.' She turned to her husband. 'How will he get to Sandness, dear?'

'He'll have to go to Lerwick first.'

'I'll hire a car.'

'Lerwick's the place for that. We'll take you, if you like. We're going anyway.'

'That's kind –'

'Not at all. It's a pleasure, isn't it, dear?'

She smiled at me. 'Anderson. I seem to have heard . . . oh, isn't that the bird man?'

'He is an ornithologist.'

'Yes, that's right. We met him once, dear. You remember?'

'I do now,' the man said. 'One meets so many new

people. We retired here, you see, a year or two ago, and . . . our name's Dennett, by the way.'

I said, 'John Sellers. How d'you do.'

We got into their little car and drove away from Jarlshof. I wasn't sure I wanted to leave the place without reconnoitring it more thoroughly, but the Dennets had met Anderson and that decided me.

'There's a rumour, you know, Mr Sellers,' Mrs Dennett said as we headed towards the road junction, 'that your Mr Anderson has found another pair of snowy owls. Of course, that was in the spring . . .'

'Really?' I said. 'Snowy owls!'

'Well, we have some already, of course. Two pairs, I think it is, on Unst, or is it Fetlar? One of the other islands, anyway. But it's only rumour, d'you see, and I expect he's very excited about it and trying to keep it very quiet.'

'Bound to be.' I thought grimly that Anderson had bigger problems now than keeping a pair of snowy owls secret.

As we drove alongside the lit-up Sumburgh runway, half a dozen black and white birds marched steadily in line ahead across the tarmac and declined even to look up as a huge helicopter roared low through the night sky over their heads. Beside me Mrs Dennett sighed 'Oh dear, all this oil. It will ruin the islands, you know. You *do* know?'

I said I'd heard a little, and she spent the next forty minutes giving me an expert rundown on the local dissension about land options bought by oil companies, the statistical certainty that sooner or later an accidental spill at sea would annihilate the local seabirds, the inevitability of all the profit going elsewhere, and so on. She knew her subject, was good and articulate about it, and determined I should be instructed. She still hadn't finished when the headlights picked out the word Lerwick on a sign and we began to drop down the hill into the little granite town.

Interrupting her wasn't easy, but I managed it in the end. I was worried about the time. 'Will I be able to hire a car at this hour of night?'

'Oh yes. You see the Shetlands aren't like other places. Not so rigid, d'you see. And *much* more friendly. People *help*, d'you see. That's why we're all so *worried* . . .' We were back to the oil again, but I'd got my answer.

She was right. About the car, certainly and probably about the oil, for that matter. The Dennetts dropped me outside a garage just beyond the harbour, and drove off, waving.

Ten minutes later I was also driving away, in a nearly new purple Mini as stiff as six planks and with brakes that might have been adjusted in a try-your-strength competition between malicious mechanics. The man who rented me the car also told me how to find the Sandness road, and provided me with a map and the advice that I should keep an eye on it, since visitors seemed to find the road signs difficult, though he himself couldn't see why.

I blinded away with my nasty Metropolitan driving habits and discovered rapidly that the Shetlanders have a few of their own. Twice in as many miles I met them on hairpins, headlights blasting and using all the road and I calmed down a bit, especially as it was borne in on me that these roads hadn't been designed in highway engineering establishments; they'd been scraped into hillsides and round sudden contours and half the bends were on the edges of sharp drops with long, moonlit, gunmetal stretches of water far below. Every so often I'd find a sheep standing transfixed in my lights, brace myself, and touch that fiendish brake pedal and slide towards the beast on locked wheels, thanking my lucky stars I was driving something as sure-footed as a Mini.

The Shetland population is thin on the ground, and by the time I was half a dozen miles out of Lerwick, there was only the occasional light from a hillside croft house to interrupt the endless dark landscape. Even these sparse friendly gleams became fewer as I worked my way steadily westward, concentrating ferociously as the road narrowed and wound, stopping occasionally to consult the map when a sign arrowed the way to a place that might or might not be on the way to Sandness.

I'd made a mental note of the mileage before leaving Lerwick, and driving as fast as I dared on that tricky road, it took me an hour and twenty minutes to cover thirty-two miles to the tiny cluster of houses that was Sandness. I opened the car door and stepped out into half a cold gale sweeping powerfully off the Atlantic Ocean less than a mile away and bringing with it a deep, damp chill.

Picking a cottage at random, I knocked on the door and asked the old woman who answered about Anderson's house. She told me, in the heavy, Norse-laden accents of the islands, that there were two Andersons nearby. Would I be wanting old Mr Anderson because he was away in Lerwick? No, I said. Mr Anderson the bird watcher.

'That would be young Mr Anderson, away up the hill.' She was old and bent, but spry and alert, and she slung a dark shawl over her shoulders and stepped out into the wind to point the way. I thanked her, began to return to the Mini, then went back to find out whether anybody else had been asking for young Mr Anderson.

'I didn't hear,' she said firmly, and there was something in her emphasis that said she'd certainly have heard. I thanked her and drove off, backtracking a little way, then turning up a rough track towards the rearing moonlit bulk of Sandness Hill with the cloud shadows flying across it. The distance from the road was perhaps five hundred yards, a very gentle rise that became steeper near the house. I turned the car round, switched off the engine, and went up the slope on foot.

No light came from the house. Blind glass shone the moonlight at me as I climbed. The house was of grey stone, small, with a couple of gabled windows to the upper floor and as I moved towards it I looked carefully at the barren, empty landscape around me, feeling a real sense of isolation. Nothing moved except the air; there was nothing to hear except the sound of my own footfalls and the buffeting of the wind in my ears. I had hoped to find Anderson there, but the lack of lights made it seem unlikely now.

The door was white-painted, so the small black lettering was easy to read. One word; the name of the house, *Jarlshof*. I nodded to myself, then knocked and heard the sound echo emptily. There was no response. I tried again, several times, sadly certain now that the house was empty, then moved away from the door to look in through the windows. What I could see, lit palely by the intermittent moonlight, was a shadowed and fairly spartan room: a wall full of bookshelves, a bare table with two or three plain wooden seats, a couple of old armchairs. It fitted with what little I knew (which was what Alsa had written) about Anderson. This was a place where one man lived and worked, a man not much interested in comfort, a man who chose remoteness and absorption and didn't care to chase the phantom satisfactions of goods and chattels. You meet people like that occasionally and usually find yourself envying them, grossly tempted to follow their example until the realization of your own dependence on creature comforts enables you to thrust the idea away. But guiltily, always guiltily.

I worked my way round the house, looking through windows. A couple were curtained, but I peered in through all the others and finally found myself standing before that white front door again, feeling helpless. There were two possibilities now. I liked neither. I could wait here for Anderson, not knowing how long the wait would be; it could presumably be days if he was off on some prolonged observation, and I didn't have days, or even hours, to spare. The alternative was to go looking for him, and that prospect didn't thrill me. He could be anywhere in this mass of islands, pursuing his solitary studies, and unless he made a practice of telling somebody where he was, there'd be no chance of finding him. I remembered what Mr Dennett said, the rumour that he'd discovered some rare birds, and scowled to myself. If he had, he'd be keeping very quiet indeed.

The hell with it then. The need to find the man was too

great for me to be scrupulous. Somewhere in the house there might be an indication of his whereabouts. I'd have to break in.

But as it happened there was no need. Trying the door without hope, I found that it was unlocked and simply stepped inside, then used my lighter to try to find the switch. No switch. There was a Tilley lamp on the table and I searched back through my memory and fumbled with it until I recalled that it was necessary to get the pressure up before the vapour mantle caught and glowed. Now, at least, I had light. I looked first at the floor behind the door to see if mail was still lying there. There wasn't any, but a couple of opened envelopes lay on a sideboard, window-fronted envelopes, one from the Inland Revenue, the other from a garage. Each bore the Lerwick postmark for three days earlier. I swore, looking at them. Were they the last mail to come to the house? What the hell would have happened to a packet posted to Sandnes, Norway? Would the post office in Sandnes, realizing there'd been some kind of mistake, forward the packet to Sandness, Shetland? Would they even know there *was* a Sandness, Shetland? And if they did, if they had redirected the packet, how long to reach this lonely spot? Was it conceivable that there *was* a Jarlshof at Sandnes in Norway? Even the bloody word was straight Norwegian, held here unchanged through long centuries of the powerful Norse link with these islands. I had uncomfortable visions of the blasted packet being shoved through the door of some uncomprehending Norwegian in the other Sandnes, whose house happened to bear the same name.

I began to ferret round the room, opening drawers and cupboards, then moving to Anderson's old steel desk and rifling through the papers, hoping to find a diary or a log; something here *had* to give a clue to Anderson's activities.

There was nothing. Circulars from the Royal Society for the Protection of Birds, letters from other ornithologists, a few still photographs, some notes. There were even a few transparencies and my heart thumped as I picked them up and held them to the light. No luck; they were just birds.

But no! By God, they weren't just birds! I realized suddenly that there was something wrong with these transparencies. I was handling them carefully, by corners and edges, out of long habit. But somebody hadn't been so careful. There were one or two fingermarks on them, sweat leaving whorl patterns on the delicate emulsion. Anderson wouldn't do that; Anderson was a pro, he'd be as careful handling them as I was. No man shins down cliff faces to photograph seabirds, then wrecks his work with careless fingering of the result.

It was tenuous enough, as evidence, but all the same my scalp prickled. I was almost sure now that somebody else had been here before me, also examining the place. Maybe the same rough fingers whose prints were on the transparencies had opened the envelopes. Maybe Anderson hadn't been here for days.

There was nothing more on the desk, nor, now, was there anywhere left in that room for me to look. I picked up the lamp and carried it over to the rough little kitchen. A few minutes' search turned up nothing there, either. There was only one other room on the ground floor and I crossed towards the door and went in. A workshop. Two benches; one with an angled drawing board and artist's materials, another for woodworking, with carpenters' tools neatly in racks above it. I looked round the room desultorily, almost certain now that Jarlshof could tell me nothing. I'd go up the stairs and see what was there, but I knew already that it was hopeless.

I turned to go back into the living room and what I saw stopped me dead in the doorway. A man sat in one of Anderson's threadbare armchairs. He was quite still, quite calm. He held a big, battery lamp in his left hand and at the moment I saw him, he moved the switch and the light came on. His right hand held a pistol.

# CHAPTER THIRTEEN

For a moment I failed to recognize him. For one thing, he'd been dressed differently the one time I'd met him. For another, I hadn't imagined I'd ever see him again. Now he wore a dark donkey jacket and a seaman's cap whose peak shadowed the upper part of his face. I heard a sound, glanced quickly round the room and saw another man step through the stairway door, a big man dressed similarly in donkey jacket and cap. His face too, as the lamplight fell on it, I recognized. He was the first Gustaffson, the phony one, who'd come to call on me at the Scanda in Gothenburg! He stared at me in mild surprise.

I looked again at the man in the chair, knowing him now. This was the man who had impersonated Schmid. He said quietly, 'Place the lamp on the table.'

I'd been thinking, but thinking far too slowly, of letting it fall. His hand lamp scotched that idea; there'd be no sudden plunge into darkness, just a target held easily in a beam. I obeyed slowly.

'Now step away from it. Stand by the fireplace.'

The pistol followed my movement, pointing low at my abdomen. 'At least,' he said, '*you* confirm that we are in the right house. Now you can tell me where Anderson is.'

I said, 'Who?'

He sighed. 'Let us not play tiresome games, Mr Sellers. Where is Anderson?'

I shrugged. 'How would I know?'

He looked at me thoughtfully. 'If you knew, you would not be here? That's it, eh?'

I shrugged again.

'I had hoped you were Anderson,' he said. 'We have been waiting for him for several hours. You can tell me about Anderson.'

'I've never met him in my life.'

'No? Yet you are here and you got here very quickly. How?'

'I have a homing instinct,' I said. 'Like a pigeon.'

'Yes. A pigeon. A swift bird, but vulnerable, Mr Sellers. I admit I was surprised to see you. Almost as surprised as you are to see me, perhaps.'

'What surprised me most was your clumsiness,' I said. 'You left dirty great thumbprints all over his transparencies. It was obvious somebody'd been here.'

'How clever. And how incompetent to be caught. Tell me about Anderson.'

'Tell me about Alison Hay.'

He smiled faintly. 'You are in no position, Mr Sellers – '

'Where is she?'

'You think she has been found? How could I know? I am not, as you must now realize, of the Gothenburg police.'

'You're here because you heard about Anderson from her. There's no other way – '

He nodded. 'Of course. The question is how *you* knew, Mr Sellers. Tell me.'

'Why should I? Who are you, anyway?'

'Who I am doesn't matter. But you will tell me because I wish to know. And because you can be made to tell me.'

'Then make me.'

'Oh, I can. Quite simply. And I know more than you think, Mr Sellers. Even about Anderson.'

I waited.

'For example. The girl Hay was to be Mrs Anderson.'

That hit me and he watched it hit. Two blows at once. 'Was to be?' I said heavily.

'You see? Whereas you . . .' He smiled. 'For you friendship. Yes, friendship. But only friendship. For marriage, this Anderson. You want proof?'

I shook my head.

'No? But you must have the proof.'

He took a photograph from his pocket and held it towards me at arm's length. I took it from him. The picture showed

Alsa with a big bony-looking man in his thirties. Alsa was holding tight to a big, fluffy, struggling seabird chick of some kind and laughing and he was watching indulgently. A very happy scene indeed; one for the family album. He said, 'I could tell you more.'

'Then tell me.' I put the picture on the table, still seeing her in my mind's eye, remembering the way she looked at me, the way she'd put me off with that stagy my-heart-belongs-to-another business. Being gentle, because she was like that. Saying it, but wrapping it up, hoping it wouldn't hurt as much. And me refusing to believe she meant it.

'You will ask me now whether she is alive or dead. Whether it was necessary to kill her.'

'I'm asking.'

'Sometimes, under interrogation, people die. It depends for instance on how much they resist, how urgent the need for information. '

'For Christ's *sake*! Is she *alive*?'

He pursed his lips. 'We can exchange information, Mr Sellers. This is painless. I have no wish to hurt you. You will tell me how you come to know of Anderson. And other things. And I shall tell you about Alison Hay.'

I said, 'She's alive. She has to be. She's your only lever against Anderson. You daren't – '

'That is merely hope,' he said in mild contempt. 'Whether she is dead or alive, she is effective as a lever, provided Anderson does not know the answer.'

I stared at him, trying to apply some grip on my own chaotic thoughts, aching to hear him say she was alive, appalled at the thought of what might have been done to make her talk, trying to unearth somehow a tiny tactical point I could use. It was his confidence that infuriated me, the ease with which he applied his bloody pressures. Already the pressures were getting to me; the need to know about Alsa had me on the rim of despair and somehow I must get back at him. I said quickly, 'I'm not alone.'

'No? You have an army perhaps? Swarming over the hillsides? Do not be absurd.'

'This morning, in London, I talked to the security service.'

'And the CIA, no doubt.'

'No. The National Security Agency.'

He stared at me for a moment, then spoke briefly to the big man.

I said, 'Russian.' I don't speak it, but it's not difficult to recognize.

His eyes flickered to me, then away again as the big man put down his rifle and unslung a rectangular case from his shoulder, flicked back the fastening studs, pulled out four feet of telescopic aerial, flicked a switch, and spoke into the machine. The reply was a harsh hiss of static. The big man muttered and spoke again and again the roar of static mush came back. He kept trying for a minute or two, then shrugged helplessly.

The phony Schmid snapped an order and the big man nodded and went out, grimacing. I understood both the reason and the grimace. Scown had had his own bright idea about walkie-talkies once, a long time ago, and I too have stood in the lee of little hills swearing at them. The big man had been sent climbing.

'What now?'

'We wait.'

'For instructions?'

He frowned. 'You are a nuisance. Anderson will return. We will be here. But for the moment you must be taken away.'

He was sending for reinforcements and I began to ask myself where they could be. To the west lay the Atlantic. A ship, then? One of the inevitable Russian trawlers that swarm round the world's seas. But there were no hills to the west so no need to climb. The high ground lay near the middle of the long island; I'd driven up and down the spine of hills on the way here. So with luck it would take time. I wished I knew more about the topography of the place. Those inlets I'd passed could probably shelter a ship, particularly a small one like a trawler. How near was the nearest? What kind of transport had they?

He didn't move his eyes from me, after that; but he didn't talk either. I was standing, he was seated, and we were both listening to the wind buffeting the windows. Somewhere up the hill the big man was struggling higher, swearing, seeking a spot from which the cross-country line was clear. I said, 'Speaking of incompetence, you haven't searched me.'

'For what? You are no danger to me. You are carrying nothing to interest me. What you have of value is inside your head.'

'You don't know that. '

'I know I can kill you before you move a foot. So be still.'

Somewhere upstairs, a loose-fitting window kept rattling, and once or twice his eyes moved irritably towards the sound.

'May I sit down?'

'No.'

He was listening, his head slightly to one side, awaiting the big man's return. Upstairs the window rattled again and he frowned.

I was assembling saliva in my mouth, stockpiling it, consciously suppressing the reflex that demanded I swallow, tilting my head back to allow the fluid to flow into my throat.

Was there enough? Could I make myself choke? Would the choking immobilize me? I opened my mouth, breathing in hard and tried to kill the swallowing movement halfway. I managed to inhale a tiny amount. Then other bodily reflexes took over and I began to cough and splutter, magnifying the effect deliberately and reaching for my handkerchief. He watched me carefully, his eyes above the unwavering pistol following the movement.

I got a coin out with the handkerchief and concealed it in my hand as I blew my nose and hawked and spluttered for a moment or two. Then I returned the handkerchief to my pocket.

'Fear,' he said, 'Sometimes affects the membranes.'

I nodded, the coin concealed in my right hand. I moved it slowly through my fingers until it rested over my thumbnail, wedged against my index finger.

'Anderson's an ornithologist,' I said. 'A bird-watcher. They spend their time in isolated places with cameras and binoculars. It could be days before he's back.'

He gave me a contemptuous smile. 'It is winter now, Mr Sellers. The migrations are over. The breeding season has not begun. I am not an idiot.'

I said, 'I understand he found a pair of snowy owls.'

'So?'

'Not migratory. Very rare.' I didn't know whether they migrated or not. Or care.

'Since you do not know him, how do you know this?'

'Alsa – Alison Hay, did a story,' I lied. 'It was among the newspaper cuttings.'

'I see. Let us hope these owls do not detain him long.'

'That's one,' I said.

'What?'

'A snowy owl. Up there.' I nodded in the direction of one of Anderson's wall charts and his head turned involuntarily towards it. For about two seconds.

He was saying, 'So elementa – ' when the coin I'd flicked up over his head landed on the stone floor beside the door.

I shouted, 'Run, Anderson!' and he swung round quickly to look at the door. The low armchair inhibited his movement. 'Run!' I called again at the top of my voice, then I flung myself towards the Tilley lamp and swept it in one movement from the the table into his lap.

Paraffin spilled and caught. Not much, but it was quick and there were little flames on his clothes and he lurched forward to try to control them. I got him once, with desperate violence slamming my fist at his neck, before the pistol went off. The bullet flicked my jacket, but I'd got him again before he could fire a second time, this time with all my strength, and on the nose. He grunted and then whimpered and I hit him again, smashing him back into the chair before I hurled myself to the door and off down the hill towards the car.

Nothing to interest him in my pockets! I had the Mini keys in my pockets and I went down the rough slope like a greyhound, climbed into the car and got it away fast, without lights, accelerating down the track towards the road.

I'd gone maybe sixty yards when something slammed into the car. The big man had a rifle, but even so it must be a lucky shot, and I knew it. I kept my foot hard down and the gear low as I bucketed towards the road, then swung out on to the metalled surface without stopping.

Seconds later I was accelerating fast away from the place. I turned my head as I went and saw a small glow from the cottage. Maybe the Tilley lamp had crashed to the floor as he struggled to rise. Good! Maybe he was frying in his own oil. Also good! I switched on the headlights, needing them badly. I hadn't seen any wheeled transport, but they might have a car hidden somewhere. Again I was thankful for the Mini; on narrow winding roads, that little car's stability is worth a lot of engine power.

I realized how much I was trembling and tried to control it, to switch my mind away from what had just happened, and began to take risks to force my mind to concentrate on driving, to concentrate on the road and on where the road would take me. There was no-one to help, no friends on the islands. I knew no-one here except the Dennetts, who couldn't conceivably help. But hang on! Who was the office stringer here? Newspapers use freelances in every corner of the country and there was certainly one here; I'd seen his name a few times, on copy. What *was* the name, damn it? I tried to visualize the sheets of copy paper. Lerwick. Something, Lerwick. But what was the something? If I'd been in the *Daily News* office, I'd have called the news desk and got the answer pat. But I wasn't in the office; I was driving like a madman across lonely peat moors with armed men not far back who would be very anxious indeed to get their hairy paws on me again.

The name, what *was* it? It was an odd name. I knew that. Something incongruous, something that didn't fit. I could remember the names of whole masses of correspondents, but not the one that mattered. I started to go through the ones I remembered, hoping to roll it out of my memory in a list. MacGregor, Kirkcaldy, I remembered him. His name fitted; Onslow, Brighton; the splendidly-named Brown, Windsor; somebody at Lincoln. Why Lincoln? Of course, damn it, Lincoln was it – the man's name here! Lincoln, Lerwick!

That was why it was incongruous: two place names. And a very English name in the far, far north.

Lincoln. I must speak to Lincoln. He'd know the islands like the back of his hand; freelances have to if they're to make a living, especially in a place like the Shetlands where the story has to be very good indeed if it's to interest the London-orientated noses of news editors.

I was going through the minute roadside hamlets like a frantic flea and a couple of times a lighted phone box was past almost before I saw it. Well, I'd wait until I reached Lerwick. There I could keep the car out of sight in case the big man had made radio contact and others were on the lookout for a purple Mini.

This time I did the trip in a minute or two over the hour, not without giving the local sheep and myself a fright or two. The only real danger was that somebody might be driving to meet me, but that was to assume good organization on land and somehow I didn't really believe they'd have things as well set up as that. Anderson was the target. I'd just come blundering in.

Lerwick isn't big, and before I knew it I was almost on the harbour front. I turned right, up a street of houses, swung into a narrow lane, and climbed out. As I closed the door, I saw a bullet hole in the body panel, a couple of feet behind the driving seat. At night, with an accelerating unlit target, that was some shooting. I shuddered and swallowed and hurried away.

There was a phone box near the town hall, I was told, and I ran to it up something Brae, a street so steep it knocked the breath out of me. When I reached the box I gave myself great offence by having to use a ten-pence coin for a two-pence call. Then I remembered that the coin I'd used in

Anderson's cottage had been a two. Well spent, I thought.

Lincoln was listed under Journalists in the Yellow Pages. His wife answered the phone with the slightly weary politeness of journalists' wives who become accustomed but never reconciled to late phone calls. I told her who I was.

'Jack's away, Mr Sellers. Can he call you back?' A Scots accent. Maybe Lincoln was a Scot, despite the name.

'No. I'm here in Lerwick, in a call box. I need to find him urgently. Do you know where he is?'

'I know where he *was* going. To the galley shed in Saint Sunniva Street.'

'If not, one of the pubs?'

She said primly, 'I feel sure you'll find him at the shed, Mr Sellers. D'you know where it is?'

'I'll find it.'

'Anyone will tell you.'

'Thanks.' I hung up and left the kiosk, looking for anyone who'd tell me, but the street was quiet. Finally I found a small boy who should have been in bed. 'Da galley,' he said. 'Away da.'

Looking in the direction his finger pointed, I could see a pool of bright light among the grey stone houses half a mile away.

'Da's da galley.' He seemed impressed.

He grinned and ran off, almost certainly not in the direction of bed.

I also grinned briefly to myself, glad to have something to grin at, then set off towards the lights. The wind still blew, but Lerwick is sheltered from the blast by the high hills and the half mile walk was an opportunity to wind down, soothing yet bracing. I turned into St Sunniva Street, still tense but feeling better.

A small crowd, perhaps a hundred people, was gathered beneath the bright television lights, and a camera dolly showed above their heads, lenses pointing into the shed. I approached, then pushed my way through until I could see inside. I ought to have remembered, of course. I'd heard of the galley, of Up-Helly-Aa, the Shetland Fire Festival, but until I looked in through the double doors the word galley hadn't clicked in my mind.

It stood there now, a big, colourful, beautifully-built Viking galley, shields at its sides, the striped sail furled at its masthead, people milling around. Half-bottles of whisky, those flat halves that fit conveniently in pockets, were much in evidence and a few people were wearing full Viking costume. I looked at the galley with interest. In the Up-Helly-Aa festival it would be dragged in torchlight procession through the streets, and burned, spectacularly. A waste, I thought, then doubted my own sudden judgment. Why a waste, when it was also an exclamation of pride?

The somebody nudged me and rattled a collection box under my nose. 'She's fine, eh?'

'She is.'

'Costs money, she does.' He was smiling. 'More every year. Inflation they call it.'

I found a pound note, folded it and slid it into the box. 'I'm looking for Mr Lincoln.'

'Oh aye. The reporter?'

I nodded.

'He's here somewhere. Saw him no more than a minute or two ago. Aye, there he is, over there.'

He pointed out a man in his late thirties, fair-haired and stocky, who stood quietly watching the TV cameraman. Earning his bread, no doubt.

'You're Mr Lincoln?'

He turned. 'Yes?'

'John Sellers, *Daily News*.'

We shook hands and he said, 'Here for Up-Helly-Aa, then? Make a nice feature. Nationals haven't done it for a year or two.' He was English, probably Lancashire from the vowel sounds.

'Not really. I want to see a man.'

'About a dog?' He laughed. 'Okay, that's why I get a retainer. Who is he?'

'How many retainers?'

'A few.' He laughed again, energetic and cheerful, a busy,

independent freelance who served many people but no master. 'Good, is it?'

I said, 'It's a story we care about. I want help, but it's an exclusive. So far, anyway.'

'Oh?' Bright and beady interest.

'A tenner for information,' I said. 'More if it stays exclusive. God help your retainer if it doesn't.'

He said seriously, 'You've been dealing with too many Southern crooks, Mr Sellers. I'm secure if I'm paid.'

'James Anderson. The ornithologist.'

'Jim Anderson. Oh yes, I know him. Don't tell me the *Daily News* is interested in birds with wings.'

'I just want to see him.'

'He was here till a few minutes ago.'

'Here?' I could hear the surprise in my voice.

'They're all here for Up-Helly-Aa. He may still be marching, I think.'

'Where is he?'

'He'll have gone. You've heard about the fire?'

'What fire?'

'His house. I got a tip-off from the police a few minutes ago and told him. Not too bad, so I understand. But he lives in the far west, you know. Takes a fire engine a long time to get there.'

'Damn! He'll have gone out there.'

Lincoln said, 'I don't think so. He went to phone, I know that. To find out how bad it was.'

'Where will he phone from?'

He laid a finger against his nose, grinning. 'Local knowledge. When he's in Lerwick he usually stays with Miss Petrie. She was a teacher here for years. Retired now.'

'Her address. Quick!'

He eyed me with interest, my urgency whetting his appetite for the story; he gave me the address and directions how to get there. It wasn't far away. Less than ten minutes' walk, he said. I half-walked, half-ran and made it in five.

Miss Petrie lived in a neat granite cottage in a small row in the older part of the town, and from the shut-down look of the place Anderson wasn't there and she'd gone to bed.

I gave a couple of bangs with the polished brass door-knocker and waited. After a moment a light came on inside, a bolt was drawn back, a lock turned. She was about seventy, white-haired and needle-thin, wearing a heavy woollen dressing gown with several neat darns in it. Miss Petrie could have modelled for any advertisement that required a face stern yet kind, authoritative yet gentle. A long, good, helpful life lay behind her and she looked at me with an incongruous sharp hostility in her level grey eyes.

I said, 'Miss Petrie?'

'Yes.' She said it slowly, reluctantly.

'I'm sorry to disturb you, but it's very urgent indeed. I *must* speak to James Anderson.'

'Then you'd better speak to him somewhere else. He's not here.' Her voice was cold.

I said, 'I have very important information for him. My name –'

'No,' she said sharply. Her hands shook slightly, from age or nervousness. Age, probably. This one would have good nerves.

'Please, Miss Petrie. If you can even get a message –'

'I don't know where he is. You're wasting your time and mine, young man. Good night.' She began to close the door.

Desperately, I said, 'If he's told you somebody's after –'

But the door was shut. The lock clicked and the bolt slid home. I raised my hand to the knocker, but let it fall, accepting the futility of knocking again. If I'd ever met someone acting out of character, it was the old lady behind that door.

Nor was it hard to guess the reason. I'd doubted, at first, whether Anderson would have gone to Miss Petrie's house. Far more likely that he'd have set off on the long drive to Sandness when he heard about the fire. But now I was sure that he either was there or had been there.

The old lady's unnatural hostility only confirmed it; she was protecting one of her own, and with determination. I wondered what Anderson could know. A fire was a fire. An accident, almost invariably. But this whole set-up said clearly that he must know there was more to it than that. He must be highly suspicious and he'd communicated his suspicion to Miss Petrie; now, already, one line of defence was mounted.

I turned away angrily, knowing the defence was, for the moment at least, impenetrable, and I hurried back towards the galley shed, hoping Lincoln would still be around. Turning into St Sunniva Street, I could see the crowd was still there, but the TV camera had stopped work. I prayed that Lincoln hadn't. Forcing my way into the shed again, I looked round for him anxiously. There wasn't a sign. Damn! I felt a sudden, leaden sense of despair, and stood for a long moment, body slackening, in the realization that the roads were closing round me.

'Sellers!'

The call came from above and I turned and looked up. There was a kind of balcony at the end of the shed above the doors, and Lincoln was leaning over, a half-bottle in his hand. I ran up the steps towards him and he held the bottle out to me. 'Here. You look as though you need it.'

'Thanks.' I took a swift swallow. 'He wasn't there.'

'No? That's funny. I was sure that's where he'd be.' He looked at me shrewdly, reading my face, my weariness, the anxiety I couldn't have concealed if I'd tried. Then he said flatly, 'This must be a hell of a story. Big-name features man tear-arsing round at this time of night with the features pages all locked up and gone.'

'It's important,' I said. 'That's all.'

'I can see it is.' His eyes didn't leave my face. 'This is a funny day. Something's on.'

'Funny?' I said.

'Two stories. Both Sandness way.'

'What's the second?'

'The post van was attacked this morning. Out by Walls. Same parish as Sandness.' He let the words come slowly, watching their impact on me.

I made myself sound like a suitably detached newspaper professional as I digested it. 'Anybody hurt? How much stolen?' But I had no doubt at all about who'd done the attacking, or why.

'Somebody flagged the van down, then coshed the driver, and searched the mail. Didn't take anything as far as I know. There wouldn't *be* much. Small bundles of letters to mum and dad, that's all. It's an elderly population, what there is of it, in West Mainland.'

I said, 'But they got nothing?'

'I told you. There were four or five registered letters, apparently, maybe with a bit of money in them. They weren't touched. There's no way of knowing about the rest. What's going on, Mr Sellers?'

I said, 'Don't ask me. I'm here to talk to Anderson. How well do you know him?'

He shrugged. 'I know most people who might make copy. I have to. Birds make copy sometimes.'

I forced a smile. 'Snowy owls?'

'Don't knock 'em. They bring in the tourists, and I've done a few pieces about the snowy owls on Fetlar.'

'Where's that?'

'One of the islands. Good distance north of here. Not many people. I expect that's why the owls are there.'

'But Anderson's found some more, hasn't he?'

'Ah, come on! You're not up here about snowy bloody owls!'

'Has he?'

'So they say.'

'Where?'

'All right. You're paying me. But don't wreck my livelihood. I was saving this one.'

'Go on.'

'They're on Noss. That's another island. They're actually on the Cradle Holm. Anderson and another bloke have been keeping observation for weeks, turn and turn about.'

'Who's the other man?'

'Dunno. Some volunteer from England. In December and

135

January! These bird men are bloody mad!'

'And what's the Cradle Holm?'

'No you bloody don't! That's a bloody good story. Worth money. Picture story in colour.'

I said impatiently, 'It's not what I'm interested in.'

'You would be.'

'Look, I swear –'

'Fleet Street promises! Not likely. I've had some.'

I heard myself sigh involuntarily. 'Do you want me to write it down? I John Sellers solemnly swear on behalf of the *Daily News* that we won't print a line about the Cradle Holm without the permission of Jack Lincoln. If we do, two hundred quid. Is that what you want?'

'It'd set my mind at rest.' His face showed he meant it.

I wrote on a page of his notebook. I'd resigned, of course, so the thing was not valid. But he wasn't to know and I didn't want his story anyway.

He folded the paper and put it into his wallet. 'It's proper name is the Holm of Noss. It's a sea stack, nearly two hundred feet high and absolutely sheer on all sides. Right?'

'Go on.'

'The whole of Noss is a bird sanctuary. The Cradle Holm is at the southeast corner. There's a gap of about sixty feet between the cliffs of Noss itself and the sides of the Holm. Dreadful spot altogether. Well, there's an old tale about it. The top's flat and there's more than an acre of it and in the old days, eighteenth century some time, one of the local landowners didn't like to see an acre of good grazing go begging. So he brought in a clever climber from one of the islands – Foula, they say – and promised him a cow if he could climb up the Holm.'

'And did he?'

'So the story goes. He started by climbing up the mast of a boat to get past the overhang, then shinned up. Then they threw a hammer and some stakes across and he knocked them in. Then a rope, and he fastened it to the stakes his end while the other end was secured on Noss itself. You follow?'

'Perfectly.'

'Well, they slung a wooden box cradle from the rope and from then on the shepherd used to put sheep in the cradle one at a time, climb in alongside and pull himself across by the rope.

'The climber. Did he get the cow?'

Lincoln shook his head. 'Would have, but he was too cocky. Wouldn't go back across the rope. Said he'd climb down the way he'd come up. He didn't make it.'

'And?'

'Fell. Killed.'

'Is it still in use?'

'No. Not for donkey's years. It's all gone now – stakes, rope, cradle.'

I nodded. 'Fascinating, I agree. But what's the point?'

'Point?' he said. 'I'll tell you what the point is. Jim Anderson did the climb again a few weeks ago. Solo. Must be nuts. Then when this other bloke came to help with the observations, they fixed up a rope contraption called a Tyrolean traverse. They go back and forward now like ping-pong balls.' He shuddered.' You should see it. Like a hole down to hell.'

'Worth two hundred any time, with pictures,' I said. 'Keep it for us.'

He grinned. 'Told you.'

'You can tell me something else. Do you know Miss Petrie? I mean reasonably well?'

'Yes.'

'What's she like?'

'Nice old soul. Taught generations of 'em. She made 'em work, but they liked her. She's a kind of monument.'

'Does she trust you?'

'As far as anybody does. Yes, she knows me well enough. I've started being local you know. After ten years I've just started. They trust each other up here, but not outsiders. Or not much.'

'Then do me a favour, will you? Tell her I'm all right. If looks could kill I'd have died on her doorstep. I need to talk to her but she won't talk to me.'

'It would come better from the minister.'

'I haven't got the minister,' I said. 'Just do it.'

'Tonight?'

'Tonight.'

He thought for a moment, then nodded. 'I'll be ten minutes or so. I've got to check all's well with the TV boys and so on. Wait for me.'

'Thanks. And –' I pointed to the bottle in his pocket.

'Want a lot for your money in Fleet Street,' Lincoln said. But the bottle came out and I took a pull at the whisky. 'Where will you be?'

'I'll wait outside.'

'Okay.' He vanished down the wooden steps, busy and energetic, enjoying his life, making for the people at the far end of the big shed. I followed a moment or two later, but turned the other way at the bottom of the stair and went out into St Sunniva Street. There were still plenty of people there, talking good-naturedly; a community engaged in community pleasure. I leaned against a wall and waited for Lincoln to finish inside.

I had just bent my head to light a cigarette, cupping the flame against the wind, when a voice said, 'It really does seem to be Mr Sellers.'

I raised my eyes and found myself looking at the broad face, with its cap of tight, fair waves, of Willingham. I began to turn, to try to get away, but the way was blocked. Elliot was standing at the other side of me.

## CHAPTER FOURTEEN

I blinked at them, looking from one to another in amazement and something close to despair.

I'd been so certain I'd got away clean, so certain nobody could know where I was! I'd been sure that message about Norway would send them off on a wrong tack.

Elliot, grim-faced, looked at me briefly. Then he said, Come with us. Don't try anything.'

I stared at him, still finding it almost impossible to accept the evidence of my eyes. 'How?' I said. 'How the hell –'

'You're so, damn smart,' Willingham sneered. 'All clever tricks.'

Elliot said sharply, 'That's enough! Let's go, huh?'

They had a car at the end of the street. Not that it was needed. We went only a few hundred yards, then drew up outside a stone-built, square Victorian building on the hill overlooking Lerwick harbour. Outside hung the familiar blue lamp with the word Police reversed out in neat white lettering. They led me inside in silence. The duty constable raised a heavy oak counter flap to admit us to the deeper recesses. After that we went upstairs to a quiet room on the first floor. Willingham closed the door behind us, locked it and put the key in his pocket.

For no particular reason I strolled across to the window and looked out over the busy little harbour. Behind me, Willingham said, 'Not this time. There's no way out now.'

I turned to face them, two contrasting men: the thin, saturnine Elliot, grim-mouthed and watchful; Willingham red-faced and angry, square and squat as a bad-tempered boar.

Elliot looked at me steadily from behind his heavy spectacles. 'It's no game, Sellers. Nobody's playing around.'

I took a deep breath. 'Least of all me.'

'You sure act that way. This isn't some ingenious newspaper story you're chasing. Not fun and games and a big by-line.'

I returned his stare. 'You'd better tell me what it is, then. As I remember, this morning you didn't know.' God, was it only this morning! London this morning? Gothenburg only this *morning*?

He said, 'We still don't. We knew the plan. We knew *how* the information was coming out. You know that. But we don't know what that information is.'

'What makes you so sure it's important? It could be some crazy misunderstanding.'

He nodded. 'Sure it could. But it isn't. Reaction's too fierce. It had to be something big or that bunch of Russian Jews couldn't use it to twist the Soviet Government's arm. And if it's that big, we've got to know, understand that. We . . . have . . . got . . . to . . . know. Your government and mine.'

'And you think I know?'

'More than you're saying,' Willingham said harshly. 'A hell of a lot more.'

'Let's cool it,' Elliot said. 'There's no mileage in hate, for any of us. Who've you come to see up here?'

I said, 'Great Aunt Gertrude.'

He looked at me stonily. 'We'll find out, Sellers. Just like we found out where you were.'

'In time?'

'Maybe not.'

I said, 'Maybe your friend could beat it out of me.'

Willingham was staring at me angrily. 'Don't think I couldn't.'

'Who did you come to see?' Elliot asked again.

'Sorry.'

'Look, Sellers, you're an intelligent man –'

'I know the penalties, if that's what you mean. Obstruction, withholding information. You'll find other things. I don't much care. It's the other penalties, to other people, Alison Hay for one, that I'm thinking about.'

'I know it.' He gave a little sigh. 'Okay, let's tackle it from another angle. Let's forget the guy you came here to see. Let's find out what else you know. See if we can get any closer.'

'And then?'

'And then we see. You found something in her room at Gothenburg. What?'

'Sorry.'

'You found out something else in London. It sent you chasing up here. What was that?'

'Sorry again.'

He said, 'It's a simple line of questioning. It can go on all night. It can get rough.'

'I can imagine.'

'I doubt it,' Willingham said. 'I doubt it very much.'

'Nice man and nasty man,' I said. 'I'm familiar with the technique. I watch TV. A punch in the kidneys from one, then a cigarette and kindly words from the other. You're on my side. He's not. Etcetera.'

Elliot gave a thin smile. 'It even works. Believe that. But we don't need it, Sellers. Listen, we finally got to the papers in the girl's room. The Swedish police didn't like it. It took time. High level talking, but we did it. There was nothing. Nothing for us. But there *was* something for you, right?'

I didn't answer.

'Okay, so keep talking. We wanted you in Gothenburg in the first place because you know the girl well.'

'You *wanted* me there?' I said.

'That's right.'

I stared at him. 'It was only by chance I was there at all.'

'Sure,' he said. 'You were in Vegas. You told me. It wasn't too convenient. Not when we needed you in Gothenburg.' There was a tinge of complacency in his tone.

I was beginning to see it, but I didn't believe it. Not at that moment. I said, 'Get out of town? Those cruisers on the lake?'

Elliot nodded. 'Neat, wasn't it?'

'Christ, you –'

'Sellers, we *had* to get you out. Right? You're a name correspondent, we couldn't just kick your ass the hell out of the United States. Too much grief that way. Bad news for everybody and maybe you wouldn't have gone to Gothenburg. You see, I'm levelling.'

I said angrily, 'I was bloody near killed!'

'Quiet place. Few guys with rifles and orders to miss. Couple of phone calls. Then you're on the plane. So am I.'

I was thinking about that desperate chase in the ghastly

heat of the Valley of Fire. The way I'd been shepherded, hunted, turned into a shaking bundle of sweaty fear, crouching exhausted among those hellish rocks.

He said, 'We wanted her found.'

'Not her,' I said savagely. 'You don't give a damn for her. You want what some bastard loaded on to her.'

Elliot simply watched me for a moment. Then he said, 'There's a half-dozen big questions about the Soviets that need answering right now. Big ones. I'm not going to give you a lot of mullarkey about world peace. But they matter. All of them. And there's something halfway out in the open here, Sellers. We've got to know what it is. When we do, if we can, we'll help you. Nobody wants innocent victims.'

'But it's just too bad if somebody *is* the innocent victim, eh?'

He hesitated and then committed himself. 'That's right. It's too bad. But I said we'll help you *if we can*. What alternative have you got? You're here. You'll be held here. You're helpless. There's nothing you can do. Right?'

I nodded wearily, knowing what Elliot said was true. I was in a little box at the end of the road and nobody was going to let me out. There was no way for me to reach Anderson now.

Elliot said, 'Help us. We help you. A deal?'

'It's a bloody awful deal!'

He thought he was winning and gave a satisfied little nod. 'Not the best. It's a sticky world.'

'What happens,' I asked, 'after all this? Do I stay locked up?'

'We'll cross that when we have to. What do you know, Sellers?'

'Very little.'

'Great. It's gonna be a long hard night.'

Willingham said, 'You can't play it soft with one like this.'

'I can try. What did you find in the girl's room, Sellers?'

'Nothing.'

Elliot sighed softly. 'Oh, Jesus! I thought –'

I said, 'I'll tell you why I'm here, though. She's got a friend up here.'

'Who?'

'I don't know,' I lied. 'I just know she's got a close friend in the Shetlands.'

'It's not enough. You didn't fly up here just because she has a friend.'

'A close friend. She was out of the hotel quite a while. You think and I think that she got rid of whatever it was she was carrying then. I think the fire in the hotel letter box had scared her off that and she posted it elsewhere.'

Willingham said, 'Who's Anderson, Jarlshof, Sandnes, Norway?'

'Who knows?' I said. 'Who's Brown, Smith Street, Cardiff, Wales? I was sending you in the wrong direction.' At least they hadn't discovered yet that there was another Sandness, another Jarlshof. They were in the police station but not using the knowledge it contained; playing things too close to their chests. If they'd mentioned either word to one of the local coppers . . . but the instinct for secrecy was too strong.

Willingham grinned. 'You were pathetically easy to follow. That call from Elstree. From Elstree! You were tracked on radar the whole way. Bloody amateurs!'

I said to Elliot. 'Are we talking seriously? Or is your dog going to bite me?'

'Go on,' he said softly.

'She's got a friend in the Shetlands. You can't get much more remote than this. Nobody'd look here. You wouldn't be looking in this direction if I hadn't led you here. Nor would anyone else.'

Elliot said sourly, 'I don't think I believe you, Sellers.'

I shrugged. 'You told me I'd no alternative. Neither have you. But there is something else.'

'Okay?'

I fished in my inside jacket pocket, pulled out the wad of photocopies I'd made and begun to unfold them.

'That's why there was nothing,' Elliot said. 'You took those papers from her room.'

I shook my head. 'This wasn't in her room.'

'Her desk, then.'

'Not there either.' I was straightening the folds, sorting out the photocopy I remembered. I put it on the table and flattened the creases with my hand. It wasn't a particularly good copy; the folds had shaken off some of the black xerox powder, and my hand brushed off more. 'This was at the printing works.'

Elliot came and stood beside me to look at it. The title *Russian Life* was blocked in sketchily across the top of the rough layout.

'Front cover, right?'

I said, 'Alsa didn't draw this one.'

He glanced sideways at me quickly. 'You sure?'

'You can see the difference. The others are her own roughs. This one was done by an artist.'

'So?'

'So who drew it and why was she carrying it?' I said. 'She didn't have an artist on hand in Sweden, so she brought it out of Russia with the rest. Maybe she didn't even know she'd got it. It's another thing somebody loaded on to her.'

'Mm.' He was studying the design, frowning. 'Those flags. What d'you reckon they mean?'

'It's a layout gimmick, I should think. You see the flags are only drawn in outline. I'd guess the idea was to put a picture inside each flag. It's not original and it's not brilliant, but that's what I think it is.'

Elliot studied the paper in silence for a while, then straightened. 'Maybe there's something. I don't see what. It looks like a layout. No more than that.'

I said, 'You've missed the point. It's a lousy copy and the lines have faded, but the flags are supposed to be stuck in a map of European Russia.'

He looked again. 'Yeah. I see it now!' There was excitement in his voice. 'Any ideas what the flags represent?'

'None.'

His excitement flattened. 'If she was gonna put pictures in those slots, what pictures would they be?'

'I don't know. Maybe the flags represent cities. But it's not accurate finished artwork. It's a freehand job.' Then I noticed something. I'd missed it earlier, in the plane, when I'd studied the thing. 'But look at these. Look at the flagsticks. The pencil lines are precise, aren't they? A neat finish to each stroke. No, hang on!' I picked up the paper and held it to the light. 'Look at the *start* of each stroke! *That's* precise, everything else is rough pencil, but not that! Whoever drew this started the stroke at the bottom, at a precise point, and drew upward only a little way, then the line goes free again. No artist would do that, until he was doing the finished job.'

Elliot turned to Willingham. 'Go get a map. Any kind of map. An atlas will do.'

Willingham looked unhappy. 'It's half-past eleven. Where the hell – '

'I don't care where,' Elliot said savagely. 'It's your country we're in. Get one.

We waited ten minutes, then there was a knock on the door. Elliot opened it and the station sergeant came in with a blue school atlas in his hand. 'You want this, sir?'

'Yeah, thanks.' Elliot took it quickly. 'That's all, sergeant.'

'Yes, sir. Just one thing, sir. It belongs to my lad. I went away home to get it. He'll be needing it for the school tomorrow.'

'He'll be – !' Elliot gave a short surprised laugh. 'Okay, sergeant. He'll have it. Thanks a lot. Where's Mr Willingham?'

'Downstairs, sir. Said he'd be up in a moment.'

'Right.' Elliot opened the dog-eared atlas, which looked as though it served more often as a classroom weapon than as an instrument of learning. 'Okay, here we have it. European Russia.' He picked up the photocopy, laid it over the map and grinned. 'Wrong scale, naturally.'

I said, 'We can work it out, I think. Fetch that desk lamp over here.'

I bent the spine of the atlas back, holding all the other pages out of the way, then told him to hold the map of Russia against the lamp. I picked up the photocopy. The paper was thickish, but it might still work. I held it up and moved it back and forth until the line of the eastern border of the Soviet Union and the shapes of the Gulf of Bothnia, the White Sea and the Black Sea coincided. Then I tried to hold it steady and see what places on the map coincided with the flagsticks. It took a few minutes. Each time I identified a city Elliot marked the atlas with a pen, then we started the alignment all over again and picked out the next place.

Finally I could put the photocopy down and together we

He was running his eyes over the names again. 'Moscow. Orel, Sumy, Kremenchug, Gorlovka, Zaporozhye, Pervomaysk, Vinnitsa.

'Well?'

Elliot scowled. 'Small places, most of these. Some I never even heard of.'

'So it's no help?'

He was running his eyes over the names again. 'Moscow. Okay, Moscow. Anything could be happening there. But these others. We'll need to get a real analysis done on this. See what collated intelligence makes of it. And that'll take time, damn it.'

I said, 'Maybe it's just a layout. No more.'

'Maybe.' Elliot's tone meant he didn't believe it. I didn't either.

'Missile sites?' I asked in my innocence.

'Ah, hell no. We know the missile sites.' He read the words aloud again, one after the other, trying to worry sense out of the string of names. The type in the school atlas was small and Elliot had bent close to the paper to read it. It occurred to me suddenly that I could hit him and try to get away. I straightened and stood listening as he pronounced the Russian names. He said without looking up,

'Don't try it. You'd never make it.'

'I suppose not. See anything?'

'No.' He straightened. 'Not a damn thing.'

But quite suddenly I saw it. Perhaps because I was looking at the map from a range of four feet rather than a few inches. I said, 'Give me your pen, quickly!'

'What is it?'

'Hand me the book over there.'

Puzzled, he handed it to me. I used the book as a straight edge and drew a line from Moscow through Orel, Sumy and Kremenchug. Then another, connecting Gorlovka with Zaporozhye. Finally a third to join up Vinnitsa and Pervomaysk. When I'd done that, I went back to each line and extended it until all three lines met.

The book's bulk prevented Elliot's seeing what I was doing until I'd finished. When I'd done, I laid the book aside and looked at him.

He was staring at the map in astonishment. After a moment he said, 'My God, it can't be that simple!'

The three lines made an arrowhead. They converged on a place close to the Black Sea. Elliot bent to look again and I saved him the trouble. 'Nikolayev,' I said. 'Does Nikolayev mean anything in your sweet young life?'

But there was no need to ask. He repeated the word slowly, with a kind of awe, staring at the atlas with wide eyes.


## CHAPTER FIFTEEN


For a few moments he stood there, perfectly still, with the kind of look on his face that Lancelot would have given the Holy Grail. Then he turned to me suddenly. The holy joy faded and his face hardened. 'Listen to me Sellers, and listen good. There are priorities and priorities. This is grade A class one, understand? Don't get in my way. Don't get in anybody's way! This is so important it's –'

I said harshly, 'Simmer down.'

He stared at me, then spoke more softly, but excitement still throbbed in his voice. 'I mean it, Sellers. You give us full co-operation, or else. I want every scrap of information you have. I want it now and I want it fast.'

'For Christ's sake! Who pointed it out to you! I'm co-operating.'

He closed his eyes tightly for a second, he was calming himself deliberately.

I said, 'What about Nikolayev?'

'Okay. I'll tell you. If you understand how important this is, maybe you'll be less of a son of a bitch. It goes like this. Nikolayev is a ship-building town. Right?'

'I don't know.'

'Accept it. It's true. They build warships there. All kinds of warships. And we've watched them for years with photographic reconnaissance satellites. A year or two ago, they roofed in one of the construction yards. Roofed in the whole damn thing. And they've been building something under that roof.'

'What?'

He grinned without humour. 'Yeah, what? That's what we want to know. What we *do* know is that it's big and that it's top secret. God knows what that roof cost. But that's all we *know*, really *know*! But we suspect, and brother if it's what we *suspect* . . .!' He drew in a long, hissing breath.

'One ship?' I said. 'Can it be as important as that?'

He gave that grin again. 'There's rumour, there's suspicion. There's conclusions and extrapolations and educated guesses. The ship they're building may be an aircraft carrier!'

I blinked at him. 'So they're building another aircraft carrier? So what?'

He said, 'Not *another* aircraft carrier, Sellers. They only have one, the *Kiev* and she's small. A trial ship, that's all. This one may be a big attack carrier!'

It still hadn't reached me. 'I'm no student of naval strategy,' I said. 'What's so significant about that?'

'I'll tell you,' Elliot said softly. 'The Russian navy has

always remained basically a defensive force. They've built it up fast. It's modern and efficient. But its chief function has been to deny the US unrestricted freedom of the seas, particularly in waters within Polaris range of the Soviet Union. And to limit US options for intervention in areas where the Soviets also have an interest.

'But understand this. If they've started building attack carriers, there's only one reason.'

I said, 'I thought carriers were out of date.'

'You did, huh? Look, Sellers, if they're building attack carriers, it shifts the capabilities of the Russian navy from defence to offence. It means the Kremlin's extending its global reach. Attack carriers mean they're equipping their navy with seagoing airpower. And *that* means they're out to contest the US Navy's dominance at sea. They haven't *had* aircraft at sea before. Now maybe they're going to.'

'I told you, I'm no strategist,' I said. 'They're changing their strategy. I see that. I even see the implications of an offensive posture as against a defensive one. But – '

He looked at me as though I were an idiot. 'Sellers, do you have any idea . . .? No, you don't do you? Listen, if it's an attack carrier, one is no damn use at all. They'll have to build six or eight, maybe more, because each of their fleets will have to have at least one, otherwise there are weak points and the whole deal's stupid. Now, the cost of building even one attack carrier is so enormous, and the technological requirements so taxing, that it's likely to overstrain their whole technological capacity, slow down the space programme, everything. That's true, Sellers, even if you do have trouble believing it. Britain's phasing out carriers because she won't, soon, be able to afford even one. You know that?'

'No, I didn't.'

'Okay, think about the decision. In the minds of the Russian leaders, it's a massive decision, right? It's a crucial, historic choice. The demand on resources would be gigantic, the project would take maybe ten years of murderous effort and concentration of materials and manpower. It means they cut down on consumer manufacture, jack up steel production – Christ knows what it means. The internal political effects are big. But more important than that, it shows their *intentions*, long term intentions. Expansion of their spheres of influence. Change of posture from defence to offence.

'Sellers, look. You asked me if one ship meant so much? *This* ship, this *one* ship, is probably the most important ever built. Not for itself, but for what it tells us. If the Russians are building an attack carrier, it means they're embarking on the next massive phase of Communist expansion internationally. It means a whole sweeping change in everybody's outlook; massive changes in international strategy.'

I watched him, fascinated, not doubting the truth of what he said. There was a sheen of sweat on his brow when he stopped. But even then he hadn't finished. 'If the ship under the roof at Nikolayev is an attack carrier, we're playing in a whole new ball game, all of us.'

I stood very still, absorbing it. Then I said soberly, 'You honestly believe Alsa brought that information out? '

Elliot took a handkerchief from his pocket and dabbed at his forehead. 'If it's from Nikolayev,' he said, 'It could be the answer. You may never have heard about it, Sellers, but this is international armaments mystery number one. And not just armaments either; it's economics on a critical level. Theirs *and* ours.'

'Ours? You said we couldn't afford – '

'You can't. Not Britain. I'm talking about the American shield, the big umbrella. Look at the other side of this and try to think some complicated Russian thoughts. They may be building the carrier. But maybe they're not. Maybe they're just pretending! Listen, they know all about photo-reconnaissance satellites. They should; they've sure put plenty up there. So some smart cookie in the Kremlin some place has this bright idea. 'Let's roof in a ship construction yard, comrades,' says this smart guy. 'They'll see it and then they'll start wondering what's going on undereneath, right? They'll wonder why all the extra secrecy. We build subs and every-thing else in open yards, so what's with the roof? They'll conclude we're building carriers,' he says. 'And if they think we are, they'll have to do something about it. Like build some more of their own.' You see the pattern, Sellers? It all works in reverse. If the Soviets *are* building themselves some attack carriers, then *we* have to build more, just to stay ahead. The cost to us is almost as stupendous as it is to them. Huge additional arms budget, big diversion of resources and material – the whole shebang. They've got us guessing and they know it. Carriers take years to build and if they've started already, we've got to start soon; strategically we daren't wait until they actually start launching.

'*But*, Sellers – and it's the hell of a big but – if all they're doing under that roof is building some tanker and taking their time about it, well then *we're* going to be spending billions of dollars. We're going to be *wasting* billions of dollars. Right now they got us both ways. If they're building and we don't, the whole strategic balance changes. If they're not building but they succeed in forcing us to build, then they smack us a real economic sucker punch. And meanwhile all the dough they *don't* spend on a carrier goes into some other little sweetheart, like anti-missile-missiles or anything else you can think of.'

'And all this,' I said, 'comes for the price of one tin roof?'

Elliot gave a little shrug. 'Those bastards don't play all that chess for nothing. So now you know the big question. Is that tin roof a little ploy with a pawn? Or is the goddam thing a queen?'

There was a knock on the door. Elliot turned, walked over and unlocked it, and let Willingham in. I didn't like the expression on Willingham's face. He opened his mouth to speak, but Elliot got in first. He said just one word: 'Nikolayev.'

Willingham's mouth suddenly opened a good deal further, then closed with a snap and he said quickly, 'I don't think we need him any more.'

'Why?'

Willingham gave me a glance of malevolent triumph 'There's an Anderson here. And a Jarlshof. And a Sandness.'

It had been bound to happen. I was so tired now, so battered by the day's rampaging events, that defeat seemed to cover me suddenly with a wet, black blanket. They knew it all now, the whole damn lot. I'd nothing in reserve, no hope to cling to. It was the finish for me and probably, and much more tragically and totally, for Alsa, too.

Then, from somewhere in my tired mind came the realization that I was still ahead. There were still things I knew and they didn't. And Elliot's argument, cogent and convincing as it was, hadn't shifted the balance of my own values.

The information was important, all right. It was important to a great many people: to governments, to politicians, to strategists. Even maybe to me. But not as important as a life I valued. If it was one life against all this, I'd settle for the one life. *If* there were some way to save her. Alsa didn't matter a damn to Elliot and Willingham. She mattered a lot less to the Russians. But she mattered to me, even if the Russians had been right and she intended to marry Anderson.

I said, 'There was a fire tonight. At Jarlshof.'

'I know that, sweetheart,' Willingham said. 'Did you start it?'

'As a matter of fact, I did.'

'Excellent. We'll get you for arson, too.'

Elliot said quietly, 'Why did you start it? '

'Because,' I said, 'the house was lousy with Russians.'

While they were still digesting it, gaping ⸱ me, while expressions chased one another across their two faces, I said harshly to Willingham, 'Did the police tell you a postman had been attacked?'

He nodded slowly.

Elliot said, 'By the Russians? That's what you believe?'

'It was on the Sandness Road. I don't have facts to prove it was the Russians. But I know it. West Mainland is full of old people. All the mail going that way will be personal. No money, or very little. Not worth the effort for any criminal.'

'They've got it back, then,' Willingham snarled.

I let them think for a moment. It was Elliot who spoke. 'What time? Which came first?'

'The attack on the postman came first,' I said. 'Otherwise they wouldn't have been lurking around Anderson's house. So they can't have got it, can they?'

Elliot came towards me, put his bony face close to mine, and said very quietly, 'Where is Anderson?'

'The Russians asked me that.'

'Where is he?'

'I don't know.'

Willingham said, 'The galley shed. What the hell were you doing there?'

'Looking for him. Not finding him.'

Elliot turned away. 'Willingham, we need police help. We need to know how the mail comes in. Get the head cop up here!'

The head cop turned out to be the sergeant, because the local police inspector was away on a three-day course in Edinburgh. Elliot was clearly disconcerted by the lack of heavy rank. 'What's your name?'

'McAllister, sir.'

'Okay McAllister. Get on to the postal authorities. If there's any fresh mail on the island now, it's got to be checked. Anything, anything at all, addressed to Anderson, Jarlshof, Sandness, or to a girl called Alison Hay, at any address, has to be found. Arrange for tomorrow's mail, when it gets here, to be checked too.'

McAllister was a square, phlegmatic man built like a shovel blade. He said. 'What do you expect to happen, sir?'

'Who knows? Maybe an attack of some kind. Just do it, huh?'

'If it's to be an attack, sir, we'd better warn British

Airways. Mail comes up by air from Aberdeen.'

'Okay.' Elliot nodded approval. 'And ask the post office people in Aberdeen to search at their end too. Get going.'

McAllister stayed where he was. 'I doubt they'd do that on my say-so sir. You'll need to get authority, maybe the Chief Constable of Aberdeen. Can you arrange for that sir?'

'I'll fix it,' Willingham said. He hurried out and I heard his footsteps descending the stairs.

'And what about outgoing mail?' McAllister asked quietly.

'Jesus, yes!' Elliot said. 'Get that looked at, too. Same names. Anderson and Hay. *Any* letters to anyone of either name are to be held for examination, right?'

'Right, sir.' McAllister turned to leave.

'How many phone lines have you, sergeant?'

'Three, sir.'

'I got to call London.' Elliot began to follow the sergeant towards the door, then stopped and turned to look at me. He said, 'Get a man up here to stay with Mr Sellers, sergeant.'

'Aye, sir. I will.'

McAllister removed the key from my side of the door and went out. The lock's click was loud in the room.

I went over and looked out of the room's other window. The room itself was on a corner of the building. I already knew one window overlooked Lerwick harbour, that it was high above the ground and that there was no easy way down from it. Disappointingly, the same was true of the other. I had a nice view of the modernistic library building and the Town Hall, but the drop was a good twenty feet. I'd break my neck if I tried it. And anyway, I didn't have time. The lock turned again and my guard was with me. Like McAllister he was a broad, hard-looking man, thirtyish, accustomed to handling drunken trawlermen, I guessed, probably two or three at a time. He gave me a little nod that somehow or other contrived to be a warning, too.

I said, 'Any chance of a cup of something? Tea, coffee?'

'When I can. Not now.'

'When you can will be fine.'

I sat down and looked across at him. 'Been in Lerwick long?'

'Five years.'

'Like it?'

'I like it fine.'

'Bit cold, isn't it?'

'Not really, no. We get the winds, but not the ice and snow like Scotland. It's a good place to be a bobby.'

'Because it's small?'

'Aye. You get to know the local people. It's no like the big cities.'

I said, 'You know Jim Anderson, from Sandness.'

He looked guarded. 'I know him.'

I smiled. 'It's okay. I understand. But everybody's looking for him. Mr Elliot and Mr Willingham, too. It may be you'll know something that will interest them, too.'

'Aye,' he said. 'It may be.'

'Somebody told me about a climb he did.'

'Och aye. He climbs fine. He was over to Foula in the summer on the high cliffs. Ringing birds, so they say.' He shook his head a little, unimpressed by that kind of unnecessary risk-taking.

'I don't know him,' I said. 'He's a friend of a friend. I gather he's a nice bloke.'

'Och aye. He's all right, Jim Anderson. Wee bit mad, you know. Climbing and all. He's a good sailor, too.' The policeman gave a tight little smile of recollection. 'I've been out with him. Fishing, you know. He doesnae get worried in the rough water.'

I asked, 'Has he a boat?' and when he looked guarded again, added, 'If he has, they'll need to know.'

'Aye, maybe you're right.'

'What kind?'

'Shetland model. They mostly are, up here. Good sea boats for men that can handle them.'

'Where's he keep it?'

'Down in the small boat harbour when he's to this side of the island. Walls, maybe, most of the time.'

'Is it here now? They'll need to know.'

'Aye. It was this morning.'

'Show me where?'

He gave me a look of amiable warning. 'You'll not be trying something foolish, sir?'

'With you?' I said.

'I'd be a handful for you.' He walked to the window and pointed. 'You can just see her, sir. See the edge of yon roof?' The harbour was silver in the moonlight.

'No. Oh, yes I can. The pale one?'

'Aye. She's twenty-six foot. Decked in. Good sea boat.'

'Lucky man,' I said.

'Aye.'

'Harbour's busy, too.'

'Always is,' he said. 'For a wee place there's a lot of boats in and out. Fishin' boats mainly, but others, too. Even cruise ships sometimes. Och, we get all kinds. They come ashore, you know, the fishermen. Into the pubs, after the girls. I've seen six nationalities in one pub.'

'Gets rough? '

'Och aye. Now and then. Some are worse than others, you know. Depends how full their pockets are. All seamen are alike. A few drinks and maybe one gets nasty. English, Norwegians, Germans, Poles, Finns, all the same. All bar the Russians.'

'Russians?' I said, startled.

'Och aye. They come in here. There's a few here now. They're the best of the lot. Never any trouble.'

'Oh? Why's that?'

'Och, I don't believe they have the money. Not to come ashore on a wee kind of rampage. Or maybe they go to the salt mines if they get in trouble.'

*Russians!* I thought. Russians in Lerwick. Legitimately in Lerwick. Part of the scenery. I said. 'Which are the

Russian ships?'

He pointed towards the mass of fishing boats tied up in the harbour near the fish quay. 'There's three or four in there.'

'And they come ashore as they like?'

'Oh aye. There's often a few Russians in Lerwick. You see 'em look in shop windows. Not buying, you understand. Not often. That's why I reckon they've no money.'

I looked at the lines of fishing boats with deep concern. Easy come, easy go. Free access. And the phony Sergeant Gustaffson has been sent to climb that hill with his radio, to find out what to do with me!

I said, 'It seems odd to be looking at Russian boats.'

'Aye. Visitors always think that. You see over there. That wee boat on a mooring.'

I followed the direction of his pointing finger.

'The little one? By itself.'

'Used to be Anderson's,' he said. 'Little Shetland model. Sold it and bought the bigger boat.'

His tough appearance was misleading. He was a pleasant man. Straight, confidence in himself, but not self-confident, strong, self-contained as a Brazil nut, happy where he was, happy to chat about this place he knew and liked. We talked until Elliot returned. When he entered the room I was careful to get in first.

'The constable here says there are Russian fishing boats in the harbour.'

Elliot's face showed surprise, then anxiety. He asked questions and got answers. Like me he was startled by their freedom to come and go. Then he said tightly, 'Thanks, constable. I think the sergeant will need you now.'

'Very good, sir.'

When he'd gone, Elliot turned to me. 'Police have only eight men available. They're mounting a search for Anderson, but . . .'

I nodded. 'You'll never find him here. Not if he doesn't want to be found. You're in a close community. They'll stick together.'

Elliot looked at me quickly. 'Why wouldn't he want to be found?'

'Like I said, it's a tight community. He'll know about the fire and he'll know about the postman. Perhaps he even knows more than that. There's a lot of space up here, a lot of tiny villages, remote crofts. He can keep his nose down forever, and – ' I thought of the implacable Miss Petrie and her they-shall-not-pass performance at her cottage door – 'and they'll form an impenetrable ring round him. If he wants it.'

Willingham had returned while I was talking. He said tightly, 'We'll find him, don't you worry.' I took no notice, nor, I saw, did Elliot. Willingham flushed and his apparently-permanent anger intensified a little. 'London will square the post office in Aberdeen.'

'Right.' Elliot looked at us both, for once showing a trace of uncertainty.

I voiced his thought. 'What next?'

'We wait. What else?'

Willingham said, 'I'll join the search. The more bodies the better.'

I said, 'Watch the door close in your face. The police haven't much chance. You have none at all.'

'You, of course, have a better idea!'

'I can think of one place to look.'

'You can, can you?'

'Anderson has a boat.'

'How do you know?' Elliot asked quickly.

'I asked a policeman, like the song says.'

Elliot said, 'Get him!'

But the constable had already left to tramp the post-midnight streets.

I said helpfully, 'I know which boat it is and where it's moored.'

'Tell me.'

'I'll do better. I'll show you.'

They didn't want that, either of them. They wanted me safe and secure in the police station and tried to circumvent me by asking the sole remaining bobby if *he* knew.

Fortunately he didn't. And a boat is such a convenient hiding place – for a man or anything else – that they daren't let it pass.

Elliot said wearily, 'Okay, Sellers. Show us.'

'A pleasure.'

We went out into the empty night. The wind had dropped now and it was cold and still. Together we tramped down the steep hill towards the waterfront and turned right along the quay. Several of the fishing boats wore the hammer and sickle flag. We continued past them.

'That one,' I said, and pointed.

The Shetland model rode easily on her mooring, wide-bellied, bow both ends in the fashion of the Viking galleys. She didn't look as though anybody might be on her.

'Deserted,' Willingham said flatly.

'How would she look if he was aboard?' I asked.

Elliot looked round. 'We need a dinghy to get out there.'

There was a small rowing boat turned upside down on the sloping ramp and we righted it and launched it. 'Shall I wait here?'

'You will *not*!' Elliot said sharply. 'Get in. I'm not losing sight of you again.'

There wasn't far to go. Less than a hundred yards at a guess. We came away from the ramp, heading between two moored fishing boats on to the shining water. There were the small clatters and bumps of a harbour's background noises and somewhere not far away, a little engine was idling. Willingham did the rowing. Elliot sat in the bow, looking towards Anderson's boat. I sat in the stern.

It was as we came by the stern of the big fishing boat to our left that what I'd thought was a donkey engine turned out to be something else. The idling note was suddenly a sharp rising roar, very close, and a dark shape drove out at us from behind the bulk of the fishing boat. There wasn't a chance of avoiding it; not a thing any of us could do. We were hit fair and square amidships, rolled over instantly, plunged into the cold water of the harbour.

The shock of sudden immersion smashed the breath out of me and the boat, as it rolled, caught me a painful blow on the leg. I splashed and struggled, got my head to the surface and glanced round. As I shook the water from my face to look round, something slid powerfully by me. A hand grasped at my sleeve, gripped tightly, and I felt myself being drawn rapidly through the bitterly cold water.

I tried to turn my head to look up and as I did so, my other arm was grabbed. Two men were holding me, each by one arm; between them sat another. I stared up at his face in astonishment. The last time I'd seen it was in the Scanda Hotel in Gothenburg. He wore seaman's clothing now but the eyes behind the rimless glasses were the same. I was looking up at Pavel Marasov, the polite Russian press attaché!


## CHAPTER SIXTEEN


Marasov bent close and low to make his voice audible above the engine's noise. 'Where is it, Sellers?' he yelled.

I shook my head. Already my teeth were chattering. The water moving by me as I was dragged along was sucking the warmth from my body.

'Where?' he repeated.

'I don't know.' It was difficult even to speak as water from the boat's bow washed at me.

'Then where is Anderson?'

'I don't kn –' My mouth filled suddenly with water. I began to choke and was roughly hauled higher. 'I don't know,' I shouted.

Marasov stared at me. I was trembling now with the brutal cold. I managed to say, 'We're looking.'

He continued to stare at me for a long moment, while the water raced by. I gaped up at him helplessly. Then he bent closer. 'Find him, Sellers. Find him. Find the transparency.

Nobody must see it, understand? Work alone! Stay away from those men. If you do not, the girl Hay will not be seen again.'

I gasped, 'Is she . . . is she . . . okay?'

'So far,' he said. 'Remember what I say.'

The best I could manage was an awkward nod of my head. The engine noise diminished suddenly and I could feel that the way was coming off the boat. Marasov said, his voice louder now that it no longer competed with the revving engine, 'Stay away from the American, and the other, the man Willingham. I cannot save you again.'

While I was still gaping at him the grip on my arms was released. I sank suddenly, my mouth filled with water, and I choked again. When I surfaced, and after I'd finished coughing, I realized I was only a few feet from a stretch of rocky shore. I swam weakly towards it and hauled myself out of the water. I was desperately cold, teeth chattering so hard it hurt, body trembling violently. Looking around, I managed to make sense of my whereabouts. I was at the south end of the Lerwick harbour a good distance from the small boat harbour where we'd been knocked into the water. And I was in trouble. There had seemed to be no wind when I walked with Elliot and Willingham down the hill from the police station. But now I realized the air was anything but still. It flowed slowly around me, working with the water in my soaking clothes to chill me to the bone. And there was no prospect of dry ones. Also, the police were on the streets, Elliot and Willingham would already have swum ashore and put out an alert on me.

Then there was Marasov. For a moment I began to think about Marasov, but there were priorities more urgent than that. Elliot's phrase came into my mind. *My* grade A class one problem was dry warm clothes! I made myself walk up towards the road. It was absolutely quiet now. Nothing moved. I looked furtively around me and began to move quietly back towards the town. Up a side street I saw suddenly the familiar end of a phone box, checked quickly that none of the local bobbies was visible, and hurried towards it.

Money or no money, Lincoln didn't like answering the phone in the wee small hours. He sounded irritable even as he spoke his own name.

I said, 'It's John Sellers.'

'Oh Christ. At this time?'

'I need a boat. First thing in the morning. When can I get one?'

'I have a boat. Where do you want to go?'

'Not sure yet. But early.'

'There's a hire charge, Sellers. Especially to you.'

'Never mind that. What kind of boat is she?'

'Converted lifeboat. Cabin cruiser now. She's good. What time?'

'Eight,' I said.

'Bloody *hell*!' Then he sighed audibly. 'All right.'

'Where is she?'

'Hays Dock. North end. See you there at eight.'

'What's her name? Just so I'll know.'

'Katrina.'

I said, 'Sorry to disturb.'

'I'm used to it,' he said wearily. 'But what the hell happened to you earlier. I waited half an hour!'

'Sorry,' I said. 'I had to move. Buy you a large Scotch sometime.'

'You'll do more than that.' He hung up.

Hays Dock. North end of town. I was a long way from it, a good half mile, and my chances of walking there unobserved, in still dripping clothes, along the deserted quayside, were nil. I'd have to lengthen the journey, work my way round the back of the town. Oh, Christ!

I climbed a bit, sticking to shadows as much as possible, then slowly worked my way north like a hunted cat through a network of alleys, slithering from hiding place to hiding place. And about halfway, climbing a narrow passageway just below the police station, I suddenly found myself with a good view of the harbour. I didn't care about the harbour at that second. I didn't care about anything but getting out of the murderous cold. But something caught my eye. An absence, not a presence. Something missing that ought to have been there: where was Anderson's boat? Not the one he owned now; *she* was still on her mooring. But the other one, the one he'd sold. That one had disappeared!

I got going again, and made suddenly incautious by the need to move fast, nearly ran into one of the coppers. Fortunately my senses were temporarily sharper than his and I managed to make myself part of the shadows until he'd gone by. Then I hurried on. When I finally reached Hays Dock, I groaned. The boat was there, sure enough, but she was moored twenty yards out and this time there was no convenient dinghy to hand. I forced myself to enter the water again and swam slowly out to her. My clothes weighed me down like lead ingots, the cold and my own weariness had drained the strength from my limbs; it was no more than swimming one length of a small pool, but it felt like swimming the Channel. As I came under the bow I saw her name was *Catriona*, but spellings didn't matter. This was the one. I scrambled up the three steps of the waist ladder into the stern well and found the cabin door locked. Too bad. Sorry, Lincoln. I kicked it in and scrambled inside.

There were curtains, but they were flimsy and I didn't dare use a light. I searched in the semi darkness until I found some sweaters, dampish but a great deal drier than my own clothes, in one of the lockers. There were also, thank God, spare trousers and sailing boots, plus oilskins, a duffel coat, and what have you. I stripped, towelled myself down with the duffel coat, then dressed quickly. I felt a bit better, now, but badly weakened.

I rummaged round, then, trying to make out what made the thing go, and came to the conclusion Lincoln must do pretty well, because *Catriona* had been nicely converted. There was a push-pull fuel switch, self-starter, a simple throttle, forward-astern lever. It ought to be simple. The starter seemed to make a tremendous noise and didn't fire her first time. I stuck my head out and looked round apprehensively, but all remained quiet so I tried again. She caught this time and the engine chugged beneath my feet with quiet efficiency. I slid up on deck, slipped the mooring chain, wincing even at the sound of the little splash, then hurried below and set her moving slowly ahead.

My instincts told me full steam ahead; logic said nice and slow. I stuck with logic and thought about whether anyone would notice, or even worse, might think the movement of the boat worth reporting. In seaports, they say, there are eyes everywhere. I came slowly out of the dock mouth.

Hell's delight, lights! An unlit boat was certainly suspicious. I hunted for, and found the switch, got the masthead lights on, and decided one light was as bad as another and put the cabin light on, too.

Still the harbour remained quiet. No other vessels were under way; there was no sign of movement, no running up and down the quayside, no pointing or shouting. I opened the throttle a bit and, looking round the cabin saw a sink, a stove, lockers. Food perhaps? A few tins. Bully beef and beans, soup, a couple of bars of chocolate, tea and coffee and a great treasure, a half-full bottle of The Grouse beautiful elderly Scotch Whisky. I had a mouthful of that, for starters, then crammed some chocolate into my mouth. It's scarcely a gourmet combination, but I felt the benefit as the whisky warmed my windpipe and the chocolate filled chilly little corners of my gut.

Nipping back and forth between the wheel and the stove, I put on a kettle of water and lit the Calor gas. I opened a can of beans and ate them hungrily, with a spoon. When the water boiled, I made tea, laced it thoroughly with The Grouse and began to feel like the man I remembered.

By this time, I'd also found the charts and was considering my route. Across the channel from Lerwick lay the island of Bressay. On the far side of Bressay lay Noss. On the far side of Noss lay the Holm of Noss. If Anderson had decided to get out of everybody's way, he could hide there as well as anywhere and the missing boat had half confirmed my guess.

But I was by no means sure of what I was doing. I'd told Elliot and Willingham that Anderson could be in any one of a million places and that remained true. All the same, I had a kind of mental picture of the man now: he had an instinct for high and lonely places, plus strong independence of spirit. Anderson would choose his own way, and follow it. And the Holm of Noss was his by conquest if not by title. More than that: scarcely anyone knew he'd done it. He'd kept it quiet because of the snowy owls. There, he would not be found unless he chose to be.

I headed south down the channel between Mainland and Bressay, watching the dark Bressay cliffs climb high and black above and sticking as close to them as I dared. I realized suddenly that I'd no idea how much fuel was in the tank and there seemed to be no way of finding out. I prayed there would be sufficient. Certainly the engine mumbled steadily enough, but then it would, of course, until the last drops had burned. I shrugged to myself. There was nothing I could do about it now.

I used more of the hot water to make more tea, added a generous slug of whisky and thought about Marasov. He'd certainly got here fast from Gothenburg. How? Then I remembered my geography. The Shetlands lie closer to Scandinavia than to Aberdeen. That accounted for the strong Norse links; also accounted, of course, for Marasov's quick trip across. A big fishing boat going flat out wouldn't take very long to cross and Marasov probably had even faster transport at his disposal. But what he *said* was less easy to understand. He knew I was in the Shetlands: his men at Sandness had radioed the information. Okay. He'd kept watch for me, spotted me, grabbed me. But *why*, after that, had he let me go? The more I thought about it, the more I returned to one, simple conclusion: that Marasov must think I was his best chance. He must believe I was more concerned about Alsa than anything else. Well, he was certainly right about that! But there was an awful finality about his warning. *The transparency must be returned without anybody else seeing it. Or else it was curtains for Alsa!* I wondered what the transparency showed. Was it, like some nineteen-twenties melodrama with a touch of technology, a photograph of the plans? Or the ship itself? Would it be possible to tell, from a single photograph, what kind of ship she was? I thought of the characteristic flaring hull of an aircraft carrier and decided it would, if construction was far enough advanced.

In which case, I realized grimly, a sight of that transparency would mean curtains for me, too. And not even a sight. To have touched it would be enough. Marasov wasn't going to say, if I did succeed in getting hold of it, 'Thanks for your help and here's your girl friend.' He was going to say to himself that if I'd had a chance to see it, I must be put out of the way, permanently, before I had the chance to describe what I'd seen. So either way we were done for, both of us. And James Anderson too, if he so much as touched the lens case addressed to him!

Marasov had himself a work-horse and knew it. As long as I believed Alsa was alive, he knew I'd go on chasing. And I daren't *not* believe it.

Ahead of me a red light glowed a warning. I checked Lincoln's chart and found a red-ink cross marked and beside it, heavily underlined, the words *oil rig wreck*. Minutes later, I passed close to a tangle of steel girders sticking out of the water, with the waves washing at them. The waves were getting bigger now as *Catriona* came out of the shelter of Bressay Sound and became exposed to the wider sea. Beneath my feet she began to rise and fall disconcertingly and I held tight to the wheel as she rolled and pitched beneath the high cliffs. Had I bitten off more than I could chew, trying to make this trip? I remembered all the radio warnings I'd heard over the years, of all the gales in Orkney and Shetland, force this and that. Even the names on the chart now had a sinister flavour; something called Geo of the Veng lay just behind me, above towered Bard Head, beyond lay Hamar and Muckle Hell. I was warmer now, but I shuddered and forced myself to concentrate as I brought *Catriona* round the towering headland and turned her slowly through heavier seas to head north for Noss.

Clinging to the wheel one-handed, I held the chart with

the other and stood swaying as I tried to work out what I must do. The chart's legend showed Noss to be all cliffs apart from two tiny sandy beaches, one on each side of a narrow neck of land at the extreme west. The island itself stretched about a mile and a half, east to west, a mile north to south. At the western end, where the two beaches were marked, the land was low, as a fifty-foot contour line showed. Looking ahead, I found I could dimly see Noss now and its dark wedge-shape confirmed what the chart showed. The land rose steadily from that low western tip towards a towering cliff named The Noup, at the extreme east. The Holm of Noss lay a little less than half a mile south of the Noup. I thought about continuing in *Catriona* to the Holm, but reluctantly decided against it. Lincoln had said the sea stack was two hundred feet high. If I got there, what would I do? Shout? The sound of the sea alone would make me inaudible. I could hardly climb the bloody thing. So the only way was to go ashore, to cross the island.

In spite of the hot drinks, the spirits, the food I'd consumed, I felt weak as a kitten. The long day had drained my physical and mental strength. I hadn't slept the night before. I ached to pull this pitching boat in somewhere, just to lie on one of the bunks and let the world drift away. But there wasn't a chance. For a start, there was nowhere *for* the boat to go except that little beach on Noss. And I must go *on*!

I needed energy above all things. Sugar gave quick energy, didn't it? And there was a container of sugar in the food locker. The remaining water in the kettle was still warm and I half filled my cup with sugar, managed to pour some of the water on to it, then half-drank, half-ate the sweet revolting result and came close to vomiting it straight back. But, rather precariously at first, then more easily, it stayed down. By the time I was bringing *Catriona* cautiously in towards the little dull stretch of moonlit sand the chart called Nesti Voe, I'd stopped thinking about my stomach and was trying to think how to get ashore dry-footed. There wasn't any way, as it turned out. I just had to run the boat up on to the sand and jump down into the shallows clutching the anchor. I found an embedded rock and dug the anchor flukes hard in behind it, tugged the chain to persuade myself it would hold, then sat down and tipped the water out of Lincoln's rubber boots.

That done, I turned and began to walk up off the beach. There was a house on the eastern tip of the island, which the chart had described as a shepherd's house. It wasn't in fact, but it looked empty and slightly forlorn and I ignored it. Instead I set off on my steady eastward climb. The land rose a little, then fell away, then rose again, a straight and steep inclined plane towards the great cliff. I kept to the south, following a narrow track worn by generations of sheep. It stayed always a few yards away from the sharp drop to my right. Even so, it was unnerving. I was alone on the island, the cliffs were getting higher with every step I took, and I had the feeling that if I slipped or put my foot accidentally in one of the dozens of rabbit holes, I'd fall and roll inexorably over. It probably wasn't true. If I fell I'd be able to grab at something and hold myself; the slope to the cliff edge wasn't as steep as my mind made it, but that didn't stop the fear mushrooming inside my head, or stop my eyes straying endlessly towards the cliff edge when I should have been keeping them firmly on the little sheep track.

Whether it was adrenalin produced by fear, or whether the sugar and the food I'd eaten were doing what I'd hoped they'd do, it was impossible to tell. But I managed to keep climbing. I was still tired, my legs began to ache as my muscles faced the unaccustomed effort of a long, hard, uphill walk; but I was getting there. Stopping and turning, I looked down and across the long slope and saw that, even if I appeared to be making no headway, a third of the journey lay behind me. I turned and plodded on, hands on my knees now, pushing my legs downward with each step, bent low and leaning forward to minimize the effort. After a few more minutes, I stopped and gave myself another breather, and, looking back, guessed I'd come about a mile. Not far now, then. A few more minutes, less than ten anyway, and the Holm should be visible. I was getting higher, and the air grew colder. Had I not been working so hard, I would have been very chilled, and up here there was quite a strong wind.

I came quite suddenly on a sharp little down slope that ran direct to a low, ruined wall. To my left, the Noup itself reared still higher into the night sky; below and a couple of hundred yards to my right, a slash of darkness cut across the grassy slope. There was grass this side, grass the other. But that black tear into the earth must be the chasm between the island and the Holm.

I stopped for a moment, looking down at the acre top of the great stack, but could see nothing on it. The surface was not entirely flat; bumps and shadowed hollows told me that. I began carefully to pick my way down the slope, which was short and steep and far more genuinely dangerous than the sheep track I'd followed. If I fell here, I'd certainly roll; there were gaping holes in that low wall and on the other side of it, hundreds of feet of empty space.

Finally, with dreadful care, I came to the gap. Lincoln had told me Anderson had rigged up something called a Tyrolean traverse. I didn't know what that was and had imagined some kind of rope network stretched across the gap. If so, it wasn't there now. Instead, there was an apparatus like the earlier one Lincoln had described: a thick stake driven deep and held by pegged restraining wires. From the stake a heavy nylon rope stretched across to the Holm. I shouted Anderson's name, but the wind up here was in my face, carrying any sound I made back over Noss, not over to the Holm. I shouted and shouted, but drew no response. It was then I knew, sickeningly, that I should have to cross. I was beginning to believe Anderson wasn't there, but I couldn't be sure. And I had to be sure. If he was on the Holm he could be sleeping; after all, he'd built a hide there from which to watch his birds, and I hadn't been able to make enough noise to reach him, let alone to penetrate sleep.

But how to cross? There seemed to be no cradle; just the rope running down and across to the stack. As I came carefully closer, I realized there was not one rope but two; the heavier was two-inch nylon, the lighter was of the same material, but only a slender line, running over a pulley on the stake and tied to a cleat below it. On the far side of the chasm, the heavy line ran into dark shadow and I could see nothing. But – and my heart thumped at the thought – if there *was* some kind of cradle, and it *was* on the other side, it could mean only one thing: Anderson had used the cradle to cross!

Quickly I untied the light line and pulled. A yard, and nothing had happened. Two yards. Hand over hand I pulled it in. There *was* a weight on the end and it *was* moving towards me.

The cradle! As it came closer I could see that it was little more than a large, deep box. At front and rear, the wooden ends rose higher than the sides, and the rope ran through holes drilled into the wood. Simple. Efficient if the rope and timber held. Lethal if the rope failed, or the stakes were uprooted.

I looked at it with an apprehension approaching horror. In a moment or two I'd have to make myself get into the thing and move out over that black chasm. What was it Lincoln had called it? A hole into hell. He'd been exactly and precisely right; no exaggeration, no hyperbole. Except that the hell below was anything but fiery.

I'd got the cradle over the cliff edge now and I hesitated a long minute before I could force myself to climb in. As I did, the rope sagged under my weight, the cradle rocked terrifyingly and I could hear my own uncontrolled grunt of panic. I squatted in the bottom of the cradle, keeping the centre of gravity as low as I could, and grasped the heavy nylon line securely. Then, drawing a deep, shuddering breath, I allowed the cradle to begin its slide down the rope.

I couldn't see what was beneath, and I was insanely glad I couldn't. There was only a vision of death down there and I was close enough, without actually seeing it. Slowly, passing the rope very carefully through my hands, I slid backward down the line, making sure every time I changed hands, that my grip was hard and firm. If my hand slipped, the cradle would bucket away down the slope and while I'd no idea what was at the other end, it seemed frighteningly probable that I'd be thrown out and maybe flung into the depths below.

The distance was only twenty yards or so, but it seemed endless; I moved only a foot with each fresh clutch at the rope and the sheer cliff of Noss was sliding into view above the end of the cradle, still very near.

Inch by inch, I made my way across, tense with fear, my mind empty of everything but that line and my own grip on it. Empty, that is, until a glance at the Noss cliff made me ask myself how I'd get back. I'd have to haul myself *up* the line, instead of merely stopping myself sliding down. It would take strength to do that, and to supply the leverage, I'd have to stand up in the swaying cradle. If only someone were standing on the Noss side, to pull on the lighter line!

That thought brought a new question stamping brutally into my mind. It was a question that made my skin crawl. The cradle had been on the Holm side. And the light line had been tied to the cleat. If Anderson had crossed to the Holm, then *who* had tied the line?

CHAPTER SEVENTEEN

I got my answer as the cradle gave a sudden bump behind me. The bump itself was, at that moment, bad enough; my first jolting thought was that something had gone dangerously wrong; and so it had, but not with the cradle. When I realized it could slide no further and that I was really across, actually on the Holm itself, I raised my body from its awkward crouch to look cautiously over the side. I was seven or eight feet from the edge, in a little cleft in the rock wall. I stood slowly upright, turning carefully to climb out, and found myself looking at the dark figure of a man.

He stood about five feet away, booted feet planted well apart. His back was to the moon so his face was in shadow but the moon gleamed on something else: on the blue barrel of the weapon in his hands.

He gave a quick jerk of the rifle, ordering me from the cradle, then stood back as I climbed gingerly out on to the Holm's thick grass surface. Another jerk of the rifle had me moving away from the edge, walking awkwardly backward, my arms raised.

He didn't speak. When he'd got me where he evidently wanted me, near the middle of the flat top of the stack, he pointed to the ground, making me sit. He bent, picked up something from the ground and stepped back a pace or two before he took a fresh one-handed grip on the rifle and fumbled awkwardly with the other hand until a slender length of metal appeared. A radio. He was one of Marasov's men.

He spoke quickly, in Russian, and I saw him look at me carefully as he talked, presumably giving a description. It didn't take long, and he snapped the aerial back in place, lowered the radio to the ground and took a proper grip of the rifle before he came closer again.

'How on earth did you know about this?' I said.

No reply. He wasn't talking. His mouth was flat and hard and wasn't going to open. Or maybe he didn't speak English. I thought about it and worked out for myself how Marasov knew about the Holm. He could only know because Alsa had told him, and Alsa knew because Anderson had told her. That told *me* two things: first that Alsa *was* probably still alive; secondly that the man who'd impersonated Schmid had possibly been right when he'd said Alsa intended to marry Anderson. At least they were very close. So Marasov, knowing about this place, had simply put a man here to wait. If Anderson came, fine. If he didn't, it was merely a short spell of sentry-go. Marasov, it was becoming increasingly obvious, was very well-organized indeed. Then another question reared in my mind. I was wearing two heavy roll-necked sweaters, the top one navy blue. Also dark trousers and boating boots. A wholly different rig-out from the one I'd been wearing when I was pitched into Lerwick harbour and Marasov dragged me away. How then would this man have described me? My clothes? Well, it was a rough working rig-out. He'd say that I was in my mid-thirties, on the fair side. Anderson was about the same age; I knew that from the photograph. Might this man think I was Anderson? If he did, Marasov would come tearing over here like a terrier after a rat. And when he got here, he'd decide that if my ideas were no forwarder than his, he might as well dispose of me now as later.

Which made it very urgent indeed that I do something. But what?

Up there we were exactly like two flies on top of a jam jar, except that one fly had a sting and neither could fly away. The only way off the Holm was by the cradle, and my captor would clearly wait until the other side of the rope-way was manned before sending me across. He was armed and standing, I was unarmed and sitting. All the advantage to him. I move, he fires. I thought about it. Wait a minute . . . would he shoot? Not if I was Anderson he wouldn't, because Anderson was vital! They wanted Anderson very badly indeed. Suddenly the memory of the men who'd shot to frighten me in the Valley of Fire came back, Elliot's men, bloody vivid in my mind. Firing dozens of shots, all going wide. Orders to miss?

Maybe.

It was a hell of a chance to take. I'd taken that chance in the Valley of Fire and been right. But you could only be wrong once.

What if I didn't try? Well, then Marasov would come and say to himself, it's only Sellers and Sellers is patently no use any more. In that case there was the nice, high cliff of a remote island all too close to hand! Farewell Sellers. And goodbye Alsa, too, because there was no-one else to care except Anderson, and Anderson could have no real knowledge of the set-up. Nor could he know that the only possible end was sudden death all round. If Marasov found Anderson and said, it's a fair exchange, the transparency for the girl, Anderson would jump at it. And thereby sentence the pair of them.

I'd screwed my courage to the sticking point before and it had taken a ghastly act of will. By rights it should have been easier this time. Same scenario. Same act of lunacy required. But it wasn't easier. It was almost impossible. One part of my mind ordered my legs and arms to move, while another part, the sensible part that deals in self-preservation, said don't believe a word of it. Inertness is the watchword. Disobey this fool! But somehow I made myself stand. And stretch. In spite of the cold, my back ran with sweat. He stared at me, stone-faced, and I'd have given everything I had to know what was in his mind, what his orders were.

He gestured angrily at me to sit down again. I pretended I didn't understand, fixing an idiot look of puzzlement on my face and looking at him with my head to one side like an inquiring dog. But it *was* a gesture to sit that he made, not a threat to fire. Significant? My God, but I prayed it was significant. I made myself stretch, as though to loosen tired muscles, then bent and rubbed at my calves, giving him a rueful half-grin. Hell climbing up the island isn't it? He was still making that sit-down gesture. If I'd obeyed it before, why wasn't I obeying it now? I straightened, shrugging my shoulders, hugging myself, doing the isn't-it-cold act, stamping my feet to emphasize the point. He scowled at me and gestured more furiously with the rifle. I pretended I suddenly understood, pointed at the ground, gave him another inquiring look. He nodded vigorously and I began to lower myself, bending my knees, letting my body bend, until almost at the point of sitting I'd got myself down nearly into the on-your-marks position. He was five feet away. Six perhaps. Two good strides while he made his decision to kill me or not.

There wasn't time to pause and ponder. I hurled myself forward, low and rising in the tackle taught to me and practised endlessly long ago and far away on greener grass than this. Get his legs! Two hard stamps with my feet, driving up from the crouch, aiming the shoulder for the thigh. What if he'd played Rugby in Rumania or somewhere and could sidestep like Gerald Davies? Crunch! Hard into the thigh with my shoulder, arms round his legs, feet driving on. No shot, and he was over backwards and we were crashing down together. I swarmed over him like six All-Black forwards and behaved much the same way, all knees and elbows, gouging and thumping. An explosion of energy I'd never have believed I could raise. Side of the hand up under his nose and a highly rewarding shout of pain, thumb to the eyeball, knee to the groin. Gotcha! He tried to fight me, but too late. It was over. I chopped at his exposed throat and he whimpered and gagged and when the second chop landed he stopped moving.

I rose, grunting, and stared down at him. He wasn't shamming. He was badly hurt, possibly even dead. And I wasn't going to waste time finding out which.

Where was Anderson's bird-watching hide? If he'd been here . . . but no, he hadn't been here, couldn't have been. All the same, John Sellers, find it, and look.

I found it and looked. It was empty. A couple of note-books, ropes, cameras, binoculars, two sleeping bags, spirit stove and Thermos, a few provisions, a torch. I took the torch, switched it on and headed back towards the ropeway.

The torch seemed to give out an uncanny amount of light, much of it in directions in which it wasn't pointing. Turning, I saw that the seaward edge of the Holm top was silhouetted in a blast of light from below. I crossed quickly towards the edge, went flat on my stomach, crawled to the edge and looked cautiously over. Instantly, the light half-blinded me. Dazzled, I lay still, waiting for the light-burn to fade from the retinas of my eyes. It seemed to take an age of rubbing before I could see at all. But when some vision had returned, I played it differently, watching the beam as it moved, choosing the moment when it swung away a little on the sea's movement to raise my head.

And what I saw brought bile into my throat, even though

it wasn't entirely unexpected; I'd half-known what I'd see on the dark water far below. But the confirmation of it sent a spasm through my insides. A Russian fishing boat rode the sea down there, and there were men on the decks, staring up as the beam illuminated the edge of that frightening cliff. Worse, one of them was pointing and seemed to be shouting.

I ducked back quickly and hurried across the top of the Holm towards the cradle. There was no time now for hesitation; I must get into it and get going!

Climbing in, settling my feet carefully in the rear corners, I stared up along the thick nylon rope. The angle looked awesome; twenty-five degrees, even thirty! I found I had to keep my weight off centre to let the rope pass my body, and that alone made the cradle lurch alarmingly to one side.

I grabbed the rope and pulled. Nothing. No movement at all! What the hell was holding me back. A scraping sound gave me the answer. My own weight grounded the rear of the cradle. I'd have to move to the front, lean out over the gorge to shift the balance.

Two awkward, fearful steps, with the cradle swaying alarmingly and I was at the front, reaching out to grab the line two feet beyond the front eyehole. And now, for the first time I could see down into the abyss, into the narrow gap where the sea, compressed between cliffs, boiled white among the black fangs of fallen rock.

Right. *Pull!* The effort needed was enormous. The cradle slid forward a few inches, desperately slowly. And as I changed grip, it slid straight back again. One hand didn't seem to be enough to hold the combined weight of the cradle and myself. Pull again! Try harder! Try a long pull and a quick grab. One foot gained, and hands burning from the bite of the twisting rope strands into my skin. Haul and grab, haul and grab! I'd never make it this way, not in a million years. What if . . . I pulled again, forced my body hard against the rope and very nearly turned the thing over. But it held! Again, then. Two feet gained that time, not one. But precarious as hell. Again. And again. Every time I braced my body against the rope, the cradle tried to roll over and hurl me into the cauldron below. The rope also burned into the skin of my ribs, turning every woollen strand in my sweater into a little scraping blade. But I moved. I was out of the shadow of the cleft. My back and arms already ached fiercely. Even fit and rested I'd never have believed I could do it, let alone in the condition I was in. The rope stretched away in front of me to the fearful face of that grey, sheer cliff. I pulled, braced my body, pulled again. My ribs felt as though they were being scoured. The little pricking agonies of strain began to appear in my thighs, my neck, my back. Pull, pull, *pull*! Less than two feet gained each time, and shortening. But the distance still to go was lessening, too. Another effort! Pull the bloody thing! Christ! Suddenly I was nearly rolled over. The cradle pivoted upward and for a dreadful moment I was suspended almost horizontally over empty space, staring down in open-mouthed horror at the greedy, foaming water. I lost three feet and about ten years of my life getting back into equilibrium, and began again to fight my way upward.

My strength was going, though. My arms and hands were beginning to exhibit the slight numbness of muscles becoming starved of blood. Each pull required fiercer efforts, greater concentration. How on earth had anyone done this trip with a sheep in the cradle! How far to go? I glanced back, then stared up the rope. More than halfway, but more than halfway to exhaustion, too. I knew if once the cradle slipped back down the rope, I was beaten. If just once my grip failed, I'd be whipped back down to the Holm with a force beyond my power to hold.

The something caught my eye off to the right. The searchlight beam was moving! The fishing vessel must be easing forward towards the north end of the Holm. Once it got there, I'd be caught in the light! I pulled and pulled again. Each heave seemed to drain more energy, as though somebody had turned on a tap to draw my strength away and each wrenching effort squirted its quota into the void below.

Twelve feet to go. Ten. Eight. Light all around me, but

not the full beam. Not yet. Six – and I was caught, almost blinded again, held in the centre of the light beam. Four, and something buzzed by me and an almost simultaneous crack hit my ears. The cradle jerked as a second bullet actually struck. One more heave! Not enough. Wood splintered just behind me. Heave! And suddenly I was over the lip, shielded by the cliff itself, holding on to the rope and clambering awkwardly over the raised front of the cradle. With a sudden zipping sound the cradle whipped away under its own weight, back down the heavy rope. I heard shots but didn't wait to look. I began to stumble instead up the short steep slope ahead of me. I must somehow reach *Catriona* and get off the island. But *Catriona* was a mile and a half away. I groaned at the thought and tried to will myself forward with promises to my weary body that if I could just get to the top, it was all downhill. I fell, forced myself up and fell again, scrambled for grips with my skinned and aching hands, dug my toes into the slope, struggled, fell and struggled some more.

I got there on my hands and knees and stayed still for a long moment, letting my eyes roam over the long incline before me. Gravity would do it, if I could stay on my feet; gravity and the wind behind. I forced myself upright and let it happen, leg forward and down, body following, leg forward. After the hell of the rope, the desperate weary upward scramble, this was almost easy! Effort was scarcely needed at all. I was swaying oddly, my body almost out of control, but gaining speed, becoming almost drunk with the sudden wonderful ease of it. That's why I bloody nearly broke my neck. Head high and eyes anywhere but where they should be, I stuck my foot into a rut and crashed down heavily, jarring bones I didn't even know existed, driving the breath from my lungs. I lay there dazed for long moments, incapable of movement, gasping, thinking almost dreamily of the endless madness I'd been through that day, hearing the shots again in my imagination. Then suddenly it wasn't a dream and I was cold and wet from the dew, shivering, thinking about that damned fishing boat and what it would be doing while I lay there. It would be heading the way I was heading, that's what it would be doing! Marasov would want to know, if he hadn't already guessed, what had happened on top of the Holm of Noss. He'd be landing men on Noss to find out. And it was fifty-fifty he would land on Noss Voe, where *Catriona* was waiting! If not there, the other beach was only a couple of hundred yards away. I *must* get moving again!

Slowly I dragged myself to my feet and set off down the slope. The slight euphoria had gone. I swayed as I stumbled on but no longer drunkenly. This was pure physical weariness, slack muscles wavering and giving, no longer under real control. Yet my mind was clear. I had no difficulty in concentrating, no difficulty in picking out the next place for each foot to fall. The difficulty lay in placing the foot there accurately. My legs were like jelly, and I was only lurching forward, yet I was covering ground, and quite quickly, too. And after a while a little control came back. Perhaps it was because each step was no longer hard labour and I'd stopped gasping for every breath. There was cool air in my lungs, oxygen flowing into me. My feet began to land where I intended them to land and I found I was in altogether better balance.

I didn't look round. Wherever Marasov's fishing boat might be, I wouldn't be able to see it because it would be hidden beneath the cliffs, and I didn't dare to look anywhere but at the next few feet of ground ahead. I fell again, several times, but never as painfully as the first time, and by now the sheer hard urgency of the need to get away focused my mind on the other need, the need to roll up again and hurry on. I was astonished by the resilience of my own body. With each passing minute it was allowing control to return to my mind. My ribs ached from the rope, my hands were badly chafed and very sore, my feet were developing blisters in Lincoln's awkward, lumbering boots. But I was getting there. Would I be there in time? Damn it, I *must* be there in time! I needed every second I could gain and quite coldly and consciously I allowed gravity more play; let my body go forward faster. I stumbled again, and was up, almost exhilarated by the speed, and hurrying down that long slope.

Then, quite suddenly, the headlong plunge had ended and I was running uphill again, climbing the little saddle that lay between me and the beach at Nesti Voe. For a few yards my momentum carried me forward, but then I was slowed to a walk and the weariness began to creep again among my muscles and tendons. God, I'd only to go over the fifty-foot contour line, and after that it was downhill again! I *must* keep going. I breasted the top of the slope, staggered forward a few yards, and let go again, flogging my weary body on.

From where I was the moonlight lit the beaches. *Catriona* was still there, and afloat not aground. Thank God for that! And then I saw something else, something that momentarily stopped me in my tracks.

For a few seconds I could see the other beach, too. And another boat lay there, a little Shetland model, the dark thread of her mooring line curving to the beach!

## CHAPTER EIGHTEEN

So Anderson was on Noss!

Oh, God!

Where the hell was he? Why hadn't I seen him on my way down the slope? But I knew why— I hadn't been looking at anything but the way down. He'd have seen me, probably. Or would he? Maybe he'd been on lower ground, working his way round the southern cliffs while I came down the great central slope.

As I forced myself to move again, my mind was racing. Marasov would land on Noss if he believed anybody was there. Maybe Anderson could hide successfully, climbing, perhaps, down some cliff chimney he knew. But his boat would be found, he'd be trapped there and sooner or later they'd reach him. The fishing boat would circle the island, men ashore would search. Anderson would be finished. I wondered briefly why it had taken Anderson so long to reach Noss.

I reached *Catriona*, pulled the anchor clear of its rock, waded into the shallows, slung it aboard and climbed over the low stern. Then I bashed the starter, swore as the engine failed to fire, pushed it again and gave a whooshing grunt of relief as it spun and caught. Did the bloody thing always fail first time and go the second?

Now, astern! I flung the lever over and heard the water swishing under the propeller blades. The beach receded slowly as I backed *Catriona* off, waited, then flung the lever forward and brought her head round.

Where was the fishing boat? I stared over my shoulder and was appalled to see she was no more than a few hundred yards away, barging across the mouth of the little bay beyond the beach, her bow wave glistening. I'd already half-decided, in a rational, if self-sacrificial moment, that if I could make it follow me, Anderson's chances would improve. Now the option wasn't even open. It was roaring towards me at full speed, big and powerful, searchlight knifing into the night. I opened the throttle as wide as it would go and slowly *Catriona* began to pick up speed. So far as I could tell the island of Bressay, only two hundred yards away across the channel, was all cliffs. Not high cliffs, but they didn't need to be high to stop me. I reached for the chart and ran my eyes feverishly down the Bressay coastline. Yes, there! A gap in the cliffs at a spot called Grut Wick. I must get there. How far? A mile, perhaps more. I'd never make it. There was only one way – I'd have to blast *Catriona* straight across the Noss channel and try to get ashore as she struck.

Glancing over my shoulder, I was horrified to see how close the Russian boat was now. She seemed to be tearing through the water. And she'd seen me, too. She wasn't slowing or turning to go into Nesti Voe; she was coming powerfully on, directly towards me.

But *Catriona*, too, was picking up speed. Poor *Catriona*!

Poor Lincoln, too, for that matter, with his boat smashed deliberately into cliffs and then probably sinking, certainly abandoned. Bressay loomed nearer. Only a few yards to go now, and I could see the waves washing on the half-submerged rocks that jutted forward from the base of the low cliff. I left the wheel and scrambled forward, ready to jump as she struck. A harsh grating noise, then she stopped with a brutal bank and I was half catapulted, half jumping down to the flat, water-covered, sloping rock below me, falling headlong into the icy water. I scrambled upright and began to climb, glancing over my shoulder. The Russian fishing vessel was only a couple of hundred yards away now, knifing forward. I hauled myself desperately upward, insanely grateful that the cliff sloped back, that the rock stratum had buckled under some tremendous pressure of long ago and afforded scrambling angles. In a few seconds I was up and clear of it, but my heart was thundering painfully with each step now, every beat hammering at my eardrums. My legs were latex cylinders, buckling in all kinds of directions at once. That last explosion of effort had done for me. My strength was gone. I stood shakily for a moment on the grass slope at the top of the cliff and looked up. Ahead of me the ground sloped high, five or six hundred feet of rearing hillside, a steep track that I had no hope of climbing, led to an escape I would now never make.

I was beaten. I'd tried, but I was done. From behind the damned searchlight caught me and I waited for the bullets to smack into me. But no bullets came. Marasov must have decided to catch me alive. Well, he'd have no trouble. I made myself stagger on a few steps more, but it was only a token, a gesture to myself that I hadn't given up. I'd keep trying until they actually caught me; until hands grabbed me and held me and I could stagger no more. The searchlight threw the slope into blinding relief ahead of me and in its great blaze I could see the long stripe of my own shadow, black against the hillside. A few more stumbling steps brought me on to a tiny plateau, and there it ended. I could go no more. The will remained, but not a morsel of strength. I simply stood still in the searchlight beam, sagging, looking at the ground at my feet. I didn't even turn to watch Marasov's men come over the cliff, just stood there, waiting to hear the footsteps come towards me.

But that sound . . . it wasn't footsteps. An engine? The fishing boat, of course. But no, it couldn't be. This was a clattering sound, and came from above. The searchlight went out suddenly and I was blind in the night, listening still, wondering what the sound could be, but too spent even to lift my head. It grew louder, frighteningly loud, and I cupped my hands over my ears to keep it away. The light came on again, but differently somehow, then I knew why it was different: it, too, came from above. I made myself look up and saw a huge helicopter quite close above my head, dropping slowly, and a man stood framed in its doorway, waving to me. What did he want? My soggy brain realized he wasn't waving, but beckoning. The wheels touched now, and the huge helicopter bounced gently on her suspension and I staggered towards the beckoning arm. I was grasped and bundled in through the doorway and suddenly there was a great roar as the floor lifted powerfully beneath me.

A voice said, 'You're such a clever bastard!' and I knew the voice, somehow, but I didn't understand why my eyelids were clamped closed. I couldn't open them and I didn't want to. Everything was sliding away.

Pain woke me. Not great pain, just a multitude of tiny agonies in various parts of my body. I tried to ease my limbs to make the tiny agonies go away, but they didn't. I opened my eyes and blinked a few times, looking up directly into a bare light bulb on the ceiling. A white ceiling; white walls, too. I was in a bed. Whose bed, where? I saw the door. Steel, with boltheads, painted a heavy green, battered and scraped. And in the middle of the door a kind of inset cone. Realization came and I sat up suddenly and painfully, grunting at the protests of flaring muscle pains. This was a cell! A cell in a prison. I looked behind me at the window. Bars confirmed it. Memory flooded back. A helicopter. A voice. I knew now whose voice. Willingham's!

I shouted and a moment later a copper came in.

'Where is this?' I demanded.

He said easily, 'You're in the cells.'

'Where?'

'Lerwick police station.' He went out again and a moment later the terrible twins marched in: Elliot and Willingham.

I remember asking inanely what time it was. Prod a reporter awake and the first thing he does, an instant conditioned reflex, is look for the clock. I knew it must be morning because there was daylight outside. Elliot didn't bother to answer. He said instead, 'Explain.'

'Let me waken up first,' I said. 'Give me a cup of tea, or something. I feel like death!'

'You're lucky you feel anything. What happened? Why were you over there?'

'Tea,' I said. 'Tea for the love of God!'

I didn't want the tea so much as a few moments to get my thoughts together.

Elliot compressed his lips, said disgustedly, 'Tea! Tea and Limeys!' He moved to the door.

Willingham said, 'Let him –'

'If tea encourages him,' Elliot said quietly. 'Tea there shall be.' He called the copper and passed on the message. I closed my eyes and thought furiously. My mind wasn't quite my own and effective lies were elusive. The tea came far too quickly, in a scalding white mug.

Elliot let me take two sips. 'Okay, you got your tea. Start talking.'

I said, 'Did you find Anderson?'

'No.'

I took another sip and felt better. 'Bad luck.'

Willingham snorted angrily. A real snort, the kind pigs make.

Elliot said, 'You got a lead.' Not a question, a statement.

'Christ knows what happened,' I said. 'I got flung in the water, then dragged away by some bloody boat. Somebody was hanging on to me, but I managed to fight loose. When

I got ashore, they were coming after me and I ran. Pinched a boat. Sailed away. They came after me.'

'There was a guy here this morning,' Elliot said. 'Name of Lincoln. He wasn't too happy. He was due to meet another guy, a guy called Sellers, at eight o'clock. At his boat. So eight o'clock he's there. No boat, no Sellers.'

'It was his boat I pinched. I knew where it was, you see.'

'Yeah. Yeah, I see.' Elliot's nostrils were pinched too, and he exhaled exasperatedly through them. 'He also mentioned several other things. About Anderson. About a lady called Petrie.'

I wondered whether he'd also mentioned the Holm of Noss. His picture story. Worth money. Probably not, unless Elliot or Willingham had let him in on the reason for the whole thing.

I said, 'Miss Petrie wasn't much help.'

'She was no help to me either,' Elliot said ruefully. 'We threatened her with everything from obstruction to the Official Secrets Act. All she said was that she'd no idea where Anderson was.'

The tea was a little cooler now. I could drink instead of sip. It's strange how effective hot tea is, even as balm for aching muscles. I said, 'I don't know where Anderson is.'

'Or where to start looking?'

'No.'

Elliot looked hard at me. 'I'm starting to know when you're telling the truth,' he said. 'It doesn't happen often. When it does, your face changes and you look kinda shifty.'

'There's only Miss Petrie,' I said. 'No other way to him that I can see.'

'I'll tell you something, Sellers. Early this morning we did what we should have done a long time ago. We talked to the postman who got held up. Know what happened yesterday?'

'Go on,' I said soberly, half-knowing.

'He met Anderson on the road, that's what. Anderson was coming into Lerwick; the postman was leaving. The postman stopped and gave Anderson his mail. Against regulations, of course, the bastard! They got him fifteen miles further on.'

He stopped and looked at me, making me ask the question. 'Okay,' I said. 'What kind of mail was it?'

Elliot said, 'There was a little package. About three by one, as he recalls it. Kind of a cylinder. Redirected from Sandnes, Norway.'

'Really?'

'Really.' His tone was heavily sarcastic, his face threatening. 'You know about that package, Sellers. I want to know how. Because he's got it now and he's missing and he's got to be found.'

I said, 'All right. I'll tell you. Do I look shifty enough to believe?'

'Just talk.'

So I told him about Alsa's contact lens case, about the optician's shop, about the fact that Alsa and Anderson intended to get married. The information was no use to him now.

When I'd finished he agreed I'd looked sufficiently shifty to be telling the truth, sat down on the bed and looked at me as though he could have garotted me.

'If you'd said this in Gothenburg – '

'To a National Geographic writer?'

'Even later. When Schmid got you. It could still have been stopped. Only just, but it could.'

Willingham entered the conversation again, in his characteristic way. He said, 'I give you a firm promise Sellers. Look round this cell. Get used to it. Because you're going to spend a hell of a lot of your life in one just like it. You have my word on it.'

I swallowed, not doubting he meant it, or that it was true, or that he had the means to accomplish it. 'Can I have a bath?' I said. 'Prisoners are always given a bath.'

Elliot groaned.

I said, 'I just might have an idea. I need to think about it.'

'Tell me.'

'After the bath.'

They didn't let me soak long, but bathtime lasted long enough and because there were bars on the bathroom window too, was private enough for me to think the thing through. But there was one little detail I couldn't remember, a detail that was absolutely vital. The hot water also eased my bodily aches and pains somewhat and a hard rub-down with a magnificently harsh white cop-shop towel helped even more. Back in the cell, I dressed in Lincoln's clothes and felt in the pockets of the trousers. They were empty.

I said, 'Where are my things?'

'They were removed,' Willingham told me with evident pleasure. 'Standard practice with prisoners. You will be given a receipt.'

I turned to Elliot. 'In my wallet,' I said, 'probably very wet, is a photograph. It was taken at an office dinner. It shows Alsa Hay and me together.'

He said, 'So?'

'So to Anderson Miss Petrie's been almost a surrogate mother. They've known each other a long time. He stays at her cottage when he's in Lerwick. Do you suppose,' I said, 'that he might have taken the girl he's going to marry to see Miss Petrie?'

'I still don't get it.'

'Don't you? He's hiding, right? And she's protecting him. Possibly even in touch with him. He's got what somebody wants. His girl's sent him a picture and some kind of warning. There's a fire in his cottage and the postman who gave him the package is attacked. Anderson can't do much except wait and see what happens. Wait for some kind of approach. But the approach has to be from somebody he can trust. Right?'

Willingham said, 'Fine. We'll take the photograph.'

'I don't look like you, Willingham, I'm very glad to say!

187

Nor does Elliot. The only person here who looks like me is me. There's just a chance Miss Petrie might trust me. *If* she's met Alsa. But *you* can't do it. The photograph's no use to you unless I'm present, nice and clean and smiling earnestly.'

Elliot looked at me doubtfully. Then he said, 'There's one more thing you don't know. Anderson has a partner in his bird-watching. Guy called Newton. He seems to have vanished, too.'

I thought I could guess how. This man Newton must have been on the Holm, doing his stint. Anderson was on the way to relieve him when the postman gave him the package. Anderson probably went to Noss, taking his mail with him. They changed places and Newton returned to Lerwick, where Marasov grabbed him in the mistaken belief he was Anderson. Bad luck on Newton, but it got us no further. I said, 'I can't see it changes anything. Now, do we show the photograph to Miss Petrie?'

Elliot nodded slowly, then said, 'Yeah. We'll see her. I'll have your things brought in.'

I had a bad moment of waiting. I wasn't absolutely certain, couldn't quite remember, whether I'd changed all my things from one set of clothes to the other aboard *Catriona*.

I was relying on the fact I usually do, out of habit. Whenever I change my clothes, my wallet goes first.

The copper brought in a miscellaneous collection of small change, keys, a soaked passport and a wetter handkerchief. And the wallet. I opened it and looked among the soggy money and indestructible credit cards for the picture. It was there. Water doesn't damage photographic prints unless they dry out and stick to something.

'Got it?' Elliot asked.

I nodded.

'Okay. Let's go!'

I slipped the wallet into my back trouser pocket and said, 'There's one more thing.'

'What's that?'

'Nature calls.'

'Jesus!'

'Absolutely imperative,' I said.

So off I went to the lavatory. There's paper in lavatories, and for anyone who wonders, some British police stations haven't introduced the soft stuff yet. Not, at any rate, for prisoners. The stock in there was lethally harsh, but plenty strong enough for writing, and my wallet held, as always, a little ball-point pen of the kind they put in the spines of diaries. I carry it because my first boss said a reporter should never be without one in reserve and the habit stuck.

I wrote my message quickly, put the pen away, folded the paper small and went out to join the other two. 'Shall we go?'

When we got to the neat little cottage, Miss Petrie took one look at Elliot and said, 'I told you. I don't know *where* he is!' Having told him, she noticed me. 'I told *you* too.'

I said, 'Miss Petrie, I'd like to show you something. May we come in?'

'I see no need –'

'It's important. It really *is* important, Miss Petrie. Please! May we come in?' She didn't want us in. She hadn't lived a life of trickery and deception and clearly felt safer with the more obvious practitioners of the arts in the street. But her manners won. She stepped back reluctantly and allowed us into her spotless little sitting room.

'Well, young man?'

I pulled my wallet out, removed the photograph and handed it to her. Alsa and I had sat side by side at somebody's retirement dinner and I'd trimmed the rest of the print away to leave just the two of us. Romantic. A little pathetic. I handed the picture to her and said, 'Alison Hay.'

Miss Petrie looked at it closely, then at me, even more closely. I said, 'I've never met James Anderson. But Alsa is an old friend. So was her father.'

She looked hesitant, unsure how to play it. I said, 'The picture was taken at a dinner. We work for the same newspaper. My name is John Sellers. I was hoping that at some time, Alsa might have mentioned my name.' But there was no reaction.

'I see. And these gentlemen? Are they her friends, too?'

'No, Miss Petrie, they're not.'

Elliot said quickly, 'Just a *minute*, Sellers!'

'It's okay,' I said. 'They don't know her, but they are involved in this.'

'Hmm.' The bright, alert eyes looked me over again. I was no beauty in those dried and creased clothes. I hadn't shaved. Miss Petrie wasn't convinced and I could do nothing more to convince her. Or could I? I said, 'She told me about Aggie-Waggie.' It was true in a way.

'Aggie-Waggie?'

I smiled. 'Three jolly workmen.'

She said, 'It's only called Aggie-Waggie in Shetland.'

'I know. Alsa told me.'

Elliot said, 'What the . . . What's Aggie-Waggie?'

'A children's game,' I told him. 'They play it in the school yard, don't they, Miss Petrie?'

'In the street too.'

I said, 'Miss Petrie, I can't offer you more than that in the way of bona fides. I can only say I'm on Anderson's side.'

'Are you? You've never met him. Why should you be?'

'Because I'm on Alsa's.' Then I added quickly, and flatly so it wouldn't hurt so much: 'I wanted Alsa to marry *me* Miss Petrie.'

She glanced from my face to the photograph and back again and for a moment it seemed to me that the frost in her eyes just might have held something else, perhaps sympathy. 'You're generous, Mr – ?'

'Sellers. Miss Petrie, I don't know whether you can get a message to James Anderson.'

She opened her mouth to speak, but I ploughed on. 'I don't expect you to tell me whether you can or not. But I suspect you can. And *if* you can, I'd like you to do so.'

She didn't answer, just stood waiting.

'It would be better if we could actually meet him, but we must at least speak to him. He can name the time and place and the circumstances, but it should happen as soon as possible.'

She thought about it for a moment, looking for the deceptions, finding none because there were none to find. Not yet. At length she said, 'I don't know if . . .'

'If you *can*, Miss Petrie.'

She glanced at me once more, then opened the door. I wanted Elliot and Willingham to precede me, but naturally they didn't so I had to force it a bit. I had the little message held between my fingers and I offered my hand for her to shake. She took it immediately and palmed the little folded paper as though she'd been doing it all her life. I smiled, thinking she'd probably *watched* it all her life: classroom notes slipped from inky fingers to grubby paws. I said, 'We can be reached by telephone, at the police station.'

She closed the door behind us and Elliot sighed. 'Will she do it?'

I shrugged. I didn't know either. I thought I might have convinced her, but my note could just as easily undo it all again. The note was a real piece of duplicity.

'We'll have to wait,' I said, 'And hope.'


## CHAPTER NINETEEN


We went back to the police station to do our waiting. There was nothing else to be done. The police were still continuing to search for Anderson, but Sergeant McAllister's occasional reports on lack of progress had a hopeless air. He knew as well as we did that if Anderson didn't want to be found, there was no way on earth of finding him.

We did a few desultory, time-passing things. I had some breakfast and later another and longer bath in the hope of easing away some of the embedded stiffness and soreness from my body. It helped a bit, but not much. Elliot went into purdah to telephone London and emerged looking as though parts of him had been gnawed. Willingham conceived the bright idea that all Russian vessels should be ordered from

Shetland waters forthwith and tried to convince Wemyss in London that it was a wise and far-seeing strategy. After listening to Wemyss for a moment, he asked McAllister whether Polish and East German boats came into Lerwick too, reluctantly agreed with Wemyss that it was the same difference, and abandoned the idea. McAllister added his jot to the general uncertainty by telling us that a squad of Russians was actually marching in the Up-Helly-Aa procession that evening. A few weeks earlier, some Russian fishermen had proved that professional comradeship overrides the ideological variety by performing a particularly heroic rescue of a dozen fishermen from a local boat wrecked off the Shetlands, and the invitation was the island's way of saying thanks. In Lerwick, at this moment, the Russians were clearly fireproof.

Noon came and went. Time drifted by. Not much talking was done. Willingham unearthed another bright idea. Now he wanted to pressure Miss Petrie really hard. 'In circumstances like these, any means are justified,' he urged Elliot doggedly. I wondered for the hundredth time what this psychopathic idiot was doing in intelligence at all. Elliot simply said she didn't look the kind who bullied easy and forget it. We stared at the phones and waited for them to ring.

It was a long wait, and its end merely signalled the start of another. The phone rang at three-thirty. Elliot answered it, handed it to me, and picked up another linked phone so he could listen, too.

'Mr Sellers? Catherine Petrie here. I'm given to understand that you should wait at the entrance to the Town Hall at six o'clock.'

I said, 'Thank you.' And asked carefully, 'He's accepted what I said?'

'I believe Miss Hay has spoken of you, Mr Sellers.'

With Elliot on the line, I couldn't take it further. I just had to hope. Miss Petrie rang off and the second long wait began.

We went to the window and looked across the street. The Town Hall entrance was a mere thirty yards or so away, and could easily be watched from where we stood. Willingham started watching at three thirty-five and kept up a shuffle of irritation as daylight died and the lights came on, inside and out. Elliot telephoned London again to say that things might be looking up now. I kept my fingers crossed and stared at my shoes, and wondered exactly where Alsa was. I no longer even considered the possibility that she might be dead. The phony Schmid had put an equation to me: that whether she was dead or not didn't matter, so long as we could hope she was still alive. The equation didn't hold any more. Anderson now had the transparency, and when he knew the rest of the story, he'd want to see Alsa alive and kicking before he even considered anything else. And the Russians would be well aware of that. They'd be here now, in the darkening streets, waiting for us to move, ready to make their play. So they had to keep Alsa somewhere near. On a fishing boat perhaps. Even one of those in the harbour. Several times I looked down the hill at the tied-up boats, and had to restrain myself from rushing out of the police station, down to the quay and on to the nearest vessel that was flying a hammer and sickle.

Towards six o'clock, the streets were filling up. The Up-Helly-Aa procession was scheduled to begin at seven and all Lerwick, plus half the rest of the population of the Shetlands and a hell of a lot of tourists, would be standing watching. People were coming from all directions, the pavements were already becoming crowded and the police had given up their forlorn search for Anderson after Miss Petrie's phone call. Tonight was whisky night, festivity night, and there were other matters demanding Lerwick's small force's attention.

At five minutes before the hour, the three of us left the room and crossed the road. People hurried past us, heading for the procession route, a little way inland from where we stood. Bottle shapes were visible in many of the passing pockets; some of the men wore elaborate fancy dress and carried long poles capped with sacking: torches to be lit for the galley procession.

We took up our position by the Town Hall entrance and waited, looking at our watches. At six the Town Hall clock boomed out above us and the carillon began to ring out a tune I didn't know. We looked at the hurrying faces, Elliot and Willingham hopefully, I no less anxiously. The difference was that I was praying no one would approach us.

'He's not coming,' Elliot said heavily at five past.

'It'll be difficult to move through the crowds,' I pointed out. 'He'll come. The message was clear enough.'

So we waited. High above us the clock chimed the quarter, then at last the half. I said, 'Perhaps there's a reason. Somebody else hanging about. Maybe he's watching us now. Maybe he's waiting to be sure.'

A few minutes later, I suggested we cross the street and come back, just to underline to Anderson, if he were watching, that the Town Hall, not the procession, was our intended location.

'Can't do any harm, I suppose,' Elliot said. 'Let's try it.' He sounded deeply depressed.

We crossed the road and stood for a moment, on the other side. The crowds were thickening fast, moving around us, jostling.

Elliot said, 'Okay, let's go back.'

'Another minute,' I said. There was a big, noisy group hurrying toward us up the hill from the quay, sixty or seventy men, laughing and shouting. I waited until they were almost on us, then said, 'On second thoughts we might as well.'

Elliot turned. Willingham turned. I began to turn, let them see me begin, then stopped, took three quick steps, slid in among the noisy crowd and hurried forward. Ahead were the two long roads on either side of the playing field where the galley would burn, and they were packed. Only minutes now remained before the procession was to begin and away to my right there were already scattered outbursts of cheering. I heard Willingham's voice shout 'Stop him!' a few yards behind, but I was in the middle of a rapidly-moving little phalanx of men and a few seconds later the whole group was merging into the crowd in the streets.

I separated myself quickly, then, and began to slide through the crowd, knees bent a little to keep my head down, praying that I'd slipped away successfully and heading now for the spot I'd specified in the note I'd slipped into Miss Petrie's hand.

Squads of men in fancy dress lined the roads as seven o'clock struck. I was too early. I moved deep into the crowd, trying to be inconspicuous, but for once in Lerwick, sweaters and work trousers weren't standard dress. People were in their best for Up-Helly-Aa. For twenty minutes I stood sweating, before the music crashed and the marching began. I made myself unpopular, then, pushing my way to the front. Suddenly a Very light soared into the sky and all along the road little lights flared suddenly as matches were struck. Then the lights grew brighter as the matches lit torches and the torches were raised high. Up-Helly-Aa had begun! I stood there in the torchlight, in the front of the crowd, trying to stick my face out. This was the designated place and the appointed moment. Miss Petrie had been given the photograph to pass to Anderson. Would he recognize me?

A squad of men in Viking costume came proudly by, torches held high, flickering flames gleaming on horned helmets decorated with glossy ravens' wings, shields bearing battle signs. Despite myself, I watched. The scene was ancient, majestic, strangely moving as a silence fell and the men marched forward in the torchlight.

I didn't see or hear him approach. One moment I was watching the marching men; the next somebody was whispering close to my ear. 'Sellers?'

I nodded.

'Follow me.'

We slipped easily back through the crowd; people were only too anxious to let someone from the front move away. A couple of minutes later, we were clear, hurrying inland, then turning and turning again, down a narrow lane and finally into a darkly shadowed yard.

Anderson was a big, rawboned, rangy man. Serious looking; physically hard. We moved close to a wall and I said quickly, urgently, 'Have you –'

Anderson stared grimly at me. 'No questions. Tell me what *you* know.'

So I told him. About the Soviet Jews who'd made their futile plan, had been betrayed, had tried again using Alsa as an unknowing courier. How she'd left the lens case in the shop, and the optician, presumably knowing only one Sandnes, must have added the word Norway before posting it and that it must then have been redirected by the Norwegian postal service.

He listened closely and carefully as I explained it. Then I told him why the transparency mattered so much, why Alsa had been kidnapped, who Elliot and Willingham were and why it was vital to keep them at bay. I told him about Noss and the Russian who'd waited for him there.

'It was you there last night?' he asked.

'Yes.'

'I saw you, from a distance. Maybe you saved my life.'

'Maybe I did. It's Alsa's life that matters. Have you got it?'

Anderson hesitated, stared at me for a moment, then nodded.

'Here? With you?'

'Yes.' He reached into his pocket and pulled out the little plastic case. 'There was a note from Alsa inside: just a few words. It said her life depended on hiding it safely. I didn't know what it meant but –'

A light blazed suddenly from the mouth of the yard. There were rapid footsteps and a voice snapped, 'Keep still!' We were against a wall already. There might have been somewhere to run if we'd had time, but the speed and surprise left us helpless.

Four of them. And Marasov's rimless glasses gleaming above the torch. 'Give it to me.'

Anderson didn't move.

'I said, give it to me.' Marasov raised his pistol slowly,

pointing the barrel at Anderson's right eye, holding out his hand. There was nothing Anderson could do. I watched in despair as the little tube was handed over.

Marasov said, 'Watch him closely!' Then he stepped back, uncapped the lens case, pulled out the protective plastic cage from inside it and extracted the tiny square of thirty-five millimetre film. He held it up against the light of his torch, threw the tube away and stepped towards us again. He was smiling. 'I knew you'd lead us to him, Mr Sellers.'

'You?' Anderson glared at me. 'You bast –'

'No,' I said, 'I didn't. They must have followed me!'

'Yes, we followed. We were patient, and now we have recovered what we lost.' Marasov fished in his pocket and pulled something out. A moment later flame flared from a lighter. An American Zippo, of all things. He lowered the transparency into the flame and we listened to the little sizzle as the film fizzled quickly to a cindery wisp. He dropped it and ground it with his heel.

Anderson was almost beside himself. 'What about Alsa?' he demanded. 'Where is she?'

Marasov continued to grind the burned transparency with his heel. Then he said, 'I have no idea who you're talking about.'

Anderson didn't speak. He simply flung himself at Marasov, smashing with his big fists at the little Russian's face. He got him, too, once or even twice, before the gun banged and Anderson grunted, reeled back against the wall and collapsed in a heap.

I listened to the running footsteps as the Russians hurried away. My eyes had flooded with tears. The whole thing was my fault. I'd been so bloody clever, playing ends against the middle, and all I'd succeeded in doing was to ensure Alsa would be killed! Through me Anderson had been shot. Maybe killed. I didn't care a rap for Elliot's big intelligence breakthrough, but even that hadn't been saved from the universal disaster. I'd lost all the way round. Everything. The girl I loved, the whole bloody lot. Everything lay in ruins around me and I alone was responsible for the bloody shambles.

Anderson groaned as I dropped to my knees beside him, groaned again as I gently turned his body so that he could lie, perhaps more comfortably, on his back. Well, at least he was alive. I'd have to leave him though; have to go for help.

As I began to rise there came the sound of footsteps again, running footsteps. They stopped in the alley outside and I could see the flash of hand torches.

Willingham charged into the yard, Elliot a pace or two behind him. 'That shot!' he said breathlessly. 'What the hell was it?'

I said dully, 'They shot Anderson.'

'Anderson?' Willingham glared down at him. 'That's Anderson? Then where – ?'

I said, 'They got the transparency, too.'

He looked round wildly. 'Which way did they – ?'

'It's no use,' I said. 'Marasov burned it.' I pointed to the little black smear on the concrete. 'That's all that's left.'

Elliot seemed to sag suddenly. He bent and looked at the tiny flakes of ash, already scattered in the wind. 'Jesus!' he said mournfully.

'You stupid bastard!' Willingham snarled. 'You pathetic bloody clown. Do you realize what you've – '

I said, 'Anderson's been shot. He needs help. Help me carry him – '

'Carry him your bloody self!'

A moment later Anderson and I were alone. The two of them simply stamped off and left us and I blinked after them stupidly, not really blaming them. The only blame was mine and at that moment the burden of it seemed unendurable. 'Alsa! Alsa!' I muttered.

Beside me, unexpectedly, Anderson whispered, 'They've gone?'

I bent quickly beside him in a sudden flood of relief. 'Yes. Are you – ?'

'It's my shoulder . . .' I could hear the pain in his voice.
'Can you stand?'

'Aye. I think . . .' Anderson held out his hand and I helped him up. He gave a sudden grunt. 'I'm all right, I think. It's just . . . let me stand still a while.'

He leaned his back against the wall and slipped his left hand inside his coat, feeling gingerly at his right shoulder.

I said, 'Let's get you to the hospital, wherever it is.'

'No,' he said.

'Come on, man! You need attention.'

He pulled out his hand. 'Bleeding, but I can manage, I think.'

'Put your arm round my shoulders,' I said. 'I'll help you get there.'

'I'll have to wait.'

'Wait? Why? There's nothing to do now.'

'Oh, but there is.' In the deep shadows I couldn't really see his face, but there was something in his voice . . .

I said, 'But they got it. Burned it. You saw them!'

Anderson pushed himself away from the wall. 'Aye. They got *one*.'


# CHAPTER TWENTY


'You made a copy of a *transparency*?' I said. To copy transparencies isn't easy. You need a good photo-lab and a deal of skill.

'We don't wear skins up here,' Anderson said.

'All right. Where?'

'There's a man processes my pictures. He's got a good lab. I used it.'

'I mean, where's the copy transparency now?'

His answer was to lengthen his stride. At the end of the alley he stopped, looked round the corner into the street. Satisfied, he walked quickly out. A hundred yards more, a quick turn down another alley, and he was knocking on the back door of a house.

A man opened the door. Sixtyish, with a face seamed by long exposure to sun, wind and sea. He looked at Anderson, nodded, then stepped back to let us in.

Anderson said, 'I have to get to my boat, Tom. But quietly.' He didn't introduce us.

The man Tom nodded. 'She's in the harbour yet?'

'Aye.'

'All right.' Then he noticed the way Anderson stood. 'What's wrong with your shoulder?'

'Nothing. Come on Tom.'

'I've seen a bullet hole before,' the man said quietly.

Anderson sighed. 'Aye. It's not serious.'

'Maybe. A little look, that's all, Jim. Let me see.'

'There isn't time!' Anderson said impatiently.

'Don't be a bloody fool!' Tom was already unfastening Anderson's blue donkey jacket. He took off the coat carefully, then peeled Anderson's sweater upward. Both the sweater and Anderson's back were bright with blood. Tom looked at the wound carefully, then moved to examine it again from the front. 'It'll no' kill you. Can you move it?'

'Not much.'

'Collar bone's gone. Aside from that it's in and out and probably clean, unless fibres from your clothes were forced into a wound. Minute, Jim.'

He opened a drawer and took out a big first-aid box, applied penicillin powder liberally, then taped big wads of gauze in place, back and front. 'I heard they were looking for you. Anything I can do?'

Anderson shook his head. 'Just hurry.'

Tom didn't hurry, but his broad, work-worn, spatulate fingers were remarkably deft as he worked. He pulled the sweater down again. 'You need a sling, man.' Then he buttoned the arm inside the coat. 'Can he sail?'

It was the first time Tom had shown he was even aware of me.

'It'll be all right, Tom. Just hurry.'

A minute later, with Anderson's right arm slung and buttoned securely, his loose sleeve hanging, Tom nodded and opened a door. He led the way, Anderson followed. I brought up the rear, thinking we were going down into a cellar. Instead we entered a low corridor, a tunnel almost, with bare earth walls and roof shored up at intervals with curved staves. We went along it, crouching. At the end, Tom stood upright, slid back a bolt, eased open a trapdoor and climbed through. From outside I could hear the soft swish of water. Anderson climbed through next, then I followed. A small fishing boat was tied up hard against the wall. Tom was already bent over at the starting handle and Anderson lay on the bottom boards.

I climbed in, too, and Anderson said, 'Lie like this.'

I crawled down beside him and waited. The engine started, then Tom spread a tarpaulin over us and the light was blacked out.

'Where are we going?' I demanded.

Anderson said quietly, 'Tom will drop us at my boat. Maybe it's being watched. Maybe it isn't. When we reach it be ready to jump.'

'But where – ?'

He cut me off. 'Until we get there, only I know. *When* we get there . . .' he paused and added after a moment, 'you'll see.'

The boat was moving off now. The engine puttered quietly, and water swished along the boards beside my ears. The trip took only three or four minutes.

Then Tom lifted the end of the tarpaulin. 'Seems quiet,' he said softly, 'but I don't know. There's a Russian purse-seine-setter half a cable away.'

'Can you see anybody on her?' Anderson asked.

'No. But . . .'

But there would be somebody. All three of us knew it. Anderson said, 'We'll have to try it. Go ahead, Tom.'

The engine's power increased for a few moments, then died back to a slow throb. 'Coming on her now,' Tom's voice said.

'Right.' Anderson flung back the tarpaulin and we sat up then stood, then jumped as the boat came neatly alongside Anderson's big Shetland model. Anderson put his foot on the thwart and stepped easily across. I followed a good deal less gracefully and a lot more noisily. But at least I was aboard.

'Get the anchor up!' Anderson ordered briskly, himself bending to the engine. Obediently I hauled on the chain, the metallic racket loud in the stillness as it fell through my hands into the little chain locker. Then the motor was going and we were off. I secured the anchor and went back to join Anderson and we both stared back at the lines of tied up vessels.

It was the second time in less than twenty-four hours, I thought savagely, that I'd been doing exactly this, trying to sneak unobserved out of Lerwick harbour. Apparent success; no success at all. I thought about the events that had followed, the ghastly cradle-ride, the desperate race over Noss, the final exhaustion from which only the helicopter had saved me. I remembered I hadn't thanked Elliot and Willingham for saving me; hadn't even asked where they'd got the helicopter or how they knew where I was. *Nor*, I realized then, *had they offered to tell me*! My eyes strayed involuntarily upward to search the night sky for lights, but it was dark and empty. The only lights were in the town. High on the hill I could see the glow of flaring torchlight from the Up-Helly-Aa procession. Or maybe it was the galley, already burning. Somehow in that moment it seemed a bad omen.

Tom's boat was already almost out of sight, and soon we were coming under the Bressay cliffs, leading south towards Bard Head. Anderson's face was pale and determined. He was fighting shock and fighting it well, but there would be a penalty to be paid. I said, thinking of the night before, 'Is there anything aboard. Tea? Whisky?'

'Both.'

'I'll make some tea.' I went into the little cabind and put the kettle on. The whole thing was like some nightmare re-run of the earlier trip. The kettle boiled, I made the tea, poured it into a mug, stirred in a lot of sugar as treatment for shock and handed it out to him. When he'd drunk half, I laced the remainder with Scotch, and watched him finish it.

'How do you feel?'

'I'm all right.'

I said, 'I didn't lead them to you, you know. They must have had a lot of men in town tonight, watching for us.'

'I know. Forget it.'

Somehow I found myself slightly in awe of Anderson, something I don't feel often for anyone. He had the solid confidence of a wholly self-contained man, a tangible authority that seemed to come from deep knowledge of his own world. Looking at him now, at the helm of his boat, it wasn't difficult to imagine other Andersons a thousand years ago, coming confidently to these shores in the same flimsy long-boats that also explored Iceland and Greenland and may even have crossed to America. I almost hesitated to speak. Almost. I told myself sharply not to be a fool, and said, 'Tell me where the bloody thing is. And why you copied it.'

He glanced at me. 'Alsa's note said her life depended on that one thing. It wasn't much, that flimsy wee piece of film, for the girl's life to hang on. But Alsa wouldn't have said it, if it hadn't been true. You'd know that. I thought, what if I lose it, or maybe damage it. What then? So I made a copy.'

'One copy.'

'Aye, one. I'd not lose two.'

'Where are we going? And when we get there, what then?'

'Later.'

'*Now!*' I said. 'You can't afford to be the rugged individualist. Not any more. You've only one arm, for a start. You're going to need me.'

He looked at me dourly, the weighing eye of the islander

on the city slicker. But he told me. 'Noss,' he said.

'The Holm? That bloody cradle!'

'There isn't a cradle any more. I cut the rope last night. But it's on the Holm, all the same.'

'Then how – ?'

He spoke one word then, and I shuddered, because the word meant a lot of things; it also flashed pictures on the screen of my mind. I didn't like what I saw. The word was, 'Climb.'

I made myself speak quietly, and reasonably, and listened to the tremble in my voice. 'You can't climb it.'

'No.'

'And I certainly can't.'

He turned to look at me and nodded. 'You can do it.'

I said, 'I wouldn't even try. I get vertigo on a long escalator. I've no climbing skill. For Christ's sake, man!'

'Take the wheel.' He went into the cabin and came out again a moment later carrying a big canvas bag with a drawstring neck. He fiddled one-handed with it for a moment, then handed it to me. I pulled the neck wide and he tipped the contents out: a pile of metal objects that rattled into the stern seat. He shone his torch on the little pile and picked out a shiny piece of metal a few inches long. 'See that? '

I nodded. 'What is it?'

'Jumar clip,' he said. 'Sooner use Heiblers myself, but the Jumar's safe and efficient and I've no Heiblers here. Now see,' he fumbled among the bits and pieces and selected three other items. The first was another identical clip. The other two were stirrups of some kind, with strong webbing through the eyelets.

'Now do you see?'

'I bloody well don't see!' I thought of that dreadful cliff, all two hundred feet of it, sheer and impossible. And I thought about Alsa, too, and my stomach churned because I knew suddenly that I *was* going to try. I had to *try*! I'd fail; I knew that, too, with awful certainty, just as I'd failed all along the line. But with Alsa still a prisoner . . .

I said soberly, through a dry, rasping throat, 'How does it work?'

Anderson said, 'In the night, before I cut the cable, I crossed to the Holm and let down a rope. It's secure, don't worry. Now, what you do is this . . .'

I listened appalled. It was safe, he said. I couldn't fall, he said. He got the climbing belt from the cabin and demonstrated how safe it was and why I couldn't fall. He told me the breaking strain of the nylon line was God knows how many thousand pounds. He didn't convince me for a second.

We moved away from the eastern cliffs of Bressay, across open water towards the southern tip of Noss. When I could tear my eyes away from the sinister wedge silhouette of the island, I glanced across towards Bressay, wondering about Lincoln's boat. Was it wrecked, sunk, what? I should have felt guilty, but I didn't. Where I was going, sins were forgiven, though I doubted if Lincoln would forgive mine. The closer we came, the more impossible the whole crazy idea became. As distance narrowed, the cliffs reared higher. From above they'd seemed big, from below, as Anderson nosed the boat in beneath them, they looked stupendous, grim dark grey walls striped strangely across with dull white. Anderson looked up at them almost with affection. He could afford to; he didn't have to climb.

He said, 'Be glad it's winter.'

'Why?'

'Big breeding grounds, these cliffs. Everything's up there at nesting time: all the gulls, gannets, razor bills, guillemots. Fulmars too. Just be thankful there are no fulmars.'

'Why?'

'They spit at you if you disturb them. Oil from their throats. It stinks, enough to knock you down. You can never get the smell off your clothes. Be thankful, man.'

I dutifully tried to be thankful, but it was difficult. Lincoln's apt phrase, a hole into hell, kept coming back to me and the more my mind repeated it the truer it seemed.

We came nosing into the black gap between the Holm and the island, engine slowed just a little, Anderson handling the boat with high skill where the water pounded between the huge walls.

I buckled the belt, then crept forward, boathook in one hand, torch in the other, looking for the rope.

'Just . . . a bit more . . .' Anderson was looking upward for the dangling rope. 'There!'

I hooked it in and passed the soaking end through my belt loop, then fastened the Jumar clips in position, one above the other. From each clip a stirrup dangled on its web strap. I put my foot in one stirrup and tried my weight on it experimentally, but there was a quick movement beneath me and the boat was gone, carried away on a swift surge of water! Anderson shouted, 'Don't panic. Other foot!'

Scared daft, I clung to the rope tightly while I felt with my foot for the other stirrup. It seemed for long moments that I'd never find it, but then my toe slid into the swinging metal loop and at least I could get myself into some sort of balance. I stood for a moment then and looked up at the silhouette sixty feet above me where a massive overhang bellied out against the sky. The sea hissed and swirled beneath me, almost drowning Anderson's shouted instruction to get going.

I still didn't believe it would work. Two metal clips and a pair of stirrups to conquer this awesome combination of height and space? It was so patently absurd!

'Get on man!' Anderson shouted again.

I swallowed and took hold of the first Jumar and tried to slide it up the rope. It wouldn't budge. I pushed and sweated, beginning to panic, before the pressure of the stirrup under my instep told me what was wrong. I raised my foot and tried again. This time the Jumar clip slipped easily upward. But was it secure? Carefully I let my weight move from one stirrup to the other. The clip held, gripping tight as my weight forced its sprung jaws against the rope. All right, now the next! I moved the second clip up until it touched the first, transferred my weight, and felt it grip. The two clips were one under the other; I couldn't move the second past the first. I moved the top clip again, pushed down hard on the stirrup, and went up another eighteen inches. Now again, left foot this time. Okay. At least it worked. As a system, it worked. I let out a deep breath of near relief that became a gasp as the rope pivoted suddenly. Vomit rose in my throat. I glanced down at the water. I'd climbed perhaps five feet; nothing against the task that remained. And I saw something else too. Anderson was leaving; already his boat was backing off at the entrance to the gorge. Why? I forced the question from my mind. He'd have a reason, even if I couldn't see it. I forced myself to climb. The strain on my legs was murderous and the pressure on my feet was just where it hurt most under the instep. It was probably correct technique to take the weight on the ball of the foot; I understood that, but couldn't make myself do it. The further my foot went through the stirrups, the safer I felt and to hell with the pain!

Slide the Jumar up, step after it, slide again. I was beginning to get the hang of it. But it remained difficult, each step upward an effort in concentration. Each movement of hand and leg must be co-ordinated, and it was impossible to achieve any kind of rhythm. So every step was a new operation, begun and considered and executed with desperate care. I fought my way slowly upward, nearing the overhang that seemed increasingly to press its weight down towards me. He shall not pass! I looked up at it, grimly. I bloody well had to pass.

All the while the rope twirled slowly and I made myself concentrate on the rope itself, trying to ignore the cliffs as they swung past, first one way then the other. Up with Jumar and foot together. Check the clip. Transfer weight. Steady myself. Now the next clip, the next foot . . .

Then I was at the overhang. I slipped the top Jumar clip up until it actually scraped on rock, then raised myself and tried to work out how to get past. I could see only one way. I'd have to push myself and the rope clear of the rock by sheer strength, hand flat against the rock-face, then slip the clip past. I brought up the under clip and secured it, balanced myself, and tried . . . A puff of wind ruined it. Just one puff that spun me out of control, trapped my fingers between rope and rock and cracked my head blindingly against the cliff face. For a moment I hung dazed, my weight on belt and stirrup, held upright only by my own trapped hand, now being ground agonizingly against the stone. I struggled frantically to release it, but only succeeded in hurting myself more. With my teeth gritted against the pain I forced myself to think. But there was no other way. I'd have to repeat what I'd done before: push against the cliff to force the rope out a little, then pull my hand away. It meant I'd have no handgrip on the rope at all.

But there wasn't time to look for subtleties, even if they existed. The pressure of the rope on my trapped hand was crushing. I gave a sudden angry push, snatched my hand clear and clouted my head again. I hung there dizzily, turning slowly in the air sixty feet above the swirling water. It was impossible. There *must* be another way. Elbows? What if I pushed with my elbows, still holding the rope? The first try failed, but the second worked and I slid the Jumar triumphantly over the rock edge. Now the other. Got it! I waited for a moment, nursing my hand, till the pain faded a little, before forcing myself up again. The going was desperately difficult now, the rope taut against a long vertical section of the rock face. I had to strain my body away from it with the toe of one boot just to make space for the Jumars to slide. But the *system* still worked. I fought for height and height was slowly being won. I was more than halfway, aching from the strain, but confident now in the equipment. And at least, pinned as I was to the face, that awful vertigo-inducing pivoting had stopped.

A few more feet and I gave myself a rest, equalizing the clips, letting my weight fall evenly on to the two stirrups. I counted slowly to sixty and started again. But by now it was grindingly hard going. My strength was diminishing; each upward thrust was a greater effort than the one before. For a while I know I even ceased to think with any clarity; at any rate, I have no memory of the next part of the climb after that brief rest.

I was within ten feet of the top when something thrust itself into my consciousness and for a moment I failed to recognize what it was. I think I must have been reliving what had happened here the night before, confusing one day with another, because at first the light meant nothing.

Suddenly, I was trembling awake again, staring in horror towards the entrance to the foaming channel beneath. A big fishing boat had appeared there. A boat with a searchlight. The nightmare was repeating itself! I was held in the bright beam like a fly on a wall!

Terrified now, I forced myself upward. Only half a dozen steps more. Only five. A bullet whanged off the rock close to me and fizzed off into the darkness. I flattened myself as close as I could to the rock and managed another upward thrust. Then another. There was a shallow cleft in the rock to my left and I forced myself into its sparse shelter as below me somebody opened up with an automatic weapon and bullets smacked in dozens against the rock and sang away. Another step. Cautious as hell, trying to stay within the crack. The firing had stopped. Empty magazine? Pause to reload? I took a chance and made another two feet. The cliff edge was close above me now, less than three feet or so from my hands. Still no firing. I got foot and hand in position and thrust quickly and suddenly and was cowering in the cleft as the next bullets cracked against the rock. One more. Just one. One more thrust and a quick wriggle and I'd be in cover. The searchlight was unwavering, my shelter desperately inadequate. I waited . . . and realized they were waiting, too. When I moved they'd fire.

That was when the next act of the nightmare began. It was uncanny and for a moment I didn't believe it, but it was there, the sound was *there*: clear and unmistakable high above. A helicopter came clattering over the Noss cliffs!

I watched it in bewilderment. Elliot and Willingham? What were *they* . . .? And then I knew suddenly, and realized that the men on the fishing boat would be watching the helicopter, too. Briefly, perhaps but they'd watch it. With a last, long desperate thrust I reached the edge, gripped it, and hauled myself over. For a moment, breathless and exhausted, I lay flat on the top of the Holm.

But that moment was all I could afford. I couldn't, daren't stay there. I stared up at the helicopter as it veered across the sky towards me. It had followed the boat! That was *how* it had got there. Now the helicopter was going to land up here. I crawled away from the cliff edge, then tried to stand up and found I couldn't. I took a moment or two to untangle the reason from my own confusion. But it was simple enough. The Jumars and the belt still held me to the rope.

Desperately I fumbled with the belt buckle, released it and set off at a stumbling run across the surface. Above me the helicopter was slowing, beginning to hover in preparation for landing. What had Anderson said? Fifteen paces from his hide towards the point where he'd secured the rope. I got to the hide, turned back and started counting. Then a shot came from above, a single sharp crack amid the engine's roar. Christ, *they* were shooting at me, too! Elliot and Willingham!

From nowhere a mammoth voice boomed, 'Stand still, Sellers.' But I didn't stand still. The helicopter must have some loudspeaker equipment. It boomed again. Twelve paces, thirteen, fourteen, fifteen. I dropped to my knees, searching, and found it. A plastic bottle, just as Anderson had said. Tucked in a little depression. I shook it and heard the water gurgle. The transparency was in the water.

'Stand still or we fire!' the great voice boomed.

I ignored it, stood up and, clutching the bottle, sprinted for the cliff edge.

# CHAPTER TWENTY-ONE

There was about twenty yards to go. Twenty-one would be a disaster and my physical state didn't make for fine judgment. Ten feet short of the edge I flung myself flat and began to kitten-crawl forward. At the edge I stopped, put the water bottle down, and turned to watch the helicopter. The thing was huge, with long rows of passenger windows along its sides; one of the oil company machines I'd seen on the tarmac at Sumburgh and which were used to carry men out to the deep sea drilling rigs. The roaring monster came down slowly and carefully, bringing its own fierce gale that seemed to be buffeting me towards the edge. Its coloured lights turned and flashed eerily in the now deafening darkness. It looked like some vast insect predator, come to ingest me. The wheels touched and the massive rotors continued spinning, but the pitch diminished, then a door in the side opened and Elliot stepped down and waited for Willingham to join him. They were both armed.

As I watched them walk towards me, I rapidly unscrewed the stopper of the plastic bottle. They stopped no more than ten feet away and stood looking down at me. 'All right, Sellers. Give me that!' Willingham bawled against the helicopter's racket.

I shook my head and shouted back. 'Get back into the bloody thing and fly off.'

They came closer, both with pistols levelled. Elliot called. 'We'll use these, Sellers. Don't doubt it.'

I held up the bottle. 'If you do, it goes over the edge. The stopper's off. It'll sink straight away.'

Elliot yelled, 'How do I know it's in there?'

'It's there,' I shouted. 'Now go. For Christ's sake, go!'

Stalemate.

Elliot and I stared at each other. I shouted, 'If you shoot

me, it falls. If you come near me, it falls. Get into your bloody helicopter and go!' It was Elliot I was addressing, Elliot who was in charge, Elliot who stood looking at me doubtfully. I deliberately ignored Willingham – and I almost lost everything in doing so. I should have expected it, knowing him, but I certainly wouldn't have expected his speed. He hurtled at me from the edge of my vision, diving to try to pin me to the ground. At the last second I saw him coming and rolled over desperately, lashing upward with my foot. It was sheer instinct that made me kick, sheer blind luck that I made contact, sheer disaster that my foot caught him as it did: hard and clean in the face. The impact was doubled by his own onward rush. He thudded to the ground right beside me, with a harsh yelp of pain. I lashed out again, heard his sudden scream and didn't understand for a second what had happened. But the scream continued and died away and I suddenly knew and felt myself shiver. Willingham had gone over!

I looked quickly at the bottle neck. As I'd rolled, had the bottle tipped? I shook it and listened to the water gurgle. No. It was still there.

What about Elliot? For God's sake, where was *he*? I looked up and saw he was still standing there, open-mouthed now, but the automatic still pointed at me. 'Go!' I yelled at him.

He remained perfectly still for what seemed a long time, then shrugged, turned and walked slowly back to the helicopter. I watched him climb aboard, listened to the rising clamour of the rotor blades, and then the chopper's wheels lifted and it soared upward.

Cautiously I crawled away from the cliff edge, then paused to restopper the bottle. The helicopter was a couple of hundred feet above me, beginning to circle slowly. Elliot had gone away all right, but not very far.

What the hell could I do now? I'd won a pause, but no more than that. Before my crazy climb up the rope there had at least been a scheme of sorts. Anderson and I would inform the Russians we had the copy and use it to bargain for Alsa's release. But now the Russians would probably have guessed why we had returned to the Holm. By now, they'd perhaps even have caught Anderson and be certain. For me, and for Alsa, the alternatives were bleak and fatal. Frying pan or fire? Americans or Russians? Either way, Alsa would . . .

I crouched alone in the darkness on top of that two hundred foot rock pillar and tried to find a way out. Above, Elliot's helicopter still waited. Below, there was the Russian boat. There was nothing, *nothing* I could do!

I stood shakily and looked helplessly around me. Then I saw a dark shadow on the grass near the middle of the surface. I frowned, remembering the Russian who'd captured me last night. I hadn't been sure then that he was dead. I walked slowly towards him. Now there was no question about it. He lay as I'd left him; those blows I'd chopped into his throat had killed him. Now Willingham was dead too! Two men dead. And Alsa would also die; they'd never release her now.

Then I saw that something lay beside the Russian. I bent to look at it. Of course – the radio he'd used! I scooped it up, switched on my torch, and looked at it. A simple walkie-talkie gadget. On-off switch, probably single wavelength. Could I make use of this in some way? I sat down and thought about it for a bit, then went quickly to the hide and found what I wanted.

A couple of minutes later, I flicked the switch and spoke into it. 'Marasov,' I said.

Nothing happened. I went close to the edge, raising the aerial so that it projected over into space. I repeated Marasov's name several times. Perhaps the damned thing had been smashed when the Russian fell?

Then a voice replied in Russian. I said, 'Marasov, Marasov,' and waited. There was a little hiss of static.

'This is Marasov.'

I said, 'This is Sellers. I have a copy transparency that Anderson made.'

'Then an exchange can be arranged.'

'You have two prisoners. Alison Hay and a man called Newton.'

A pause, then, 'That is true. Climb down the rope, Mister Sellers. Give it to us. I undertake to land the two people you name on one of the Shetland islands.'

I said, 'Get stuffed.'

'It is a promise.'

'Made to break,' I said. 'I have a better idea.'

'If the transparency reaches the Americans,' Marasov said grimly, 'no deal is possible.'

'It won't. Now listen. I will deliver this to you *after* you have put Miss Hay and Mr Newton on to Anderson's boat. When I see they are safely aboard and that the boat is well under way, you get the transparency.'

The walkie-talkie crackled. Marasov said, 'You do not trust me, I do not trust you. Why should I?'

'Because,' I said, 'I will offer myself as hostage.'

'How?'

I hesitated, then committed myself. 'I will climb a few feet down the rope . . . damn!' I had to stop talking as the helicopter suddenly roared low over the island. I waited for it to go away and started to talk again. 'I will climb a few feet down the rope. The transparency remains here on top. It's in a bottle. Quite safe now. I shall have a long string tied to the bottle. When I see Miss Hay and Newton are aboard Anderson's boat, I'll pull the bottle over the edge and let it fall. It's polythene. It won't break. You can pick it up.'

There was silence for a moment; comparative silence. The helicopter still clattered somewhere near, though for the moment I couldn't see it.

In my ear Marasov's voice said, 'If I transfer them, what is to stop you breaking your word and leaving the bottle there? The helicopter, after all, is waiting.'

The helicopter was suddenly doing more than waiting. It must have been lurking near sea level, because abruptly it again tore up over the cliff edge and passed low over the Holm top. I swung round to watch it go, trying to discover what Elliot was up to. For some reason tear gas came into my mind: tear gas, or that other stuff – Mace – they use to stun people in riots. Would Elliot have things like that available up here in the Shetlands? I pictured myself staggering round up there blinded and helpless. As the roar died, I said quickly, 'I'll be ten feet down the cliff, hanging on the rope. You can shoot me very easily, if I don't keep my word.'

I waited tensely for his answer. I'd offered him all I had to offer . . .

Marasov's answer was hesitant. 'How can I trust you?'

'If I don't keep my promise, you kill me. It's that simple.'

Still he hesitated. There was only one thing to do. I stood up, showed myself at the cliff edge, and said, 'Look at me now. Look through the sights of a rifle. I'll come ten feet down the cliff. Could you miss?'

Below me on the lighted deck of the trawler I could see men looking up. 'Well, could you?'

His voice crackled in my ear. 'I accept. I warn you, we shall not miss.'

I looked down at the sea far below and swallowed. I'd proposed, but I was appalled by what I'd proposed. My guts felt slithery at the thought of venturing again into the void. And the feeling of revulsion grew worse with every second I stood there. I said, 'Where I climbed before, at the south end. Understand?'

'I understand.' I could pick out Marasov now, walkie-talkie in hand, head bent back as he looked up at me. A second later the bow of the big fishing boat began to come round and water foamed beneath her stern. I stepped back, picked up the water bottle, and tied the string I'd got from Anderson's hide firmly round the bottle neck. Then I crossed the Holm, using my torch to find my discarded climbing belt, and buckled it on. Finally, I hooked the strap of the walkie-talkie round my neck. I was ready, possibly able, very far from willing.

I had to force myself to sit on the edge of the cliff, force myself to dangle my legs into space until I'd fitted my feet into the stirrups and adjusted the Jumar clips. This was the moment. I placed the precious water bottle a couple of feet back from the edge in case of accident, lowered the string over, then turned my body and let myself slide carefully downward until the stirrups took the strain. Lowering the bottom clip, I felt my foot move down. The edge now pressed against my chest. Next the upper clip. Then the lower again. My eyes were level with the bottle. Beside me the slender thread of string dangled limply.

I went down slowly, glancing every few seconds at the entrance to the channel, where Marasov's boat would appear at any moment. I wondered how he would have contacted Anderson. Well, it was *his* problem and there was always Morse. Anderson would be bound to know Morse!

Yes, there it was! Deck lights on, the big fishing boat came nosing cautiously in. I lowered myself two more steps down the rope and waited.

There came a sudden unearthly roar – magnified a dozen times as the sound smashed back and forth between the cliffs – and Elliot's helicopter roared over. Christ, what was he doing? He was up to something; must have some idea, some plan, but I couldn't begin to imagine what it was! Hanging one-handed on the rope, I fumbled for the walkie-talkie hand-set, and glanced down. The Russian fishing boat was almost directly beneath me. When I released the bottle, it would probably fall straight on to the deck.

'Marasov?'

'I'm ready.'

I said, 'Where are they? I want to see them.'

'Look down.'

I looked. Three figures stood in a little group at the stern. 'Let me speak to her.'

I saw him hand over the walkie-talkie. There was a brief pause, then a voice came. I'd have known it anywhere. Relief thudded through me: Alsa said uncertainly, 'John?'

'Is that Newton with you?'

Another pause, then, 'Yes, John, it is.'

I looked back towards the entrance. Anderson's Shetland model was entering the narrow channel, coming in towards the Russian boat's stern.

'Let them go aboard,' I said into the handset.

'John. Be careful.'

'I'll be careful,' I said. 'I have to be. Let me talk to Marasov.'

'They're going now, Sellers,' Marasov said, 'Can you see them?'

I could see very clearly. I saw the man go first: Newton, who'd nearly paid for his love of birds with his life. Then Alsa. With Anderson's good arm around her, she turned at the rail and waved up to me.'

In my ear, Marasov's voice boomed suddenly. 'They're on the boat. Did you see?'

'Now we wait,' I told him, 'until they're out of sight.'

He said, warningly, 'There are three men with automatic rifles here, Sellers. They are ready to fire if you make the slightest movement.'

My throat was dry, my stomach knotting with anxiety as I hung there, swaying a little on the rope, watching as Anderson's boat moved slowly, stern first, back out of the channel. I could see the three figures in the stern as she came about, now under forward power, and began to pick up speed.

My mind raced. Had I allowed enough time? When I let the bottle fall, would Marasov have time to retrieve it, get out of the channel and *still* catch them before they reached Lerwick? I'd have to wait as long as I dared.

By now the boat was gone. Half a minute passed then Marasov said, 'Now. It is time.'

I didn't reply.

'Do you hear me, Sellers?'

'I hear you.'

'I shall count to ten,' he said slowly. 'If you have not then kept your promise, my men will open fire.'

I gritted my teeth and argued. 'It won't help you. I'm not

holding the string. It's hanging beside me. The bottle would stay up here. We wait until they're well clear. Five minutes at least.'

I half expected to be shot at that moment, but nothing happened. I hung in space against that awful cliff, sweating and waiting as I counted five minutes slowly away.

Marasov's voice came with startling suddenness. 'Now, Sellers! Now or I call up another vessel to intercept them.'

'How do I know you haven't?'

'You don't know. But I assure you that I will. I will order them killed, you know that?'

This was it then. Another Russian boat might already be intercepting Anderson; God knows they had enough of them in Lerwick! But I'd reached the end, played my weak hand for all it would stand. I couldn't do more.

Marasov said, 'I am *only* interested in the transparency. *Only* that. Remember it. If you let the bottle fall now, they will be safe.'

I took a deep breath of doubt. But now I had to do it. I said, 'Coming now. Watch out for it!'

I reached out my hand to the thin, dangling string, raised my eyes to the cliff edge and pulled gently. It was tight, perhaps lodged against some tiny obstruction. I pulled harder . . . and watched in horror as the slack string came limply over the edge. There was no bottle on the end!


CHAPTER TWENTY-TWO


Marasov's voice rasped, 'What's wrong, Sellers?'

'No bottle,' I said. 'There's no – ' I was going to die. Now. This moment. Rifles were aimed at me. I said, 'Please, let me – '

Brilliant light suddenly flooded the chasm below me, a bright, white ball of light. I was gaping down, waiting for the bullet, but already blinded by the flaring brilliance, when a voice above me shouted, 'Quick, Sellers! Get up here, quick!' *Elliot's voice!*

But I couldn't go quickly. Climbing with Jumars was desperately slow. I felt the rope move in my hands and clung to it, as the cliff face scraped against my knuckles. I heard the sharp crackle of rifle fire from below, heard bullets smack against rock. Somehow I wasn't hit, and I couldn't understand why. I couldn't see at all. That suddenly exploding, flaring light had destroyed my vision totally. I simply hung there, helplessly, aware that I was being dragged slowly upward, knowing Elliot must be doing it, but with no idea what had caused the light, or why I hadn't been hit.

'You're at the edge now.' Elliot's voice was little more than a series of straining grunts. 'Grab it and climb over!'

'I'm blind,' I yelled. 'I can't see!'

'Christ, put your hands out. Help me pull . . .'

I felt forward at the cliff face, slid my hands up and felt the edge, where cold rock turned into grass, reached up, found a grip, and pulled. The edge was level with my chest.

'Christ, make it fast!' Elliot grated.

I pulled desperately, hands now nearly at waist level.

'Fall forward, Sellers, you're okay!'

But I didn't fall forward. I was smashed forward, by a rifle bullet which, although I didn't know it at that instant, blasted half the flesh of my shoulder away. All I knew then was that my shoulder was suddenly numb, that my face was in wet grass. I tried to crawl, but my arm wouldn't support me. I wriggled on my stomach, and rolled, until I felt grass instead of space beneath my feet.

Shock, it must have been. Exhaustion. The burning redness in my eyes was darkening, then dying . . .

I woke in the helicopter and looked up at a dim shape very near. Somebody spoke, and I assumed the shape must be a head. 'Don't worry. Keep still. You'll be at the hospital in a few minutes.'

I nodded, hoping it was true. My shoulder felt as though it was being cremated. If the pain went on much longer I'd . . .

But it didn't. I blacked out again and awoke much later, blinking at the daylight. I looked round me and tried to move, but one arm was immobile. I was in a strange room, too. I was making a habit of awakening in strange rooms. This room had a nurse in it.

I must have grunted or something, because she turned and gave me one of those reassuring nurse-type smiles. She said, 'Before you ask, you're in Aberdeen General Hospital.'

I blinked. 'How?'

'A combination of things. Morphia and a helicopter. You're all right, don't worry.'

Stupidity was rolling away. As far, at any rate, as it was ever likely to roll. Realization came back too. I sat up awkwardly, swore at the sudden pain, and said 'Alsa! What happened?'

The nurse said, 'Everybody's all right. I was told to tell you that.' She laughed gaily. 'I don't know who's all right, but they are, it seems.'

I sank back. 'Thank God!'

She came over. She actually mopped my brow. I'd heard of it so many times, but this was the first time it had actually happened to me. It felt wonderfully soothing.

'Now,' she murmured. 'A little more sleepytime.'

I woke again and it was dark outside. My shoulder was throbbing. Another nurse was on duty. I asked her, 'How am I?'

She was the brisk kind. 'You're fine,' she said. 'Damaged shoulder, that's all. And maybe you're a wee bit run down.' She advanced on me with a syringe.

Next day I learned that I was officially ambulant, but all the same I didn't feel like walking. The brisk nurse would probably have made me, but she wasn't on duty. It was the angelic one who fed me, bathed me and finally told me she had a nice surprise waiting. She pushed me in a wheelchair down a corridor, opened a door, said, 'There's your friend,' and left discreetly.

The friend was Elliot. He lay propped up in bed, wearing

a weak smile that sat awkwardly across his lantern jaw. He was also wearing a lot of bandages on his chest and a bottle of plasma was draining into him.

I said, 'What happened?'

'I got shot. Just like you. Two ribs busted. Some loss of blood. Gonna be okay.'

'I'm glad you're all right,' I said with perfect sincerity. 'But what happened before that? I saw a ball of fire come from somewhere.'

Elliot said weakly, 'Not that I'd like to try it again. There was a ledge on the north end of that damn rock, maybe ten feet wide, just below the top. I got the helicopter to drop me there.'

'And then?'

'I looked for you. You weren't visible, but there was only one way you could get down. When I found the rope, I found the bottle and cut the string . . . I could hear you talking.' He grinned, but the grin was tenuous with pain. His voice was noticeably weaker when he spoke again.

'What I did, I brought a flare from the chopper. That was the ball of fire. Nobody can aim a rifle through a flare.'

'They did,' I said. 'They hit us both.'

'Lucky shooting. Unlucky, I guess.' He was very weak; his wound was far more severe than he'd admitted.

I looked at him, trying to find words. Finally I said, 'You were nearly killed. Willingham *was* killed. I did everything I could to keep that transparency away from you. You could just have taken it and left me hanging there.'

He no longer had the strength to grin, but he smiled a little. It was very weak, but very real and I suddenly realized I had a high regard for Elliot. He said, 'I was . . . tempted. I really was. Then I got . . . to thinking. You know . . . Sellers . . .' I could barely hear him now, '. . . I thought . . . that a dope like you . . . who just wanted . . . to get your girl back . . . is what it's . . . all about.' He was almost asleep as he finished.

I said, 'She's Anderson's girl, but I suppose the principle's sound. Go to sleep. I'll see you later. And thanks.'

I was trying to turn the wheelchair away, one-handed, not wanting to disturb him by shouting for the nurse. Then, from somewhere he found the strength to rouse himself a little.

'Sellers . . .'

'Later. Go to sleep.'

'Anderson was . . . here . . .' Elliot's voice was only a murmur. 'Message . . . for you . . .'

'Oh, I wasn't sure whether or not Elliot was now talking in his sleep. His eyes were closed and the muscles of his face were slack.

'Yea . . . about gen . . . genetics.'

'Genetics?' He must be rambling.

'Told me . . . second cousins . . . shouldn't . . . they shouldn't . . . marry.'

I stared at him. 'Second cousins?' My heart was thudding suddenly in my chest.

His eyes came open but he didn't speak. He seemed to be listening. I listened too. Footsteps were coming down the corridor. And then the door opened and things became confused, because Alsa came in and both of us ignored poor old Elliot until the confusion had eased and Alsa was wheeling my chair softly to the door. I turned my head to look at him.

His eyes were still open. Then one of them closed. Just one. And he whispered, 'Dopes like you . . .'

# Duncan Kyle

'One of the modern masters of the high adventure story.'
*Daily Telegraph*

GREEN RIVER HIGH   £1.50
BLACK CAMELOT   £1.25
A CAGE OF ICE   £1.50
FLIGHT INTO FEAR   £1.50
TERROR'S CRADLE   £1.25
A RAFT OF SWORDS   £1.25
WHITEOUT!   £1.50
STALKING POINT   £1.75

FONTANA PAPERBACKS

# Fontana Paperbacks

Fontana is a leading paperback publisher of fiction and non-fiction, with authors ranging from Alistair MacLean, Agatha Christie and Desmond Bagley to Solzhenitsyn and Pasternak, from Gerald Durrell and Joy Adamson to the famous Modern Masters series.

In addition to a wide-ranging collection of internationally popular writers of fiction, Fontana also has an outstanding reputation for history, natural history, military history, psychology, psychiatry, politics, economics, religion and the social sciences.

All Fontana books are available at your bookshop or newsagent; or can be ordered direct. Just fill in the form and list the titles you want.

FONTANA BOOKS, Cash Sales Department, G.P.O. Box 29, Douglas, Isle of Man, British Isles. Please send purchase price, plus 8p per book. Customers outside the U.K. send purchase price, plus 10p per book. Cheque, postal or money order. No currency.

NAME (Block letters)

ADDRESS